SIX GUYS

A COLLECTION OF SHORT STORIES

SIX GUYS

A COLLECTION OF SHORT STORIES

WAYNE J. LANDRY

gatekeeper press
Columbus, Ohio

This book is a work of fiction. The names, characters and events in this book are the products of the author's imagination or are used fictitiously. Any similarity to real persons living or dead is coincidental and not intended by the author.

Six Guys: A Collection of Short Stories

Published by Gatekeeper Press
2167 Stringtown Rd, Suite 109
Columbus, OH 43123-2989
www.GatekeeperPress.com

Copyright © 2021 by Wayne J. Landry

All rights reserved. Neither this book, nor any parts within it may be sold or reproduced in any form or by any electronic or mechanical means, including information storage and retrieval systems, without permission in writing from the author. The only exception is by a reviewer, who may quote short excerpts in a review.

The editorial work for this book is entirely the product of the author. Gatekeeper Press did not participate in and is not responsible for any aspect of this element. Library of Congress Control Number: 2021940893

ISBN (paperback): 9781662916038

eISBN: 9781662916045

also by Wayne J. Landry
8 Short Stories

For SALLY

Contents

Perfect   **1**

Destiny   *1*

By Accident or By Design   *4*

In the Beginning   *7*

Disaster   *9*

The Letter and the Act of Contrition   *12*

The End   *14*

The Wage Earners   *15*

For Love   **17**

The Invisible Man   *17*

The Journey   *20*

The Negotiation   *23*

The First Installment   *27*

I Am Not Who I Am   *32*

The Second Installment   *40*

Thoughts during a Late-Night Drive Home   *67*

Excitement Anticipation Monday   *68*

Confusion   *76*

Home   *80*

The First Task   *82*

The Second Task   *86*

The Third Task   *90*

The Fourth Task	*92*
The Interview	*99*
My Goodbye	*100*
Two Years Later	*102*

Moochie — 103

Together in a Church — 105

Pig Bones — 113

The Cast	*113*
The Proposal	*115*
The Trap	*128*
The Interview	*131*
Gumbo	*140*
The Lucky Star	*143*
The Premier	*144*
Prayers	*147*
Prayers Pt. II	*150*
The Hound Dog	*153*
Money	*158*
Endings and Beginnings	*163*
The Obligation	*169*

A Good Sunday — 177

The Family	*177*
The Story (Sunday Morning)	*180*
The Story (Sunday Afternoon)	*193*
The Story (Sunday Evening)	*210*

The Power to Define the situation is the Ultimate Power.
Jerry Rubin

Perfect

Destiny

Elaine

Elaine sat on the edge of her bed waiting for the first morning light to burst through her bedroom window. She had spent many hours deciding how to dress the most important window in her apartment. She had positioned the bed so that she and Benjamin could be awakened each morning with soft natural light coaxing their eyes open. The light pastel pink curtains with an open weave design allowed pinkish daybreak to smile on their faces as she and her love lay in bed. Elaine had spent considerable time making their apartment warm, cozy and stylish. She wanted her husband to be comfortable; to be content when he was home. She wanted everything to be perfect.

She had spent the night feeling protected in the silky-smooth, ultra-cozy sheets that she and Ben both loved. All night she thought about the past four years of married bliss. While watching the movie in her mind Elaine decided to make the biggest decision of her life. But, for now, breakfast was her mission. She decided to make the breakfast that she and Benjamin savored on long lazy weekend mornings. Crepes by the dozen, wrapped around fresh fruit, Ben's favorite or spread with sweet butter and a teaspoon of crunchy raw sugar, Elaine's favorite.

Elaine carried her morning feast of buttery crepes to the small bistro table and chairs that she had strategically placed outside the balcony door. She sat at the table to enjoy her breakfast knowing the only people that could see her in the white and pink kimono robe, that

Ben had bought her, were at least a block away. She knew for certain, because she had made Ben sit at this very table while she went to the street below to determine when pedestrians could see her and her love enjoying the beauty of the day on their second story balcony. The Lovers lived on G Driver St.; which ended with a train station. The daily horde that migrated into the city each morning parked in the nearby parking garages and walked down G Driver to catch a train that would, in about twenty minutes, allow the wage earners to access any part of the great city. The old elegant apartment on G Driver St. was the perfect place to live. For work and entertainment, the city was a short train ride; but the happy couple's apartment was located in an area that had a small-town vibe. She closed her eyes as she bit into the rolled-up crepe. The only sound that her mind was interpreting was the sweet crunch of the sugar and a few barely audible mumbles from the mostly silent human mass moving below. The young wife turned her face upward so that she could feel the warmth of the early morning light as she savored the taste of her sweet buttery crepe. It was a beautiful morning but Elaine's forehead creased when she thought about all she had to do that day. First on her agenda was to sew together the two white sheets so that she could come up with her message.

Benjamin
Ben had not slept for the third straight night. He spent most of the night sitting in a comfortable chair looking out of the bedroom window at the street below. He missed Elaine; the last four days was the longest he had been away from her in the last four years. After each stressful eight hours of work, he would reach his temporary address, strip off his cloth armor, take a moment to meditate and hopefully wash away the day's stress. Minutes into meditation his wife's beautiful face would appear and feelings of peace and sadness would awaken storms of emotions that fueled his continual reminiscing of the best four years of his life. Whenever he thought

about the first time he saw and spoke to Elaine he was convinced that some higher power had planned their chance encounter.

He had just spent four enjoyable years of campus life and was spending a few weeks at his parent's small vineyard before going out into the real world to start working at a real job. After a couple of weeks of lounging around, visiting family and friends and eating too much of his Mom's great cooking, Ben decided to take a bike ride to get his muscles moving again. Since there would be very little traffic at this time of the year, he decided to take the old Harvest Road to the river. His plans were to go at a steady pace for the twelve miles to the river then head back home at a blistering quad-screaming speed. When he had almost reached the river, he could see a cream-colored convertible fish-tail off of the river road onto the Old Harvest Road. The convertible was easily going twice as fast as the posted thirty. As the convertible sped by, the driver, a female wearing a ball cap tooted the horn and waved as she rocketed down the road. Ben smiled knowing that the old road used mainly by farmers and vintners had a few potholes that could easily devour that small convertible. When he got to the river, he laid his bike down and climbed onto some rocks that looked over the river. He just wanted a few minutes to think about what was next. He knew he had lived a charmed life and the spell of youth was wearing off, but what was next. An old crow flew by and pecked at Ben's head. The old bird knocked him out of contemplation and threatened to attack again. He considered throwing a rock at the crow but instead abandoned the scenic view to the winged bully. That old bird had driven him away; pushed him onto the road of his destiny.

The shoulder of the road was smoother than the pitted asphalt allowing Ben to get his speed up and at a steady tempo; his homeward bound race was nearly half complete, his legs were still strong but he was having a difficult time controlling his breathe. He was beginning the long rise in the road when he sensed a wall of resistance, felt his back-end rattle and knew without looking that he had a flat tire. He knew the vineyard was at least six or seven miles away and his only option was to walk his bike down the desolate road. The morning mist had burnt away and the sun was beginning to show her strength. The walking cyclist smiled; the busted tire was just a minor annoyance. Deep inside he felt self-satisfaction; his mind was at peace, the breezy sunny morning felt glorious. Climbing up the rise in the road his pace began to quicken, he could feel this magical optimism, this unexplainable pull to something, someone or some answer that was on the other side of the hill in the road. He crested the rise and in the distance was a cream-colored car.

By Accident or By Design
Elaine

Elaine walked into the small intimate TV room, decorated with her favorite portraits and landscapes that she'd painted and turned on her thinking music. Elaine had painted the pictures when she needed to disconnect from Ben. Sometimes there was a need to be alone with her thoughts and painting had allowed her to keep her own council and to express her intoxicated emotions on a canvas. She knew it was good for their relationship to each have their private time. She had recorded an adagio that would end with another adagio beginning and continuing for hours with the same wave of emotional graceful music. The instant she heard the first note of music she knew she had to look at the photos, the visual history of her life. Elaine quickly thumbed through all of the constantly smiling pictures from her happy childhood. She was seeking one picture that marked the real beginning of her life. She turned the page and there was the picture that always brought a smile to her face. There was Ben smiling that beautiful, hypnotic smile. He was putting a tire on a jacked-up cream-colored convertible.

"Hello there. Need any help?"

Elaine had been so intent, grunting and yelling at tire nuts she couldn't budge she hadn't noticed the man that had walked up on her little catastrophe. Startled, Elaine rattled, "I jacked up the car and took off the hubcap but I can't seem to budge the bolts. I'm in an awful hurry. I can pay you for your help."

The man walked his bike closer and said, "They're called nuts."

"Beg your pardon!"

"You're trying to take the nuts off of the bolts."

"OK genius; how much?"

"I'll make you a deal. I live about six or seven miles down this road. I'll fix the tire, if you give me and my bike a ride home."

His eyes were hidden behind large wraparound sunglasses, but Elaine couldn't take her eyes off of the big dangerous smile. She put on her best indignant look and then broke free from the smile. "Is there no chivalry in this Kingdom? Do I have to negotiate for help? What do damsels in distress do in this foreign domain?" The walking cyclist continued on his journey, but the smile was still there combined with a teasing laughter. "OK! OK! I'll give you and your crippled a ride. But be snappy; I'm in a hurry."

The cyclist laid his bike in the grass and took off his gloves, sunglasses and helmet. He turned and faced Elaine. Elaine suddenly felt fire on her face. "Wow! With that little pointy helmet and the darken windshield wrapped around your face I thought I was dealing with a space alien. I must say this strange kingdom has handsome road-side service." Elaine could feel her heart beating faster, her usually focused mind went static, but her eyes unabashedly went from his gray eyes to the hypnotic smile to the muscular body draped in a damp T shirt.

The cyclist leaned into the tire tool and cracked the first nut. "You cannot possibly be in a hurry if you're on this road. In fact, one of the laws of this Kingdom, this Kingdom of Camelotnots, is that no one within its domain can be in a hurry. My name is Benjamin, but of course, most in this kingdom call me Sir Benjamin."

Elaine thanked God that this beautiful man was not a grunter or a blushing introvert. The cyclist wasn't cocky; he looked loose, free, and confident. She knew that the smile was enslaving her heart; the heart that had been dormant or dead for the last few years. Elaine pulled her phone from her skirt pocket and said, "Hey, let me take a picture of my road-side knight; Sir Benjamin from the Kingdom of Cameltoes."

The road-side knight couldn't break the next nut because the giggles were sapping his strength. "I said the Kingdom Camelotnots."

Elaine took a picture of that moment. She would always have the moment frozen in time. The moment that the ice began to thaw in her chest and the aloofness that had protected her had begun to float away.

Benjamin pointed his finger at Elaine and said, "There will be a charge for that picture.

Elaine stared at her knight for a few seconds. Her face was a mask of delight, everything was perfect, and then she cautiously said, "I hope the charge is very expensive."

Benjamin

Ben finally got up from his perch overlooking the street below and ambled into the kitchen to get a cup of coffee. He had taken the day off to just relax and settle his exploding thoughts. He was exhausted physically and emotionally. He wanted to look his best when he finally saw his love later in the day. Ben sat at the kitchen table, sipping coffee, his only sustenance for the last few days. His thoughts continually reverted back to the first day of his life. The day had been beautiful, comfortably warm, and breezy and embraced in a soft golden light. Sometimes he saw that sunlight captured in paintings. But that day could only truly be pictured in the mind. When he had crested the hill, he saw in the distance the cream-colored convertible on the shoulder of the road. He approached the car and saw the ball cap wearing woman working on a flat tire. His first thought: Was this an accident or by design; two flat tires at the same time of day on the same desolate road. Then he heard her.

"Turn you bastard." Then she let out a frustrated yell.

He cleared his throat so that she would notice his presence. But the woman was too busy cursing her tire. "Hello there. Need any help?" His first vision of his future wife was the back of a faded blue ball cap and from it flowed thick wild and tangled raven black hair. She was wearing a long jersey skirt tie-dyed purple, green, black and white and a loose grease stained white Tee shirt. When the ball cap turned in his direction the surprise was a delicate but startled face. From that moment on, memories of that glorious day differed. Elaine remembered that he started negotiating within ten seconds of magically appearing. He remembered being stunned silent by her beauty. Her pale skin amplified the color of her turquoise eyes. Her regal nose pointed to full rosy lips that were fixed around a confident smile. When the sylphlike woman spoke, it was with a coy sensuous lilt. He remembered apologizing if he'd upset her. He remembered his feeling of excited anticipation more than any words spoken.

In the Beginning
Elaine

All her preparations were complete except the letter she wanted to write to Ben; but before sitting at her desk to pour out her emotions, she wanted to sit for a while longer thinking about those first marvelous days. The bike would not fit in the car's small luggage compartment so she drove her car slowly while Ben guided his bike alongside the car. Elaine couldn't take the smile off of her face and she couldn't stop looking at her passenger "Don't you dare let that rickety old bike scratch my car."

She remembered a feeling of melancholy when she turned her car into the driveway, until, "Hey, my Mom is a great cook. When she finds out that you rescued me, she'll insist that you stay for dinner."

Elaine accepted the invitation. The food was simple, but excellent, the wine was glorious and the dinner conversation was fun and exciting. After numerous glasses of wine, Ben's parents had insisted that she use one of the spare bedrooms. She stayed the night, helped Ben's mother cook breakfast and spent the rest of the day with Ben as a guide to his parent's vineyard. The invitation for dinner turned into a new life. A chance encounter turned into revived emotions, excitement, giddiness, and a peace deep inside, a soul-satisfying feeling. It took three days before the first kiss. The third day was a perfect day. Ben woke her when it was still dark and together, they prepared and enjoyed a silent breakfast. They ate their buttered toast and stole peeks of each other and when their eyes met, wordlessly they both knew the person that they had been waiting for had arrived. They then saddled the vineyard's two old mares and spoke softly as the old horses ambled down a green grassy path on that cool dewy morning with the first pink light peeking over the horizon. Their destination was a trickle of a waterfall that pooled into Ben's childhood swimming hole. Their first kiss was just a brushing of their lips; then slow and steady exploring. She loved kissing Ben, his lips, his eyes, his ears and neck. She knew that this was the first time that she was not trying to satisfy someone; instead she was truly enjoying kissing and caressing this beautiful man. In all ways he was perfect.

She had always been so proud to introduce him to everyone. Everyone always enjoyed meeting Ben. She could still remember her extremely finicky Mother's exact words after meeting him a few times.

"I can't believe you've found the perfect man. He's drop-dead gorgeous; just so good-looking. Some days he's a sleek Ivy League shark, then the next day he's a competitive jock and then on other days he's laid back and dressed like he's the child of hippies. He's always so easy and fun to be around."

She had wanted to marry right away but it took four months before holy matrimony. Every day, every month after the nuptials the relationship grew and became unbreakable. Everyone said they were a perfect match. Everyone was jealous.

Benjamin

Ben made himself a sandwich and sat at the kitchen table reminiscing about those first magical days. He hadn't really expected her to accept the dinner invitation; it was just an attempt to not let the encounter end. Elaine's charm hypnotized his parents. His Mom had finally found a daughter and his Dad couldn't stop smiling. His parents had insisted she spend the night and the next and the next. She had a smile that made her buoyant, light, sensitive. She laughed easily and the joy was contagious. When she moved, she had a combination of innocence and sensuality.

Ben walked over to the fridge, opened the door, and blindly stared into the fridge. His mind was drifting to the happiest day of his life. His wedding had turned into the best party he'd ever attended. Everyone was happy and excited.

His friends, his relatives all said that he and Elaine were a lucky couple; a perfect match. Minutes before he walked into the Church to change his life forever, his Dad straightened Ben's tie and said, "Thanks Benjamin, thanks for turning into a good man and for making good decisions and for marrying a wonderful woman. She's a perfect addition to the Family."

Ben mindlessly sat at the table. His smile was mismatched with a far-away stare. He once asked if meeting Elaine was just an accident. But he had now known for years that his beautiful wife was his destiny. She made him a good man.

Disaster

Elaine

Elaine walked over to her desk to look for the fine sea green writing paper she'd bought especially for her letter to Ben. As she passed the balcony, she saw the expensive white sheets she'd sewed together to form her very large message flag patiently waiting to do their job. When she saw the sheets, a cold wave washed away her fond memories and put a cold fear in her heart. She knew that she would have to revisit the darkest day of her life before she would make her final decision. She walked over to the ladder and positioned it exactly where she would need it.

The dark day was last Friday. The slow moving cool front promised rain and mean dark clouds twisted, coiled and threatened. She signed out of work early on that fateful day and hoped to treat her lover to lunch at their favorite café. The sidewalks were crowded with people scurrying to get to their destination before the demon-clouds grew tired of threats. She had almost reached her husband's office when she saw the lobby door open and out walked Jessica and then Ben. Her legs suddenly felt heavy and sickly slow. She followed Ben and the Bitch and spied. Jessica clung to his arm as they smiled at each other. With every step her heart grew heavier and her stomach sicker; then the first tears began to appear when the thief kissed her husband. The clouds were finished with their threats and began to lightly dampen the world. Elaine followed the intimate couple to Jessica's apartment. She knew Jessica's apartment and she knew the room where the whore closed the blinds was her bedroom. Elaine stood in horror on the opposite side of the street and the rain attacked. She could feel a deep soul stretching deadly scream building but it would not come out. Her throat had closed and she was now breathing from her nose sipping quick shallow breaths. The rain was ferocious; she could barely see the window to Jessica's bedroom.

It was late afternoon and the rain had stopped when Ben walked out of Jessica's apartment. Elaine still stood across the street, wet, her lips blue, and her body was trembling. Her mind was a storm of confusion; she couldn't focus on anything until she saw Ben. When Ben crossed the street, he looked at Elaine and didn't recognize her and then it clicked. His face turned into a mask of horror and his only words were, "Oh, nooo!"

When Ben got near, Elaine raised her hand, palm facing outward, to shield her from his vision. Her lips were trembling but her voice was hoarse and laced with hate when she said, "Stay away. Please stay away from my home." Elaine turned and walked away her legs stiff and trembling.

Benjamin

Ben was growing anxious. He knew that if things didn't go well when he met Elaine this evening his life would be altered for the worse. He was trying to think of the best way to say I'm sorry.

Whenever he thought about that destructive day, he felt intense agitation, panic, and then crushing depression. Elaine's beautiful smile had been replaced by a blank stare, but her voice was filled with hate and despair. He had wandered and cried for hours; eventually knocking on the door of his best friend's house. When Wayne opened the door, he knew something was seriously wrong.

He sat at Wayne's kitchen table and told the devastating ruinous story. He cried, then asked his best friend for help. Wayne was shocked, perplexed and angry. His first words were yelled,

"You idiot! How could you trample on Elaine's love and trust? How would you feel if she'd done this to your stupid ass? You risked hurting the love of your life for an hour with Jessica St. Paul a dull wanton slut; the local lying whore." Wayne walked over to the fridge, opened it and just stared inside. He knew that a perfect union had been destroyed. He knew that love could repair a hurt; but the bruise would always be there. "Ben you always lived a charmed life because you always made the absolute perfect decisions. When you finally made a bad decision you radically altered something that married couples yearn for and are jealous of those who have that special beautiful bond that you and Elaine possessed. You had a relationship that always sparkled."

Ben looked like a miserable suffering man. His elbows rested on the tabletop with his hands cradling his distraught face. He looked through his barrier of fingers and tried to focus on Wayne. "I don't know if I can live without Elaine." His breath increased trying to suppress another cry. "Man, I'm scared; I don't know if I want to live without Elaine."

Wayne looked at his fallen hero. He had always been proud to have him as a friend; someone to emulate. "First thing, you need to shower. You can wear some of my clothes. I'll fix you something to eat. You can stay here until the Gods and Elaine forgive you. You'll have to explain to Sally why you're staying here. She's going to be really upset. She really likes Elaine."

It was only a few hours before he was to see Elaine for the first time since the disaster and he still had not decided how he was going to ask for forgiveness.

The Letter and the Act of Contrition
The Letter
Elaine sat at her small writing table that she had stained a comfortable shade of mahogany. The desk and the chair both had the same amateur stain that she had lovingly applied. She pulled the desk drawer so that she could get one of her favorite writing pens. When she placed the sea green stationery on the mahogany colored desk top she had to pause for a moment, the colors were a perfect combination. She thought about how much of her life had been boring and dreadful, but the last few years were like waking up every morning in the middle of an unfolding fairy tale. The worst had happened but she still wanted to convey her thanks to Ben for making her life golden for a few years. She knew she was better at conveying her thoughts, feelings, her emotions on paper than in person. She was forever scolding herself for writing the perfect letter of condolence instead of being strong and offering the bereaved a shoulder for support. But she wanted Ben to have no doubts. She wanted him to know that she loved him. She sat

at her desk with a tight smile and tears covering her vision and she started to write.

My Dearest Benjamin,

On a remote and badly torn road I met my destiny. I fell in love with you the moment I saw you. These last years of my life have been beautiful; I've been a princess, an adventurer, a lover, an equal. Every night was bliss. Your warm body coiled protectively around me allowed for the sweetest dreams. Morning showers together were a daily highlight. Each day with you was a new shared adventure in learning and loving. I want to thank you for giving me a life that most women live only in dreams. If I could live a hundred years or a day; I would take either as long as you were there to hold me. My love for you is stronger today than it was the first time I kissed you. I miss you.

Ben---I love you. I will always love you.

Be my pilgrim; follow me.

She sat at her writing table crying, tears dropping and staining her letter.

The Act of Contrition

Ben had showered, shaved and was wearing some of Wayne's clothes. He kept pacing back and forth, rehearsing his intention to ask for forgiveness without showing extreme remorse. He knew he couldn't speak to Elaine about excuses and he couldn't seem too emotionally distraught. His lover never liked crybabies or complainers that threw out excuses regardless of their guilt. He hated that he couldn't just be himself; but any words without thought could ensure that the wound would never heal. He needed her to know that the Ben she knew was the result of having her in his life. She made him a better man. He liked who he was, he was confident, because he knew he was never alone in this world. He had a bond with Elaine that he had never had with anyone else in his life. He couldn't go back to being alone surrounded by many friends and family and the whirling societal chaos. He needed her. He knew what he broke was irreparable. He knew that even if the wound healed there would always be the scar. If Elaine could accept a new beginning, he would willingly wear the scarlet letter and do any penance to show her his remorse, his regret. He tried to be upbeat, confident; instead he just felt swirling darkness surrounding him, gripping his body and mind. Ben had always told Elaine to not follow fashion because her most alluring attire was her smile and now the darkness was even fading the smile. He picked up the bouquet of flowers that he had got for his wife. Elaine had always liked Spring meadow wildflowers and the florist tried her best. Before leaving on his mission Ben looked in the mirror one last time so that he could speak words of encouragement to his reflection. He saw in the mirror a face of fear, apprehension and disappointment.

The End
Elaine
Elaine's body stiffened when she heard the knock on the door. She thought that she had been drained of all emotions but when she heard the second knock and Ben's voice her heart started to cry. She had changed into her favorite white chiffon maxi skirt and when she turned to run to her balcony the skirt swirled and floated like when Ben twirled her on the dance floor. Elaine ran onto her balcony, checked to see where she had tied her expensive sheets to the balcony's railing. Once again Ben knocked on the door. She gathered up the sheets and threw her message flag over the side of the balcony. The breeze lifted the sheets like sails; the message flag gently rippled like white waves. Ben rang the doorbell and she thought she heard keys. She ran from the balcony and up the ladder she had placed under the stairway banisters. She grabbed the noose that she had tied to the upper railing and then closed her eyes and took a deep breath.

Benjamin
Ben had parked his car in one of the parking garages on the lower end of G Driver St. so that he could walk-out the anxiousness that was

churning his stomach. When he reached the door to their apartment, he paused. What should he do? Should he use his key to open the door, should he ring the doorbell or should he just knock on the door?

Ben softly knocked and waited in anxious anticipation for the door to open. When the door stayed shut, he knocked a little harder and said, "Elaine it's me, it's Ben." He nervously stood erect waiting to see Elaine's face. The door remained closed; the silence was overpowering. He knocked then rang the doorbell; but the barrier stayed shut. He knew something was wrong. His anxiousness turned into cold fear, into panic. He used his key to open the door. As he slowly pushed the door open, he felt the need to cry, to scream her name but instead his dry mouth blurted out in a loud whisper, "Elaine it's me." Ben stepped into the foyer, looked to the right and said, "Elaine, where are you?" He then looked to the left and saw a shadow near their bedroom door that was swinging slowly like a pendulum.

The Wage Earners

On G Driver St. the nomadic horde of workers were exiting the trains nearing the completion of their daily migration. Each moving part of the human mass was an individual in his tiny private moving space. Most were thinking about the day's events; others were excited about or dreaded going home, but all were appreciating their nightly freedom. The walking river usually flowed perfectly smooth with very few obstacles or distractions. But this day was going to be different. Something had halted the river and a large pool of commuters were standing still, heads raised reading something above and hundreds of arms were stretched overhead seeking a good camera angle.

The white message banner with glossy red lettering gently rolled in the breeze. People were beginning to read the message aloud.

> MY BEAUTIFUL HUSBAND BROKE MY HEART
> AND NOW HE HAS KILLED ME.

The low early evening sun channeled a warm glow on the forest of arms. An anguish cry came from the second story apartment. "Elaine! NOoooo!"

In unison, arms came down, fingers stabbed at their phone. "911. How may I help you?"

For Love

The Invisible Man
Some people instantly reach for a cigarette, others hurriedly tip toe to the toilet, chamber pot or bush and many, in a sleepwalker's walk stumble or maybe in a Frankenstein stiff-legged gait waddle toward that first cup of coffee and still others wash away their sleep or the burdens of the night and then there are those that relive that night's dreams or horrors. These are the ways that most people experience the beginning of a newborn day. Hugo always robotically walked to the window, shoved aside the curtains and let the sunlight turn his brain on. He always liked greeting the first light and watching the morning glow climb, then spread and finally embrace. He had trained his mind-eye to see and greet the Morningstar even on the cloudiest of days. On this morning, after a late night, a very late night, Hugo pulled back the curtains and felt the warmth of the mid-morning star. He was expecting a ball of glowing yellow but instead was awakened to a soft light encircled in candy pink, Grecian blue and light orange. Hugo smiled; it was going to be good day.

After having buttered toast and coffee for breakfast, Hugo turned on his tablet to watch the video of the man that he was to interview that day. Sitting at his kitchen table enjoying his second cup of Community coffee, Hugo leaned closer to the tablet so that he could hear every word that the clearly stunned man was saying. A shiny, greasy, damp face appeared close-up on the screen, a drunken smile sat on the bottom of the picture and wild jutting hair framed the top border. The man's eyes were big with fright but his grin expressed a different emotion as he spoke to the camera.

"Oh man, I was two or three-sheets-to-the-wind. I was just minding my own business, content, waiting for the show to start." Fingers passed through the close-up as the aged face turned in profile. "Then this nut, dressed in black and wearing a mask jumped out of the restroom, yelled something to the crowd and started shooting. Without thinking and since I'm usually invisible, I jumped on the idiot, wrestled him to the ground and then others held him until the police came."

The smiling, leering lips once again filled the whole picture. "Now I'm going to the hospital."

The voice behind the camera said, "Are you hurt?"

The grin stretched from one edge of the tablet screen to the other. "Oh no, I'm just shook up. I'm hoping that I can score some pharmaceuticals."

Hugo sat back and took a sip of his steaming dark roasted coffee as the face on the screen grew smaller and the smiling man turned to leave with his new found friends, the EMT workers. This was the portrait of the world's new temporary hero. A shooting had occurred at a comedy club two weeks ago and this smiling unexpected superstar was the current conversation on social media. That twenty-two second dialogue had been viewed millions of times. The man, whose name is Elijah Cayenne, had turned down all further interviews. Multiple times each day reporters had pounded the door knocker to ask or to plead for an interview. Many times, the only response was an old white dog that slowly walked to the old rickety screened door, took a few sniffs of the outside air, turned and slowly disappeared into the darkness of the house. Occasionally a stunning petite blond answered the door. She always swung the wooden screened door open, but stayed in the doorway and with neither a smile nor a frown she spoke slowly with an Eastern European or German accent. Her dark blue eyes mesmerized all and she always spoke the same words.

"Mr. Cayenne is resting. He wishes you would only contact him by phone." Then she would close and lock the old wooden screened door, turn and the light of her beauty would be swallowed by darkness. Hugo scrolled through pictures of the keeper of the door and he couldn't help feel excitement knowing that he would soon be in the presence of the beauty.

His one fruit for the day was going to be a banana and as he peeled the fruit, he couldn't help thinking about how events intervene to change one's life. He had seriously thought about resigning, quitting his job at the City Advocate. His degree in English had helped him find various writing jobs but he had disliked them all. His dream was to write a novel. He had been thinking about changing jobs and had even begun his letter of resignation. Last Thursday when Mr. Doucet called him to his office, he had presumed he was going to be given another boring assignment.

Hugo carried his naked banana to the sugar bowl so that he could crystalize it with a coating of sugar.

When he had stepped into Mr. Doucet's office, Mr. Ellington, the paper's editor and Ms. Simpson, the office manager, were there smiling and excited to see him.

He took a bite of his sweet treat, his breakfast dessert, and recalled how confused he had been when he had entered Mr. Doucet's office. The hero of the Comedy Club tragedy, Mr. Cayenne, had called asking for Hugo to go to his home to negotiate an interview. No one was sure what was meant when he said to negotiate an interview. The big question in the room had been why the silent Hero had selected Hugo.

He was finally excited about his job. He was loaded with nervous energy; he could feel the excitement in his jittery stomach. It was a three-hour drive to the town of Flat Hill and he had been instructed to arrive no later than two in the afternoon. Hugo dressed in his blue suit and matched it with a plain brick-red tie; he wanted to look professional. While checking in the mirror to see if he looked like a serious reporter the question everyone insisted he ask was zipping around in his excited mind. "Mr. Elijah Cayenne, what did you mean when you said that you were usually invisible?"

The Journey
Hugo arrived early and as he drove through the small village of Flat Hill he had a good feeling in his heart; the sky was a dome of perfect blue, everywhere the trees and fields were a late-winter brown and tan, the bright but gentle daylight felt like the anticipated spring was near and the traffic had been unusually light. He turned right onto Sweet Faith Street and started looking for Mr. Cayenne's address. He stopped in front of one zero eight and saw a house built of roughhewed light gray stones, with a green metal roof. The lawn had been cut but the front gardens needed help. It was obvious the flower beds had not been planted in years. But there was neatness about the place; it was a clean messiness. The land surrounding the house on three sides was heavily forested with massive oak trees. Everywhere the bright sunshine shone but the house stood in shade. He had already seen the house on TV. Many reporters had been to the home hoping for an interview. He hadn't expected the embracing peace he felt when he saw the house. He felt like he was coming home from a long journey. Hugo drove down the drive and then eagerly walked to the front door. The door was open but the doorway was protected by an old wooden screened door painted dark blue. Nervously Hugo stood staring through the screened door only seeing darkness. He raised the gold colored metal knocker and slammed it down twice. No one came to the door so he was about to raise the doorknocker when he heard the tap of claws on the tiled floor. Hugo waited for the animal but the tap of claws sounded slower and slower. Then suddenly a large white dog was sitting on the other side of the screened door. Hugo squatted to be on the same level of the old dog. "Hey there old man." The old dog's eyes had the clouds of cataracts but his nostrils were sipping in information. Satisfied, the ancient canine slowly turned

and disappeared into the darkness. Two more times the doorknocker announced his arrival and still no one. Hugo turned the door handle and found that the screened door was not locked. He opened the door and stuck his head inside the house.

"Hello. Hello" His eyes penetrated the darkness and could see a very large room. A room for entertaining, decorated with formal antique furniture. Eighteenth century European manors would have had such rooms. He looked at his watch and saw that it was one fifty-nine. Hugo took a step into the large room and said,

"Hello, anybody home?" Silence, only the ticking of a distant clock as Hugo took another step into the tomb-like blackness. Smell was the only sense given a job. The antiseptic smell of alcohol with blast of iodine and ammonia halted his slow encroachment into the room. The smell jolted his mind and took his other senses off of alert. Then he felt her; he quickly turned and there she was, their faces only inches apart. Eyes wide, heart pounding, Hugo blurted, "You startled me."

"Sorry Mr. Hugo Richard, Patrick informed me that you had arrived. I wasn't expecting you to be so prompt. That definitely is a good sign."

Like a Caravaggio painting, the beauty stood before Hugo and the arresting vision create a soft light in the darken room. He could feel energy emanate from her, the atoms surrounding her were as excited as his galloping heart. Her lightly tanned skin glowed. She was willowy, almost frail, with sandy hair and haunted sapphire blue eyes. Her pinkish lips shaped into a friendly smile but her eyes were scanning, assessing.

"It's Ree Chard. Hugo Ree Chard, but you can just call me Hugo."

"Oh sorry, I didn't realize that you were French. I thought you were American. My name is Quinn."

"I am American; Quinn that's a very lovely name."

"Lovely! I always thought it was so very ordinary."

Hugo could see that the searching eyes had found the dampness above his lip; assessing the meaning of his anxiety. He cleared his throat to put a little steel to his voice, "I can't place your accent. Is it Eastern European?"

The beauty abruptly answered, "My accent is unplaceable." The blue eyes were uncomfortably penetrating but the smile was friendly, inviting and maybe a little flirtatious. Quinn turned to lead the way and said, "Follow me Hugo, Elijah is waiting."

Hugo followed the keeper of the door through the darkest of darkness. She wore a red and blue floral, loose kaftan dress which was sometimes cloaked in the darkness, but her bare feet were always visibly ploughing through the thick blackness. If she did disappear into the blackness Hugo knew he could follow Quinn's fragrance. Her perfume was a new scent for Hugo, zesty, sleek, cold, and clean. Yes, clean, an absolute pure sterile that somehow awoke the senses. Quinn kept a quick pace and Hugo followed. After walking for a few minutes Hugo said, "I didn't think the house was so large."

Quinn slowed her pace so that Hugo could walk alongside her, "Hugo nothing truly is as it seems. Am I correct?"

Hugo had not really heard the question; his mental picture was of him holding this beauty, kissing her pink lips and drinking in her exotic smell. "Yes, I guess." His foot hit something that was cloaked in blackness, he tripped and nearly fell. When Hugo looked up the shift from darkness to light was immediate. "Whoa." He had stumbled into a large cluttered kitchen illuminated by a shaded light filtering in through open windows and near the opposite door the old white dog was lying on a pile of rags.

"Patrick! Patrick you should be outdoors on this beautiful sunny day." It was more of a command than a suggestion, but the old dog continued to lie on his pile of rags, only his tail spoke. Hugo stooped to pet the dog and before his hand could touch Patrick, "Hugo! Stand up, you must focus. This meeting with Elijah is very important." The goddess beauty had left Quinn's face, she turned to walk through the door and Hugo could see a mask of concern. He stepped through the door into a room the size of a tennis court enclosed with walls and a ceiling of green tinted glass. These colored windows to the outside world were spotless, unsoiled, not a smudge. The room itself was chaos. In the left-hand corner on a greasy table was a partially assembled engine with stray parts scattered on the table and floor. Hugo scanned the room and as he slowly turned his vision from left to right, he saw a leather heavy bag hanging from metal bars, a number of dirty beat-up motorcycles, and a mound of dirt, bicycles and tools thrown together in a pile. Piles of junk and treasure were everywhere. In the right corner were file cabinets with drawers shut, half opened or fully opened jammed with paper or some prized nest egg. Then the enormous carved desk came into view. The desk top glistened like a wooden mirror reflecting its three occupants: a pen, paper and a bright dark blue red-rimmed coffee cup and saucer. Standing next to the desk was the Hero.

The Negotiation
The area around the desk was lit by a soft light from four six-foot tall ornate lamps with each shade a different pastel color. Quinn rushed ahead and stepped into the shaded light. She locked eyes with the Hero and the mask changed to delight; Quinn turned to Hugo and rattled, "Elijah, this is Mr. Hugo Ree Chard. He prefers the French pronunciation."

The Hero stepped into the shadows and extended his hand to Hugo. Hugo instantly recognized those eyes from the video, big puppy-dog eyes that were wide, brown and curious. The thick impenetrable wiry bramble of black hair was still savagely wild.

"It's nice to finally meet you Mr. Reechard."

Hugo shook the man's hand and said, "Yes, it is nice to meet you Mr. Cayenne. You can just call me Hugo."

"Quinn, please get Mr. Hugo and I a snifter of cognac so that we can soften the edges before negotiating. Please Hugo have a seat here on the davenport or in one of these comfortable chairs."

Hugo chose a huge padded chair, next to the desk, that was covered in torn, faded-red velvet. Elijah's tanned face smiled but his eyes were scanning, assessing Hugo. The Hero waited until Hugo was seated then chose a simple backless wooden chair with winged armrest. "Hugo, hopefully we will be working together so please just call me Elijah."

Quinn rushed in with the glasses of cognac. Quinn made eye contact when she handed a glass to Hugo. This beautiful woman was making him uncomfortable; he could feel her eyes reading his thoughts. He had yet to taste the cognac, but he felt a little tipsy from the four eyes voyeuristically dissecting him. He felt like a future meal.

"Hugo, your cognac."

When Quinn handed the glass to Elijah she said in a soft submissive voice, "We're having an early dinner. Maybe Hugo could join us for baked pecan-crusted trout."

His back regally erect, Elijah held the snifter in the palms of both hands and said to Hugo. "Yes, Hugo if all goes well you must try some of Quinn's epicurean miracles."

Surprised by the invitation Hugo blurted, "Uh! Oh yes. Yes. Thanks, I like fish."

Elijah lifted the snifter to his nose, closed his eyes and inhaled the flavored air. Hugo had never tasted cognac and was not sure if he should be a sipper or a guzzler. He watched and imitated Elijah.

"Hugo this brandy is from the best vineyards near the banks of the Charente River. It's not robust or floral. Enjoy the lightness, finesse, the woody flavor that embraces your taste buds and lingers."

Hugo moved his glass in a light circular motion to stir the aroma. His nose lingered in the glass enjoying the earthy scent. He sipped the amber hued cognac, held it in his mouth, swallowed, and then smiled, "I'm a lucky man. My first taste of cognac is of the best quality. Thank you, Elijah. I think I've become a cognac enthusiast." Hugo could see that Elijah was delighted with the compliment. For the next few minutes, they swirled, sniffed and sipped in silence.

Hugo was the first to break the silence. "So, what's this talk about negotiating an interview?"

Elijah slowly rose and then walked to the other side of the desk. The Host's face replaced the smile with a somber serious gaze. "Hugo, I appreciate that you dispensed with the frivolous formalities. You and your employers want something from me and I need, very much, something from you and your employer. A fair and honest contract should be advantageous for both parties to the bargain."

A tight smile formed on Hugo's face. His hunch was right; the negotiation was going to be a shake-down for money. Hugo thought, "Poor Elijah, he is going to be really disappointed. At least I had the opportunity to drink some really fine cognac. I wonder if the dinner invitation will be withdrawn."

Hugo cleared his throat, slowly turned his head side to side and in an apologetic tone said, "Elijah…. I'm sorry but the City Advocate's policy has always been to never pay money for interviews."

Elijah sat in his quilted mid night blue velour throne. His serious gaze turned into an amused stare.

"Hugo, I like you. I like a man who is direct. Honesty makes negotiating easier, more pleasant. Of course, we both know that men are rarely totally honest."

"Elijah, more cognac?"

The voice startled Hugo. He had not heard Quinn enter the room. He could see that Quinn's sudden appearance also surprised Elijah. Elijah's big eyes had gotten bigger but they continued to focus on Hugo.

"Thank you, Quinn, but the negotiations are just about to begin. We can't have any distractions at the moment."

Quinn's amiable demeanor disappeared and was replaced with a steely stare, her jaw clenched and her back straightened. In a voice devoid of her previous joy, Quinn growled, "Dinner will be served at four o'clock. Do not be late." She turned away from the desk, took a step and vanished.

Hugo stammered, "What the heck just happened? She just disappeared, vamoose."

Elijah's eyes never wavered; they continued to probe and to read Hugo's eyes, his posture, and his movements. "Quinn is unusual. She can be a distraction."

"A distraction? She evaporated. I've never witnessed such a magical exit."

"I don't want money. Hugo you have something more valuable. I have a story that must be told to as many people as possible. I need the whole world to know my story. If your paper prints my story; I will grant you an interview dealing with the incident at the Comedy Club. I will agree to any terms."

"Stop!" Hugo hands flew out as a barrier to Elijah's sudden terms. "Elijah, I was sent here to do an interview not negotiate for a storyline."

"You were sent here to negotiate for an interview. But an acquaintance of mine has already spoken to your Mr. Doucet. I just gave you my terms. I need a good writer. My acquaintance has recommended you. I need my story to be read by the world's population. It has to be legend so that even future generations will read and marvel at the story that you have crafted. Why you ask? Why is this story so important? Hugo, all the whys will be answered in my story. In a brief summary, I need someday for someone to tell my story to a certain person. If you say yes, then I need you to call your employer and tell him that I want the story and the interview told in four or five installments. Each installment will be given the top half of the third page of the Sunday edition. If an installment needs more print space, the story will continue on the top quarter or half of the page facing the opening page of the obituaries. Hugo, I sense something in you; I hope we can work together."

Hugo allowed his body to comfortably sink into the protection of the chair. His voice, wrinkled in confusion, murmured, "I knew today was going to be different. Do you mind if I walk in the garden when I call Mr. Doucet?"

The First Installment

It had been a strange week. When he had returned to work everyone had congratulated him for a good job getting the Hero to agree to an interview. Mr. Doucet had been eerily quiet. He agreed to all additional terms that Elijah had bluntly demanded. He seemed so subdued, like a scared hostage, that Hugo asked him if he was OK. Mr. Doucet had meekly responded, "Hugo, I've been awakened to something that I don't understand. But to answer your question; yes, I'm OK just a bit confused with a heavy melancholy. I'll be OK; I just need you to write your best. Make the people eagerly anticipate each week's Sunday paper. I need you to turn the story into a mania. It's an almost impossible job, but Mr. Cayenne's story is an ingenious plan for a virtually unachievable task. But I now believe in love again." Mr. Doucet's shoulders slouched a little more and he hung his head a notch lower, took a deep breath and quietly walked back to his office.

Hugo exited the Interstate onto Highway 24 that dead ended in the town of Flat Hill. He had spent the three-hour drive to Elijah's home recalling all the details of last week's encounter at one zero eight Sweet Faith Street. After Elijah made his demands, Hugo had walked into the walled courtyard to make a phone call to Mr. Doucet. While speaking with his boss he paced the length of the courtyard breathing in the gentle aroma of sweet olive and then when he strode to the other side of the courtyard he was met with the intoxicating essence of jasmine. He could still recall his confusion when Mr. Doucet quickly gave a yes to each demand in a voice with an odd timbre. When the phone call was over Hugo noticed that Patrick had been sitting in the courtyard watching, listening. When he had told Elijah, that Mr. Doucet had approved all terms he had felt faintly offended when Elijah had added more terms after the phone call. Hugo hadn't been given a chance to protest because after loudly insisting on the new demands Elijah's tone got much softer, almost a whisper, "It's almost four. We can't be late for dinner. Quinn can go to great lengths to express her anger."

The dinner had been a five-star meal. The trout had been painted with a seasoned egg wash with crushed pecans and then baked. The crispy fish sat on a bed of sweet caramelized onions. A bold but clean white wine prepared the tongue for each mouthful. A crunchy fresh salad was next, then warm baked bread torn into bite size pieces. The bread was used to soak up a bowl of savory seasoned stew. But his favorite had been the dessert; a soft moist cake covered in warm sweet custard.

The dinner conversation had been hilarious but strange. Quinn had been very chatty. She had directed her conversation toward Hugo only. When Elijah added to the conversation or made any comment Quinn had a quick reply, but directed the retort to Hugo with one eye flashing in Elijah's direction to see his reaction. The humor that eventually brought him to alcoholic giggles was Elijah's lack of reaction to the beautiful woman's caustic comments. He had been so focused on his meal enjoying each mouthful, letting his taste buds control his mind. He continually gave Quinn complements on the meal, telling her that God would definitely want her in his heavenly kitchen as she continued to hurl flirty adolescent insults. Quinn's beauty was addicting; her beauty gripped Hugo's vision and forced him to happily stare.

When Hugo turned onto Sweet Faith Street, he started to feel giddy, excited. He checked his watch and saw that he had arrived with plenty of time to spare. It was one forty-five; one of Elijah's demands had been that he arrived at one zero eight no later than two o'clock PM. every Monday. The other demand was that Hugo had to stay as long as Elijah had a story to tell.

When Hugo turned onto the driveway, he could see about a dozen deer on Elijah's front lawn. The deer stood so still they looked like lawn ornaments. When he got out of the car, he looked and the deer had ceased to exist. When he got to the blue screened door Patrick was waiting.

Hugo bent over to look at Patrick's blank stare. "Hey Patrick; hey boy whatcha doing?" Patrick sniffed the air, turned, walked a few feet into the darkness then returned to the screened door.

"Patrick, go get Quinn. Go tell her that I'm here at the door." Patrick backed his body into the darkness but his face was still in the sunlight. The big dog gave a whimper then an explosive bark. "Hey boy do you want me to follow you; do you want me to come inside?" Hugo opened the blue screened door and stepped inside. "Hello Quinn, Elijah; hello, is anybody home?" Patrick leaned his body into Hugo to force him to release his tentative stance and to enter the darkness. "OK Patrick, I guess you want me to follow you. You're going to be my guide today? Good boy!"

Patrick trotted into the darkness and Hugo followed. Within seconds Hugo could faintly hear a Bach Piano Concerto, and then suddenly he was passing through the cluttered kitchen tinted in shadowy sunlight. The journey to the green glass-enclosed room took less than ten seconds. When Quinn had been his guide the journey had taken at least five minutes. That thought was racing through his mind when he focused at the far end of the room and saw Elijah sitting in his quilted blue velour throne with a fire glowing in the fireplace behind him. Fireplace…. there had only been the quilted chair behind the desk.

"Hugo, I see Patrick welcomed you." Elijah sprang from his throne and took quick strides toward Hugo. The two men shook hands and then Elijah guided Hugo to the red chair that had been pulled close to the desk. "Quinn fixed us a small meal, and then we can work for a number of uninterrupted hours before dinner." Pointing to the torn chair Elijah muttered, "Sit here; we have folded crepes containing a thick spicy seafood etouffee and a glass of a cleansing rose'. We'll eat, then some coffee, then cognac and then get started. I'm excited to be working with you."

Hugo dropped into the huge padded faded-red velvet chair. The seat cushion rose to hold the sitter high, but the back cushion enveloped and protected the occupant. Hugo could feel his muscles loosen; the unexpected tightness disappeared. He was relaxed and hungry. He devoured the crepes and exclaimed a number of times, "This is, by far, the best crepes I have ever eaten. I need this recipe." When he had finished savoring the last bite of crepe, he heard Quinn wheeling in her kitchen cart. He glanced in her direction and saw her from the backside. She was wearing a long-sleeved, fitted, black knit dress with black stockings and black dress pumps. Something seemed odd. Hugo looked down at his plate and wished for more. He heard Quinn approach the desk and in a thickly accented command she barked, "Dishes please so that I can serve the coffee."

Hugo's eyes were transfixed on his plate, wine glass and dining tools when he saw two pale hands reach to pull them away. Keeping his eyes cast downward, protecting his vision from Quinn's glaring beauty he stuttered, "Quinn, may I have a glass of water before the coffee?"

In a blood-lusting growl Quinn snarled, "But of course, Mr. Ree Chaaaaard."

Stunned Hugo looked up and was frightened by what he saw. Quinn had his dinner knife in her fist and it was pointed at him. Her long blonde hair was now short and black, her face was powdered a smooth Geisha white and her lips squeezed together were painted blood red. But it was her bare unpowdered, unpainted eyes that were terrifying. They were red rimmed and the whites were mapped with red lighting. The watchful eyes were spying from behind a mask examining their prey.

Quinn turned and cast her gaze downward as she walked to her kitchen cart to get a red-rimmed blue cup and saucer and a beaten silver pot of coffee. Her gaze remained downcast as she placed the cup and saucer before Elijah and silently poured a cup of coffee. Elijah's face was a frozen rock with a blank stare. She returned and wheeled her cart closer to the desk. She wordlessly placed a cloth coaster on the desk and then a frosted glass that she had taken from her ice bucket. The only sound that prevented total silence came from the fireplace. Quinn slowly poured water into Hugo's glass; he ventured a peek and the eyes met his, ready to do battle. Hugo quickly looked away. Two pale hands placed a badly chipped yellow and blue cup and saucer, then a thicker cloth coaster and on top was placed the silver pot of coffee. Quinn stepped into the darkness and was gone.

In a hushed tone, Hugo lifted his pleading hands and said, "What just happened? What the hell did I do wrong?"

Elijah held his finger to his lips to quiet Hugo. He looked into the darkness and whispered, "Quinn is having a bad day. It's best to ignore her. Speak to her only if she asks a question. She'll be fine. Preparing dinner usually settles her emotions."

Hugo's confused thoughts became alert when Elijah said dinner. Would this psychopath serve a salad seasoned with arsenic? He had followed this woman through a tomb-like darkness. He was going to insist that only Patrick or Elijah could escort him through the house.

Elijah smiled, took a sip of his coffee and began to speak like nothing had just occurred; just a normal day in the Cayenne household. Elijah's speech had an old-world formality to it, elegantly demanding and commanding. He raised his hands and gracefully proceeded to explain exactly how the interview was to be conducted. "Hugo, I'm comfortable here, so I think I should stay in this chair. You look comfortable in that chair so you stay there." Elijah pulled a small piece of paper from his khaki colored, beat-up, corduroy jacket. "I've written a few notes as a reminder; I have so much I want to tell you, so much to tell the world. I see you brought a digital voice recorder."

Hugo had already placed the recorder in its docking station. He stood up and pushed the device toward Elijah. "When you're ready just push the silver button with the red arrow."

"I will start from the very beginning. Each week will be about the progression of my life. I see you have notes. I would prefer if you not ask prepared questions. If you need me to clarify anything, just ask. I will have much to say each week and I know a half page article is about twelve hundred words. I'm an amateur story teller and just an average writer; that's why I need you. I need you to captivate everyone. I'm sure you have questions why it's so important for me to tell my story and that will be told as the story progresses."

Hugo's vision recoiled from Elijah; he cautiously peered to the side of the desk. The maniac was back; she had silently arrived. Quinn retrieved the cognac from a small writing table near the fireplace. Wordlessly, she poured drink for both men, stepped into the darkness and melted away. Once again, he could hear a faraway melody; six piano notes slowly played over and over.

Elijah pushed the silver button with the red arrow, took a sip of cognac, and his left hand massaged his forehead. He sat in silence, took another sip of cognac, and when he removed his hand from his forehead his skin seemed brighter, less wrinkles, less stress lines; he looked younger. He wore a smile of melancholy and spoke cautiously, "I am not who I am."

I Am Not Who I Am

Hugo hadn't slept well. He was wrapped in a blanket sitting on his balcony waiting to greet the Morning Star. The events at the Cayenne house kept racing through his confused mind. He took a sip of his steaming coffee and the picture of Elijah, loss in thought, reliving his life was colored into his mind. Elijah had spoken for four hours only interrupting his narrative to wet his lips with cognac. Hugo had not asked one question; he just listened and took a few notes of events that he knew had to be in the story. He recognized instantly; the title of the piece had to be the first six words that Elijah had tentatively spoken. Hugo had been fascinated and pictured Elijah's adventures as they raced through his mind. He would have gladly sat for four more hours. Listening to Elijah made him eagerly want to hear more; but the dinner was a different story. Dinner was truffled scallops topped with crabmeat and caviar served with a sparkling wine. The meal was legendary. Hugo could not think of the right words to describe the wonderful feast. Dessert had been miniature bite-sized pecan pies with a glass of port. The dining room had been illuminated only by candlelight which made the mood feel primitive but intimate. The deeply scarred and stained wooden table was surrounded by a thick darkness that hid everything, even the doorway they had entered had been swallowed by the impenetrable gloom. He couldn't stop thinking of that very faint smell of fruity pipe tobacco; it was chilling, someone was watching. Elijah and Hugo concentrated on the excellent meal exchanging polite conversation and trying not to look in Quinn's direction. When Hugo had cautiously glanced at Quinn, he saw that the long blond hair was back and pinned into a messy pile on top of her head. Her beautiful face had been cleansed of all cosmetics and her breasts were barely concealed by a gauzy white blouse. She pushed her food around the plate, loudly sighed, and then looked off into the vacant distance recognizing visions that are seen only by the insane. She never spoke a word but her eyes were always searching, threatening, looking for a victim.

Hugo had told Mr. Ellington that he was going to stay home so that he could concentrate on his story. He wanted to listen to Elijah's adventure once more before he started putting any words to paper. He walked into the apartment and gathered his voice recorder, a tablet and pen. He placed everything on his kitchen table and got another cup of coffee. He stood next to the table, took a sip of coffee, stared at his recorder and then gently pushed the silver button with the red circle.

Elijah's voice was mellow, rich, pleasing to the ear and slightly accented. "I am not who I am. I was born in the year 1708 in the tiny, cold and hungry village of Beaubassin on the shores of Bassin Bay. This was French territory called L'Acadie but is now called Nova Scotia. By the time of my birth my father's family had been surviving on this land for almost a hundred years. The villagers of Beaubassin were descendants of peasants from the Old World; so hard work, hunger and danger were expected; it had always been part of their lives. They fed themselves by farming and hunting. My father, Jean Landry, was a fisherman. He fished for cod, salmon, shad and anything else he could catch. He cast his nets and lines in Bassin Bay, the Bay of Fundy and sometimes the Atlantic Ocean. He was forty-four and the widowed father of two adult sons when he met my mother on a trip to a coastal British colony to sell a cargo of dried fish. My mother Alice Bullock was sixteen years old and the daughter of a barely successful owner of a dry goods and feed store. The arrangement between my mother and father was not a bond of love but an agreement to satisfy each other's needs for survival. My father did not need another mouth to feed; so, I was an unwanted surprise. When my mother was a little girl, she had heard Homer's epic tale *The Odyssey* and never forgot the story of adventure and enduring love. She preferred Odysseus's Latin name of Ulysses; that's how I came to be called Ulysses Landry. My father, a busy and hardworking man, was unconcerned about my existence until I was about thirteen; when he deemed me capable of working on his fishing vessel, the Madonna. I hated working on that cramped, stinking boat and wearing, for days, salt crusted clothing. I hated the ocean or any body of water that made land invisible. The ocean was a watchful creature, surrounding, waiting, always ready to swallow the unwary. At night the creature turned black, slapping and rocking the boat. When the beast was angry it tossed the fishing vessel into the air and wildly crawled over the deck. I knew that I would never be a fisherman. When I told my father about my fear of the watery monster and pleaded with him to allow me to work with the village farmers draining marsh and building dikes, I experienced my first encounter with invisibility.

I had two friends my age: Plum Boudreaux and Amen Aysenne. Plum's father had married a woman from the Micmac tribe. He was as dark as a plum and so the description became a name. Amen was more of a mystery and his birth had provided the village with years of gossip and rumor. The story that was told most often began with a cold snowy night. An old man knocked on the door of Henry and Camille Aysenne's cabin seeking help. He helped a woman out of his horse drawn carriage into the Aysenne's home. The mystery woman was in the last stages of giving birth. Camille and other women from the village helped comfort the woman and gave assistance with the delivery. When the healthy baby boy had experienced his first independent breath, his mother, the Mystery Woman, stood up, look at her new born and said, "Amen!" She never touched the child; she put on her coat, walked out the door, climbed into the carriage and disappeared into the snowy night. Did the woman name the child Amen or was she just giving thanks that her ordeal was over? Henry and Camille were childless and they gave thanks for their son, Amen. Thus, began years of rumors and gossip. My two friends were my brothers; we worked and worked together; then rested and dreamed together."

Hugo looked at Elijah when the monologue had paused.

The man was deep in contemplation; he slowly raised the snifter to wet his lips. Hugo was surprised that he hadn't before noticed the gray hairs at Elijah's temples. Elijah turned to look at Hugo and said, "All that I have said is of no consequence as far as the story I want told. I thought that maybe you might need a little history to understand. The story I need told begins now. Do you need anything? Should I call Quinn to get you more drink?"

Hugo could hear his indistinct gruff voice coming from the voice recorder, "I'm fine, I had wandered into your story." Hugo pushed the pause button and started writing notes; he knew he had to include some of Elijah's early history to capture the readers. After jotting down his notes, he laid the pen to the side, sat back and chuckled to himself. Hugo liked Elijah but he couldn't understand his motive for such an outlandish and bizarre story. He knew that for now his job was, not to understand, but to convince readers that the main character of the story was a three-hundred-year-old man.

Hugo occasionally smoked a cigarette. Sometimes he'd have a smoke while having a few beers with friends. He also enjoyed having a cigarette when he was deep in thought. When there was a conflict being battled in his mind, the rush of nicotine had a calming effect. Hugo took a sip of coffee, lit a cigarette and inhaled deeply. When he exhaled, he reached across the table and pushed the silver button with the red circle.

"My Uncle Rene gave me the opportunity to live a different life. He set me free; he helped me unlock the shackles of village life. He was my father's younger brother. The young man disliked the brutal life of a fisherman and he couldn't accept the slavery of being chained to the needs of a farm. My uncle became a trapper for furs. At first, he only trapped and sold his prepared furs to French companies who then sold the furs to European clothing manufactures. Eventually the French companies became a monopoly and dictated prices and would confiscate any furs if a trapper negotiated with the English. Rene had two options: remain a lowly paid trapper or be a servant for the Company.

The Company supplied Rene with New World merchandise that had become a need, an addiction for the Indians. Warm blankets, metal axes, sturdy clothes, iron pots, and junk were traded for beaver, moose, mink, and bear furs. At the beginning of each month, Rene was in charge of three canoes loaded with trade merchandise and he returned weeks later with three canoes loaded with furs. Rene made much more money than the average trapper; but he envied the wealth that the Company owners were accumulating. The most Rene could do was to fantasize about having the wealth of the Company owners until one Sunday, after church, he met Jean Phillippe.

Jean Phillippe was a schemer, a man that was always making a financial plan. Jean Phillippe and my Uncle formed a company. Mr. Phillippe would provide the merchandise and Rene would provide the expertise and the man power. The Plan was simple. Rene and his hired workman would build two large flat boats on the banks of the Ohio River and load them with merchandise provided by Mr. Phillippe. They would float down the Ohio and then down the Mississippi River stopping at each village to barter for furs. They would build more flat boards when needed and when they reached their destination, Nouvelle Orleans, Mr. Phillippe would have English merchant ships waiting to buy the furs. The English companies were paying a much higher price than the French. The profits would be split evenly between Jean and Rene.

Amen, Plum, myself and three other men were the workman my Uncle hired to work on the flat boats. My brothers and I were so excited. We were barely fifteen years of age and embarking on a great adventure. We knew this journey was going to change our lives and, hopefully, put some money in our pockets. I've often wondered if we'd known, in advance, how much this expedition was going to change our lives; would we have cautiously stayed tied to our life of hard work and tenuous security.

The journey from our village to the Ohio River was an arduous epic undertaking. It took us almost six months to get to our destination. We experienced many hardships, trials of endurance and a few near-death experiences. Before we got to the Ohio River, everyone in our band of adventurers had doubts about Uncle Rene's plan.

"Soon after we arrived on the Ohio, we built the flat boats, loaded each primitive vessel with the merchandise provided by Mr. Phillippe and began our Odyssey. We hadn't anticipated the difficulty of steering flat boats. The Plan had been to stop at villages along the Ohio and Mississippi Rivers. Being novice boatmen, the struggle to stop two flat boats on a river with a current became a terrifying dilemma. Because of our deficient navigational skills, we would choose an area where the river bank was low to tie up the boats and build a camp. This became our market for the Indians from the different villages to come and barter. We couldn't stop at all the villages, so we let the natives come to us. By the time we got to the Mississippi River one flat boat's cargo of furs was at capacity and we soon had to build a third boat."

"Then the fateful day; the early morning light was innocently new and soothing; the light breeze was cool and calming. It was early November and we were less than a week away from Nouvelle Orleans. We had made camp at a major fork in the Mississippi River. This was the day that the four flat boats loaded with furs were to leave for their rendezvous with the British ships. Plum and the other three boatmen plus four Indians that we had hired were to keep the boats close to the river's edge and begin the final part of our journey. Uncle Rene, Amen and I were going to take one of the canoes down the opposite leg of the fork. Many of the elders from the tribes that came to barter kept telling a similar story. They all said that when we reached a fork in the River; we had a destiny decision to make. If we took the fork that coursed southeasterly, we would reach our destination in a few days. If we took the more westerly fork that flowed straight south, we would either: die, become slaves or return as an unusual man and wealthy."

"Wealth, a poor man's dream of an elusive drink and once tasted never slakes the unquenchable thirst. We would have made more money than we'd ever seen in our lives if we had just safely brought the furs to Mr. Phillippe. But the stories of wealth intrigued us. Uncle, brother and me in a canoe looking for that elusive drink. We were to travel down the westerly fork for two days and if we didn't find golden mountains we would return to the flat boats. When I reminisce, I can still see Plum's dark lips smiling, his hair burning bright in the rising sun. If I'd known that I would never see him again my handshake would have never let my brother go. When we pushed the flat boats away from the river bank, Plum gave one last wave and shouted, 'Good Luck! Come back and make me wealthy. I want to be a king.' My brother was a king."

"The first day was uneventful, except for the two times we startled massive flocks of ducks, creating a pounding explosion of thousands of frightened fowl. In many areas the westerly fork was not confined by river banks. Sometimes the waterway flowed through groves of trees, then turned into a small lake and then back into a confusing tangle of large streams. It was difficult to know if we were in the main channel of the river. The one constant was the fast-moving current. The River was in a hurry to reach its destination."

"Before dawn of the second day, Uncle Rene had decided we should head back upstream because the current was picking up momentum. There had been a four-foot-thick blanket of misty, smelly fog covering all land and water that crept in soon after we had set out for the return trip. Rene had to stand in the canoe above the blanket of fog to direct our paddling and the tone of his voice betrayed concern.

We would furiously paddle to a tree, grab hold, rest, and then repeat the exhausting routine. Whenever our grip on a tree faltered the river would carry the canoe further downstream. The fog was moving as fast as the River and in the same direction. The faint hum that we had been hearing days before entering the westerly fork was now a faraway roar; quickly getting louder. We all started panicking and yelling. Rene, Amen and I knew that the roar and the fast current meant that we were in the grip of a waterfall."

"We wedged the canoe against a small stand of trees. That ingenuity proved disastrous because the force of the current broke the canoe in half. We clung to a tree but the young sapling couldn't handle the extra weight. The current ripped the young tree from the soil. We clung to the tree as the current sent us rifling to our destiny. The churning current slammed us into some rocks then it swelled up and pushed us downward. When my head broke the surface, I was gasping for air and looking for Uncle Rene and Amen. They were gone; I was going to face death alone."

"I struggled to straddle the tree so that I could ride it like a horse. My legs wrapped tightly around the tree trunk. I held on to branches for balance and rode high out of the water. When I looked ahead to see my fate, I saw the black monster. I was being carried to an enormous vortex of rotating darkness. The spiraling, swirling disc of gloom was so large it blocked most of the sky. The roar was the water and land falling into the gaping vertical hole. The closer I got to the black hole the faster the river carried me to my death. Fear had paralyzed me. I could barely breath, my mind was in total panic and I kept mumbling the same words, 'Please God, Please God.' When I was sucked into the monster I fell into blackness. I didn't see water or broken trees or Uncle Rene or Amen. My fall started picking up velocity until I was traveling as fast as a bullet. I struggled to tuck my chin closer to my chest so that the ferocious air current didn't force my mouth open. The typhoon of wind ripped my clothes from my body, hair was torn from my head and it felt like my skin was tearing. The blast of air was suffocating and the lack of air in my lungs caused me to lose consciousness. Before my mind went blank, I was wishing for death to come quickly."

There was silence coming from the voice recorder; then Elijah barked, "Let's eat! Hugo are you hungry? *Mangeons*!"

The Second Installment
Hugo was driving to Flat Hill to meet with Elijah for his weekly Monday midafternoon meeting. This Monday was like the previous Mondays, sunny, cool, and unusually light traffic on the Interstate. Interstate One Eleven was notorious for bumper to bumper slow moving traffic. Hugo made a mental note to remember to travel the usually traffic-clogged highway only on Mondays after lunch. He was

excited to be seeing Elijah again, but there were so many conflicting emotions colliding in his mind. The day had started in a panic. His usual routine of meditation while the morning sun embraced him was shattered when he awoke hours later than usual. He ate and dressed at a frantic pace because he couldn't be late for his nine o'clock meeting with Mr. Doucet and Mr. Ellington. It had been a wild and frenzied dash to arrive at work on time, but the meeting had been all positive. The City Advocate's Captains were extremely pleased with the article he had written for the Sunday paper. They had both gotten an abundance of praise from readers and all were eagerly awaiting next Sunday's edition. Many in the newsroom told him they enjoyed his piece and Ms. Simpson had told him that their sister papers in Tittleburgh and Port Thunder had asked permission to add the article to their Wednesday evening edition and then to follow the story each Sunday. He had been proud of the piece when he'd turned it in for the Sunday deadline. Hugo was excited by all the praise but he still had an itch in his brain. Why had he failed to greet his morning friend? He'd always felt that his writing abilities, his storytelling were at their best when he stayed on his routine. He could feel a subtle change in his life: contentment edged with excitement or was it eagerness for success blended with confidence or was it just the realization that all routines eventually must be altered. He couldn't stop smiling. He was happy and felt inpatient to continue the story.

    He had stayed too long standing in the glow of bravos and now he was going to be late for his encounter at one zero eight Sweet Faith Street. When Hugo turned onto Highway Twenty-Four, he slowed to the speed limit and admired the rolling hills that bordered the highway. Most of the hills were covered in tall swaying golden grass, some hills were thickly forested and a few were bare rock. The rural scenery was majestic and isolated. Whenever Hugo drove down Highway Twenty-Four, he had a weird sensation that he was traveling on the edge of another world.

When he had reached his destination and turned onto the driveway, he could see Quinn and Patrick waiting in the doorway. Hugo's demeanor quickly changed from cheerful to wary and alert. He was only fifteen minutes late, but was now worried his tardiness might cause a problem. He had asked Elijah if he would greet him at the door so that he would not have to risk a deadly encounter with Quinn in the shadows. Elijah insisted that everything would be O.K. and he would make sure that Patrick was there to protect him. He was now recalling Elijah's solemn expression and his words.

"Hugo, you will always be safe in my home; but we can't offend Quinn and we definitely don't want to make her angry."

Hugo quickly threw the gear lever into park and grabbed his satchel containing his pens, tablets, recording devices and camera. He practically ran up the walkway keeping his eyes on his potential assassin. "Sorry I'm a little late; the traffic was a little heavier than usual."

"*Bonjour mes ami.* You are usually so punctual. Patrick and I were a little concerned."

Hugo's fear evaporated. He was always mesmerized by Quinn's bewitching beauty. She seemed so graceful, aristocratic and he usually acted like a mumbling high school sophomore. Dressed in a sleeveless shimmering silk black dress, Quinn looked like a red-carpet celebrity. Her sandy blonde hair looked windblown messy and Hugo thought it was wonderful. But it was the radiance of her sapphire eyes that paralyzed him. The beautiful hostess handed Hugo a frosted glass.

"I thought you might want some iced tea after your long journey."

"Oh, yes! Thanks!" Hugo took a sip of tea, smiled and stammered, "I love sweet tea. This is really good. Thanks, I appreciate the kind thought."

Quinn took a step and entered his space. Her head tilted a little to the right and her gaze softened as she looked into Hugo's eyes. Hugo was excited, his smile was wrapped around his face, but he was speechless.

"Hugo, Elijah has told me that I have made you uncomfortable. I want to extend my apologies to you. I know sometimes I behave badly. But Hugo, I want you to feel relaxed, to enjoy your visits. I've noticed that for the first time you are not wearing a coat and tie. I hope that is a sign that you are beginning to feel comfortable around me and Elijah."

Hugo nervously sipped his tea, and whispered, "I'm always excited when I come here. I'm always happy when I see you." He took in a deep breath and again in a whisper he said, "Can I ask you what is that unusual fragrance that you are wearing. My mind keeps saying zesty and clean, sterile and cold like a Nordic glacier."

"But of course, Hugo. You can ask me anything. I never wear perfume. Elijah is probably concerned that you are late. We should make our way to him."

The seductress slipped her arm around Hugo's arm and guided him down a long dimly lit hallway lined with flickering candles. Hugo could feel Patrick, his protector, brushing against his leg as they entered the hallway that stretched beyond sight. Quinn's lips were near Hugo's cheek when her soft confident voice tickled his ear. "Patrick told me you didn't like the dark. I hope you don't mind me giving some advice. You must seize, embrace, and live every moment. If you think rationally, fear and dread and even depression can be welcomed and adapted."

Hugo was deaf to advice. He could only concentrate on the breast that was massaging his arm as he was being led down the hall with no end in sight. Every time Quinn spoke, she would lean into Hugo, pull his arm to her breast and caressed his neck with her warm, tangy apple scented breath. He was wishing that he had not worn jeans because his erection was becoming uncomfortable in the tight pants.

"O.K., this is where we take the short cut to the kitchen."

Hugo looked to his left and saw a floor to ceiling framed painting of inky blackness.

Quinn released Hugo's arm and stood in front of him only inches away. He could smell her sweet voice before he heard its sultry tone. "I didn't have enough candles to carve a tunnel of light through this chamber. Don't be frightened; I'll lead the way; you hold onto my waist." Quinn turned her back to Hugo and grabbed one of his hands and placed it on her waist. "Hold me Hugo." The captain of the expedition took a step into the ebony painting and disappeared. Hugo couldn't see his hands that were gripping her waist. He could feel Quinn's hands holding his hands to her waist and when she took another step, he disappeared into the blackness. They moved quickly and in silence. They were traveling through a thick darkness that was void of any features. Hugo couldn't see or hear anything. He could feel Quinn's waist and her hands gently massaging the tops of his hands. Her fragrance was like a narcotic. His nostrils were inhaling her drug; but there was also, a slight and intrusive smell of fruity pipe tobacco. The expedition took a few seconds. He stumbled out of darkness into the large familiar kitchen lit by natural light shining through open windows. At the far end of the kitchen was his protector, Patrick, lying on his bed of rags.

"Patrick, what are you doing here? Some protector; you're here sleeping on the job."

Quinn swirled into view and aggressively poked Hugo's chest with a dagger finger. Her eyes were closed into sultry slits, her lips in a tight smile. In a sensual snarl she growled, "Patrick knows I will always protect you. He knows that when you are with me, you will be protected like a mother protects her baby, like a lover protects her dream, like a poor man protects his gold coin. Besides, Patrick is old; he likes to conserve his energy for his nightly adventures."

Hugo's smile was comically large. His emotions were surging and he didn't know if he wanted to cry tears of happy relief or scream with joy. The day's root had been confusing, but it had steadily grown into a fascinating blossom. He was speaking to the most beautiful woman that he had ever known and she had just declared her intentions to protect him. He wanted to kiss Quinn.

Quinn grabbed Hugo's arm and in a halting voice tight with tension she murmured, "Come Hugo, Elijah is waiting."

Their arms tightly linked, Hugo and Quinn entered the green glass-enclosed room. The room was packed with more junk and near the desk were potted lemon trees brought inside for protection against any frost. He hadn't remembered the fireplace being that huge. Last week there had been a small fire with very little heat. Today there was six-foot flames' dancing in a fireplace large enough to park a car between its stones and next to it was a mountain of firewood. The room felt cozy warm. In front of the fireplace was Elijah hunched over the great desk reading a newspaper. He looked thinner, grayer, older.

When the happy couple approached the huge carved desk, Quinn savagely shouted, "Elijah!" The sudden vicious scream froze Hugo. He saw a blur of flesh and then felt the whack to the side of his face. Quinn had slapped his face hard enough to bat saliva from his mouth.

Pointing an accusatory finger at Hugo, Quinn angrily roared, "Elijah! Your noble newspaperman did not pet, grope, tease or even attempt a kiss." She turned to face Hugo. Venom dripped from her words. "Do you think I'm a pig? Maybe you think I'm Elijah's cheap whore. Forgive me for being bruised by your mockery. Elijah, please excuse this dejected woman, I must take leave to calm my emotions." Quinn turned her back to Elijah and faced Hugo. She gave Hugo a smile that was holding back laughter, a wink and her lips curled into a kiss. Hugo was a statue listening to the click of her heels as she slowly disappeared.

Before he could fully awaken from his concussion, Hugo felt Elijah's arms embrace him in a hug. "Hugo, my friend, I was speechless the first time I read the story. Your ability with words is extraordinary. The story began as an Alexandre Dumas novel and ended as a Jules Verne fantasy."

Hugo struggled out of the embrace and looked quizzically at Elijah. "What just happened?" He pleaded, "Tell me Elijah. Who is Quinn? Does she just work for you; is she your lover? Is she insane? Has she ever maimed anyone? Has she ever been confined in an institution?"

The laugh began as a giggle; but the joyous humor couldn't be adequately released with a tiny chuckle. Elijah looked at Hugo's two-toned face and when he inspected the hue of the beaten side the laughter roared forcing Elijah to sit on the desk and hold his stomach.

"Oh, this is funny? This is how guest are typically treated in the Cayenne home." Like an exhausted man Hugo dropped his body into the padded red velvet chair and smiled. "Damn that woman is crazy."

Elijah's laughter dwindled to a big grin. "Quinn is a good woman, but different. She's part of the story and I will explain Quinn, if I can, when she first appears. We need to have a drink to celebrate a task well done. Do you drink whiskey?"

Hugo's consciousness was cluttered with images of Quinn when he thoughtlessly answered, "Yes."

Elijah hadn't waited for an answer; he had already placed two small rock glasses on the glistening desktop. "I have a nice blended scotch. Many scotch drinkers prefer single malt; but I favor a blended whiskey. This whisky is from a small family enterprise called Eden Distillers; its smooth, nice flavor, just a hint of smoke." Elijah poured whiskey into each glass. He raised his glass and said, "Hugo, to a job well done. If each installment is as good as the first; the world will know my story."

They both took a sip of whiskey. Hugo held the whiskey in his mouth for a moment before swallowing. "Oh yes, this is good scotch."

Elijah poured more scotch into each glass and before Hugo could take another drink of the fine scotch, he heard soft delicate footsteps approaching. He turned toward the kitchen and saw Quinn carrying a tray. Gone was the black dress, heels and jewelry. Her feet were bare; she wore baggy stained white shorts; a large faded maroon jersey turtleneck and it was obvious that she was not wearing a bra. Hugo's heart started to beat faster, his heart didn't feel normal, his breathing was rapid and shallow and, as usual, he was speechless.

"Elijah, I cut some smoked cheddar and blue cheese to enjoy with the scotch. Hugo, after you eat some blue cheese, hold the scotch in your mouth for a moment before you swallow the whiskey. The cheese and scotch are perfect companions."

Hugo was able to mutter, "I don't…. blue cheese….no, maybe the smoked cheddar."

Quinn gave Hugo a motherly smile and tenderly said, "Hugo never pass up an opportunity to try something new. Live your life like you write, boldly. Elijah and I only want the best for you." She turned to face Elijah and grumbled, "Because our guest was late, dinner will be served at eight unless you think you will need more time. You look tired. Would you rather do this work on another day?"

Elijah was smiling. He looked happy but exhausted. He slowly walked to the other side of the desk and eased himself into his blue velour throne. "I'm fine, my dear Quinn. Thank you for your concern."

Hugo turned his gazed from Elijah to Quinn and she was gone. She had disappeared. He shook his head thinking that every time he was near Quinn, she did something that was shocking.

"Are you OK Elijah? I can come back tomorrow."

"I'm feeling fine. I'm feeling happy and very satisfied with the work you have done for me. I've fought the Battle of Life for centuries but now my body is beginning to lose some skirmishes."

Hugo pulled from his satchel the voice recorder, set it into its docking stand and moved it across the desk closer to Elijah. He put his phone in a small book cradle facing Elijah but near his side of the desk. He placed his notes, notepad and pen to the left and his glass of scotch to the right.

"Hugo, why the phone?"

Hugo lifted the phone from its nest and said, "This little beauty can do so many things. It records and the play back has superb clarity. But I'm not sure if it can record for hours. I'm just experimenting today. Technology is still a mystery." He picked up a piece of blue cheese and laughed. "I'll sit here and try to enjoy blue cheese and sip on this wonderful scotch. Whenever you are ready, you know what button to press."

Elijah pushed the silver button with the red arrow, closed his eyes and rested his head on the back of his throne. He was still smiling, but his face looked tired and sad.

"When I fell into the black whirlpool, I thought I was going to die. Hope quickly perished. I gathered speed as I fell. I was falling faster than any bird had ever flown. The rush of air ripped my clothes from my body, tore hair from my head and patches of skin were peeled away exposing muscle. The pain was unbearable and mercifully I lost consciousness. I remember looking into caves and seeing human remains. Bleeding crushed arms, heads with smashed faces, legs torn and twisted, blood and guts piled in these macabre caverns of gore. It seemed so real. I hoped it was just a dream. The first conscious moment I can remember was one of pain. I attempted to open my eyes. My eyes felt raw and burnt. I could only see a blurry light and then a shadow. I'm not sure how many days I laid there senseless and paralyzed. My next recollection was a pale icy blue sky with tiny yellow fractures that meandered, partially encircling the periphery. A few of the yellow fractures snaked a trail to a large black hole in the sky. Sometimes that black hole was near and large and there were times when the hole was small and far away. My body was immobile, my mind was still in a dormant state; my whole world was watching a black hole come near and then fade into fuzzy confusion. It would be weeks, maybe months, before I realized that the black hole was the pupil of the eye of the woman that I was blessed to meet, to know, to love and it was because of this love I made some horrible mistakes. I lived in an illusion. I've done dreadful things to have the opportunity to possess this woman and her love for all eternity."

There was silence so Hugo looked across the desk and saw Elijah's head still resting on the back of his throne, his eyes were closed, but the smile was gone. His lips were tightly pressed together holding back the words. He was thinking, reminiscing, regretting.

Haltingly Elijah spoke softly, "When my consciousness awakened, it was sudden. My mind switched on and the current of life started pulsing in my head. My first thought was to question why I had taken so long to allow the spark to arouse my senses, my spirit; it had been so easy."

"The very moment my thoughts shifted from dark confusion to rational thought, I was being fed soup. At first, I thought it was my mother feeding me spoonfuls of watery broth. I strained my eyes to get a better view of my feeder and was astonished, then stunned and finally elated. I was dead and in heaven. Sitting before me was an angel. My thoughts became confused; I felt a heaviness and sleep protected me."

"Day after day I laid on a soft bed and in my moments of consciousness, I stared transfixed at beauty. The brightness, the shine of her short golden curly hair gave me hope. Her creamy complexion kindled desire and her big wide-set pale blue eyes brought me happiness. When the light shone on her elegant neck, I felt the need for touch. The angel spoke often; but her words sounded metallic, vibrating, confusing. It was weeks before my awakened, but exhausted brain, could deal with communication. My first attempts to speak were just grunts, then simple words and eventually sentences that matched my thoughts."

"The angel spoke my language and quickly dispelled my theory of heaven. I couldn't pronounce her name; she said it was really a number. I started calling her Fleur. I'm not sure what kind of flower. I had only seen nameless wildflowers. In my young inexperienced and confused mind; I could only equate beauty with a flower. I truly had never seen female beauty. All the women I'd known had been attacked by the ravages of a life struggling to survive. Fleur was a heavenly apparition. The two words that best described her were radiant and magnetic. She always wore pale-tinted gossamer slips. The cloth of her daily attire was cool to the touch, smooth and silky and excitingly scarce in size. I was nearly sixteen years old and had never seen a woman's naked body. The stronger I grew in my recovery the more my eyes wolfishly gorged on her flesh. My eyes explored and I fantasized.

Hugo looked up when he heard the voice recorder click off. Elijah was shuffling along the edge of the desk carrying the bottle of scotch. "More scotch Hugo?" He didn't wait for Hugo to respond; he poured about a dram of scotch into the newspaper reporter's glass.

Elijah perched on the edge of the desk; a wistful boyish grin shaped his lips as he took a sip of whiskey from his glass.

"Hugo, you know about lust. My Angel, my Flower taught me about sex, about lust. We practiced often. I was uncontrollably single-minded in my pursuit of pleasure, but later mastered the ability to make two become one. She taught me to be aware, conscious of each brief moment of orgasmic bliss. That fleeting release of pure youthful ecstasy is a reward for successful completion of the act of reproduction. Who created this addictive need? Some people say that this supreme bliss is a small sample of heaven. If heaven is eternal ecstasy, I would truly miss life."

Elijah slowly walked back to his blue cloth throne. Hugo checked to see if his phone was still recording. He watched the old Hero sit with a thud, take a deep breath and slowly aim his finger to push the silver button with the red arrow.

"Elijah! Before you get started again; one question please. Why did you change your name?"

"When everyone around you ages thirty or forty years and you are wearing your years very, very well, questions are asked. I had an answer that I could not give; so, I found it easier to eventually disappear. I would start a new life in another part of the world, a new identity, a new family and friends, a new occupation and of course a new name. I went from a Ulysses to a Jacques to a Saul. Just recently I was a Wayne and now I'm Elijah. I have notes to give you tonight that might answer some of your questions."

Hugo took a tiny sip of his scotch and blurted, "You may not have aged much in the past, but now, you are aging right before my eyes."

Elijah's shaky finger pushed the silver button with the red arrow.

"Yes, I am aging and that will be explained, but I want to continue talking about Fleur. She was always interested in my past, my feelings, and my thoughts. She made me explore questions I'd never considered. During these conversations the bloom of love blossomed into spectacular happiness. Each day was as good as or better than the day before."

"We resided in a windowless abode. The living quarters were luxurious in comparison to what I had always known. At certain times of the day a wall would disappear into the floor revealing a dining table laden with a large variety of delicious foods. There were two doors. One door was unlocked only when Fleur was summoned; the other door opened to an extensive walled garden. It was a garden created for a king: tinkling water fountains, colorful flowers, scented tree blossoms, low hanging ripe fruit, insect free and there was always soft morning sunlight. This is where I fell in love with Fleur. This is where I began a pathless journey that is now very near the end. I never reached my ultimate destination. It's taken me a few hundred years to realize that I should never have embarked on this quest."

"When I asked Fleur about her world and how I had become part of it; she became the patient teacher answering all of my questions. I couldn't understand her native tongue. When she spoke her language, it sounded like a spoon hitting the side of a drinking glass. It was a series of sharp ringing sounds. Sometimes her speech was a dull clang or a steady clatter that exploded into an ear bruising shriek. When she spoke, you could feel the vibrations. Fleur became alien, unknown, when she spoke her language. I always felt uncomfortable when she voiced those dreadful sounds. Because of my inability to understand the simplest word in her form of communication, she used earthly words to describe her world. She became my Scheherazade, as we sat in the garden and she told me a thousand and more stories."

"She said that her world was called The Kingdom. Fleur said that her people were an ancient species. Many times, they had built great civilizations that ultimately failed. Each failure was so complete that her people had to relearn lost knowledge. After many catastrophic collapses of enlightenment, her species began meticulously gathering and storing the Collected Knowledge. Total destruction of a civilization could not destroy the accumulated knowledge of past generations; all that would be necessary for survivors to access this Collected Knowledge was to possess the Key. After the last collapse of their civilization, survivors knew about the Collected Knowledge, but had lost the Key to the Adversary."

"The Kingdom was divided into three Nations. Two of the Nations were populated with Fleur's people and the third Nation was a forbidden and alien land separated from the rest of the kingdom by a wide swift moving river. After the last collapse of civilization, many believed that chaos was bred by unbridled ambition that caused envy and ultimately, violence. These people, who were the majority, believed absolute conformity was the only path that would lead to permanent peace and prosperity. They believed that all should be the same in body, mind and spirit. Everyone should follow the same laws and live by the same habits. Every child was born with the same hair, eye and skin color. Religions were eliminated; they were to worship and care for each other. Their thirst for knowledge was their occupation. They called their home the Nation of Light. These seekers of peace and knowledge were called the Traditionalists and they lived in a confederation with the other nation settled by Fleur's caste."

"Fleur always smiled when she spoke with pride about her people. She called her nation the Land of Struggle. Her tribe was a minority in the Kingdom. Her ancestors had decided thousands of years ago that free-will would rule in their world. She called her caste the Dreamers. They knew that the absence of conformity could and probably would lead some of their brothers and sisters to envy, prejudice and malice. They also believed that a life that overcomes obstacles is a stronger spirit. Someone that struggles through the seasons of life has lived and not just existed. Some in her tribe were farmers, others worked in small factories producing products and food to trade with their brothers, the Traditionalist.

Fleur's family had always worked with the Portals. The black whirlpool that I had fallen into was a portal or corridor of travel that had been created by an ancient and forgotten civilization. The Portals had been a means of intergalactic travel. The ability to control the Portals was lost a few millenniums ago. They were meant to be traveled in vessels, not as free-falling flesh, as I had experienced the Portal. These nearly invisible hollow tubes of energy devoured land and creatures from our planet and then whipped away to another planet only to return to Earth one hundred or two hundred or five hundred years later. The Portals emptied into the Dreamer's part of the Kingdom. They consistently disgorged ordinary rock and soil that had to be hauled away from their farms. Sometimes toxic materials were ejected and Fleur's extended family was in charge of keeping their Nation safe from the Portal's debris. There was always excitement when the Portals spewed water, shattered trees, rocks and torn flesh from Earth. Occasionally a reluctant, badly battered, but living traveler would be hurled out of the Portal. The women of Fleur's family nursed these lucky survivors back to health. These survivors were encouraged to breed amongst themselves and to birth many children for the Kingdom. When generations of the survivors had multiplied into a small army they were sent on a mission for the Kingdom. Unfortunately, I had arrived when a decision had been made to send most of the survivors and their descendants on the Kingdom's mission; and I was to be included."

The fierce dancing flames had lent a wonderful nostalgic glow to the junk filled room. But now the flames were beginning to wilt and the shadows were growing and getting darker, the cold temperatures had easily invaded the glass enclosed room as the heat retreated. Hugo reached into his coat pocket to retrieve a glove and cleared his throat for attention.

"Elijah! I'm sorry to break your train of thought but can I put some wood on the fire to get the room toasty once again."

"Hugo, are you cold? You poor baby. I'll get you a heavy blanket." Startled, Hugo quickly looked to his right and there was Quinn standing next to the desk with a sarcastic smile for Hugo. She was dressed in a moonlight white satin gown buttoned to the neck with large carved ivory white buttons. The candle she was holding cast a warm glow on her face. Her normally sandy blonde hair looked as white as her gown and for a second, he could smell a whiff of sweet fruity pipe tobacco.

"Did you dye your hair white?"

With an audible gasp Quinn feigned surprise. "Hugo, are you so uncivilized that you would interrogate a woman on how she decorates herself. It's for you to behold, to study, to admire and maybe dream. Elijah would you like me to bring you a blanket? Do you have ultra-tender skin like Hugo? You've thrown enough wood into the fireplace, come…. sit. I have an appetizer for you and the brute."

Elijah had walked over to the fireplace and threw enough wood to get the flames rising again. The fire's heat was once again winning the battle forcing the winter cold to retreat and compelling the shadows to melt away.

"I've got a quilt next to my chair. Did you cook the Chester White?"

"Now remember the landlord paid for her half and I put your half on the rotisserie; but it needs to cook for hours longer." Quinn pulled the metal cover from a tray and placed the platter in front of Hugo. "Come…. Sit, I grill-roasted some oysters." She pulled the cover from another platter and placed the steaming oysters under Elijah's nose. "Eat these oysters and chat a little while longer then we will dine. We'll start with a cup of seafood okra gumbo and a salad of roasted beets, then I poached red fish, oysters and shrimp in a court bouillon and then for dessert sweet custard with fresh berries and some Port wine. I picked a California Riesling for the oysters and the court bouillon. Do you agree Elijah?"

"I've said many times that God should have you in his kitchen."

"Hugo lifted a warm oyster shell and with his tiny three-pronged fork raised an oyster to his lips. Before the oyster parted his lips, he garbled, "Who is Chester White?" His eyes closed as soon as the oysters touched his tongue. Lemony, salty, a blackened cheesy crunch were the flavors and sensations racing along his taste buds before he swallowed the mollusks. He tilted the shell to his lips to sip the salty oyster juice. Hugo opened his eyes and said, "If God doesn't hire you; you can work in my kitchen anytime."

"Hugo, I'm sure a blind woman would be an improvement in your kitchen." Quinn walked over to Hugo's side of the desk and poured wine into his glass. She leaned over until her face was only inches from his. She whispered, "The blanket is on the floor on the other side of your chair" and stared into his eyes.

Hugo didn't need a blanket. This woman had given him a roaring fever. Thoughts of Quinn had raced through his mind all week and now he knew if she would have him, he'd marry her tonight. He knew that a marriage to Quinn might last just a week; but oh, what a glorious and wicked week.

Quinn pulled away but her eyes held his eyes captive. Her lips formed a small sensual smile but her voice was stern, "Really Hugo, a look of lust at the dinner table. Elijah, I will leave the bottle with you. Eat and enjoy your oysters. Resume the story you were recalling before Hugo began sobbing about the hardships of cool temperatures. In about forty-five or sixty minutes I will have the table set and the food served."

Hugo had wolfed down four oysters and was sipping his wine while watching Quinn slowly push her kitchen cart to the kitchen.

"Elijah, you eat like a king. Every morsel I've eaten here has been delicious."

"Yes, I've been fortunate. I've always had a woman in my house that could cook."

"Is it my imagination or do I hear a piano? I hear passionate music from a great distant that drifts in for a moment and then fades."

Elijah swallowed his second oyster, and then slid the platter of uneaten mollusks to the side. "That's old Crazy Sally; she's the proprietor of this property. When you stand in the driveway, you can see a hill with a clump of trees on the other side of the road. Her house is in that stand of trees. She plays the piano at all hours of the day and night. On silent winter nights we sit on the front lawn and listen to her beautiful and inspiring concerts. When the wind blows the music has a tendency to wander and float with the current."

Hugo was nearly finished his platter of oysters and was eyeing Elijah's platter. "You're not hungry?"

Elijah looked at his tray of uneaten oysters and then at Hugo's pile of empty shells. "I don't have much of an appetite these days, but you look like a starving refugee. The best compliment for Quinn is an empty plate."

"Do you smoke a pipe? Sometimes I smell a sweet fruity pipe tobacco that drifts in like the music then it fades."

Elijah took a sip of his wine and closed his eyes. "No, I don't smoke a pipe, but I know the smell and I've come to dread it."

Hugo waited for a further explanation, but none came and Elijah's eyes remained closed, "Maybe you can tell me about the mission before we go to dinner. Let's turn on the devices and whenever you are ready."

Elijah opened his eyes and his shaky finger pushed the silver button with the red arrow. He started to speak and then stopped and stared into space. He began tentatively and each word was coated with sadness.

"When Fleur delivered the news, I knew my perfect life with her in our garden of paradise was over. I was being forced to leave my Heaven. Fleur cried as she tried to explain the Mission. All survivors of the Portals and their descendants were to cross the Disappearing Bridge into the Third Nation. She said there was no Earthly word for the name of the Third Nation. She called it the Land of Doom. I always called it the Third Nation. The Mission was simple. We were to cross into the Third Nation and confront or negotiate with the Adversary. The Adversary had taken the Key needed to retrieve the Collective Knowledge. We were to acquire the Key and bring it back to the Traditionalist. The reward was a long healthy life of comfort, safety and privilege. No one could tell us anything about the Third Nation or the Adversary; because no one had ever returned from a Mission. Thousands of men and women had been sent on similar missions over a period of a few thousand years and no one had ever returned dead or alive. Fleur asked if she could be by my side on the Mission, but the Dreamers refused. I tried to calm her fears by telling her that my mother had named me after a great Greek warrior and adventurer. I assured her that I would return, like Ulysses had always returned from his adventures. He fought through great trials and tribulations to always return after each quest to Penelope, the one woman he loved. I pledged to her that I would come back from this forced service to be with my Penelope; my Penny. I had made it through the deadly Portal and I was now prepared to fight in Hell, if necessary, to be with my Penny Fleur."

"The morning of the Exodus was a gentle sunny day with an endless blue sky. The Portal survivors and their descendants gathered on the banks of a river, called The Wall, an angry raging current of black liquid. The Wall separated the Third Nation from the rest of the Kingdom. Everyone looked scared, confused and wore masks of disbelief. We were all being forced from our homes into the unknown.

Large carts were being pulled to the River's edge loaded with supplies, the old, the infirmed and the very young. We were not allowed to bring beast of burden into the Third Nation, so everyone had to help push and pull the carts. We gathered at the designated river crossing and where no bridge had existed earlier that morning, now stood a shiny metallic bridge. While crossing the bridge we kept looking back at our home to see if any Dreamers had come to bid us farewell or to threaten us if we didn't cross the bridge; but no one appeared. When the last exile stepped off of the bridge it disappeared and as we journeyed into this foreign land, each of us took our turn to look at our home for the last time. When I turned to say a private final goodbye to my paradise, I saw her. Fleur, my Penny Fleur was on the distant river bank. We stared at each other and then she closed her eyes, bowed her head and walked away. To see her disappear again was an unbearable heartbreak. That voiceless scream in my aching heart was crying."

"The first weeks in the alien land were hopeful. We traveled through a vast treeless vacherie that was carpeted with tall emerald-green, velvety soft grass. The sea of green was punctuated with solitary long stemmed white flowers or an occasional bright yellow flower bowing in the breeze. The land seemed fertile and was stone-free. Some wanted to settle there in the ocean of tall grass. But we all knew we had to push on to seek out others that had made this journey and the Adversary had to be found."

"We traveled for weeks unmolested in this broad grassland and then on a day, just like the last thirty, it all ended. Our journey had led us out of the prairie to the edge of a desert. Where the tall grasses ended faded ochre sand began. There were a few stunted and gnarled trees, stones everywhere, but not a blade of grass. The light reflected from the sand radiated a toasted brown hue to the wasteland. A light dusting of ash coated everything and it wasn't long before we all had the skin color of a working coal miner. The prize that drew us into the desert was a pulsing ball of yellow light impossibly far away. That glowing light had to be where other survivors were living and maybe the homeland of the Adversary, friend or foe."

"Three days into the nameless unknown desert our destinies suddenly changed. On our left and on our right were hills of rock piles, maybe ruins. From behind those hills came the monsters; with the appearance of humans, the beasts were eight, nine, ten feet tall. The creatures had swollen lumpy faces, with huge sausage lips and small unblinking red-rimmed eyes. Most were an ashy black, some had splotches of grey and many had gashes of raw red. When the monsters attacked, they focused their attention on one or two prey. They fought the men, but their first victims were the women, the children and the old. The creatures would grasp their prey by an arm or a leg and then disappear into the piles of stone with one our companions. We had been allowed to bring a few farming tools, shovels, saws and axes; our tools became our weapons. We were able to slay four or five of the predators, but our weapons were too few and our attackers were too many. It wasn't long before all women, children and the elderly had been dragged into the mounds of boulders. For about a quarter of an hour we stood in shock and then they came back for us. We fought on but the beasts were too many and one by one my comrades were taken. It didn't take long for me to realize that once again I was invisible. I hadn't been this obscure since my father had decided to erase me from his field of vision for not wanting to be a fisherman, or when Indians attacked our encampment on the Mississippi river. The savages had just blindly run past me. Soon I was alone in the desert. The hideous brutes continued to search for survivors. They knew there was one more; they could smell me; they probably could hear my heart beating. I bolted for the rock pile and negotiated a maze of rubble. The maze continually shrank until I was on my hands and knees crawling through a tight tunnel. First, I felt the cool air and as the tunnel got larger, I could smell the rotting scented vapors and then I was in a subterranean world of moss-draped boulders, white and green ferns, lichen covered dwarf oaks shrouded in a light fog that left a dampness on everything. In minutes my world had adjusted radically. I cautiously explore the stinking underworld. I heard what I thought was voices and was drawn in that direction. The closer I got to the incomprehensible voices the terrain changed again. The ground was littered with piles of grey and white and on closer inspection I realized that the large mounds were accumulations of deteriorating bones and human skulls. While crouched down looking at the bones I noticed that I was breathing with such force that my breath was stirring the bone ash and then I heard my first scream and then a moan. Anxiously I followed the sounds. I climbed up some boulders covered in slime and peered over the top to spy on whomever or whatever was making those sounds. When my sightline cleared the edge of the boulder, I could see a few of the beasts covered in blood, lazing about, and napping. My attention was diverted to a far corner of the huge cavern where I heard shrieks, moans and crying. Many of my friends were caged in a wooden corral in that part of the cavern and then I witness something that will stay embedded in my memory until the day I die. Two beasts dragged a young man from the corral. He weakly tried to resist, his eyes were wide with terror, his lips trembled and when he opened his month to scream his tongue was paralyzed silent. They roughly threw him face up on a large blood covered table. One beast put a hand on the young man's chest to hold him on the table and with his other hand he grabbed the man's arm twisted it right, then left and finally ripped it from the man's body. The other beast did the same with the left arm. Each monster sat on his haunches gorging on human flesh. The young man's dead eyes were looking up for answers as his corpse lay on the table between the two cannibals feasting on his flesh. Those eyes will always be with me."

"Excuse me Hugo. I must put more wood on the fire. I use to like the cold weather; but now low temperatures make me feel vulnerable, helpless."

Hugo watched as Elijah shuffled over to the wood pile, "Do you need some help?"

"No, I needed to stand and stretch."

"Elijah, your story is sounding more and more like weird science fiction."

"Hugo, many times truth is far stranger than fiction. The many unanswered questions we have about our world have answers that we probably couldn't even understand."

Elijah shuffled back to the desk and fell into his throne with a thud. "Stay with me Hugo. When the story ends many of those questions racing around your brain will be answered. But unfortunately, some of those questions can only be answered with more questions. Quinn will be coming for us, so I just want to explain how I escaped from the monsters and then we can relax and eat and then maybe talk a little more if I have the strength."

"I have more than enough material for this week's installment. It will probably take me a day to go through all the written notes that you gave me."

"Ah Hugo, the notes are just to clarify or interpret some of what I am saying. Some memories come to me and they may not even be important to the story so I just write them down. Good if you can use them, if not, you can commit them to the fire. Now my escape."

"I was stunned and, in a panic, as I watch the horrific scene before me. I was tired and dizzy and for a moment my consciousness went black. My mind woke up when I felt myself sliding down the slime covered rock. The beasts that were sleeping stood up; the savages that were eating flesh paused. I'm not sure if they even saw me because as soon as my feet touched the cavern floor my shaky legs propelled me away from the cannibals. I saw a huge keyhole-shaped opening in the rock wall and ran through the welcoming hole into a darkened chamber with a sandy floor. I saw a smaller keyhole opening and ran through it into a smaller chamber and that patterned continued until I stumbled through an opening and entered a large cave of moving shadows created by a small contained fire. I got down on my knees so that I could catch my breath and surveyed my new surroundings. All was quiet, not even the small fire was making a sound. The fire-created shadows danced in silence. My day had begun battling monsters and then the sight of cannibalism had left me exhausted physically, emotionally and mentally. But I was drawn to the fire for security, for something familiar. My legs were unsteady but they slowly carried me towards the fire. When my eyes had adjusted to the dim light, I noticed a forest of tall intricately carved stone columns holding up the cavern's roof. Between me and the fire was a massively wide, but short column of carved coiled green and yellow stone. I cautiously walked around the column to get nearer the fire. The firelight revealed a giant serpent's head, its unblinking eyes staring at me. A slight movement of a dagger tongue alerted my senses. It was not a carved column or image. It was a massive snake. I could feel a hysteria pounding in my chest. The sound of my pulse beating in my ears was deafening. My terror had paralyzed my body. My bravery had disappeared. I stood there like paralyzed prey waiting to be devoured. When I accepted my fate, my breathing slowed and I felt strangely calm. Then I realized the voice in my head was actually the snake speaking to me asking, "Am I scaring you? Should I greet you in another configuration?"

"In an instant the serpent was gone to be replaced with a ball of heatless boiling fire. I stood there dazed, closed my eyes and heard the voice again. I opened my eyes and a man stood where the snake had laid coiled waiting for me. I still remember each word of our initial conversation."

"Is this better for you? I've been waiting for you. You're safe Ulysses, so try to calm down."

"Before me was a man six feet tall, maybe a little taller. A lanky physique with brushed-back curly black hair and a silly small black chapeau perched on top. He wore the clothes of an aristocrat; black tailored woolen pants, vest and jacket and a tightly woven white shirt with sleeves cuffed by small ruby links. His light gray eyes were set into a ruggedly handsome face aged to the beginning of manhood. This man had a Gallic face, not unlike my own. His most distinct facial feature was his eyebrows. They began low over his nose and ended high at the outer end. They worked in cooperation with his mouth to express his words. They were always cocked to exclaim surprise or to feign hurt or to hood his eyes in fake anger. He wore a happy, delighted smile. That smile, like so many I've experienced, was sometimes real and sometimes just a hypnotic camouflage. His clear richly toned voice was soothing, reassuring."

"Are you OK? Are you hungry… thirsty?"

"When I heard that tranquil voice saying those caring words I woke up. Yes, I woke up from a nightmare. I went to my knees and let out a rush of air that had been trapped in my chest. I surveyed my surroundings and for the first time in my life, I felt that elusive feeling of total peace. I felt safe."

"I looked up at the stranger. We both remained mute while our eyes examined each other. Finally, I said, "Who are you?""

My savior, my friend spoke slowly with a crafted clarity to each word. He said, "Oh, I go by numerous names and titles. That's not important. What's important is helping you continue your journey. I will personally see that you and the Key make a quick and safe return journey."

"I had forgotten about the Key. This kind man said that he was giving me the Key and helping me return to my Fleur. My momentary state of bliss evaporated. I could hear him saying something about being a hero, but my swirling emotions prevented me from concentrating on his words."

"This good Samaritan stood before me and placed a deteriorating grass-woven bag into my hands, stepped back and let out a wild shriek of laughter. He was excited, but also seemed relieved when he said, 'The Key is in the bag. You can take it out of the bag to examine it; but you'll have no idea what you're holding in your hands. Tell me when you are strong enough to travel and I will get you safely back to Fleur. Give the Key to your lover; she will know where to deliver it. Now eat this to build your strength.'"

"I turned to my left and next to me was a small low table. On the table was a steaming bowl of meaty broth. I hadn't realized that I was starving and attacked the bowl of food. I stopped eating long enough to ask the questions, "How do you know my name? You said you had been waiting for me? Those two questions began a conversation that would last over four hundred years."

"The kind stranger had a look of concern on his face when he answered my questions. "Ulysses I've always known that you were destined to go on a journey or a pilgrimage. I knew before time was measured in years that you were going to wander and I always hoped that an accidental destination for you would be here. I've always known about your origin, your source, and your beginnings. All beginnings have an ending, but I'm not sure how you will end your odyssey. That will be your choice. I do know that for thousands of years, Fleur's people have said that someone, not born of their world, would return the Key to them. Take the key out of the bag, hold in your hands that which will make you a hero for a short period of time. Yes, they will love you for a moment in time; but almost all heroes are eventually turned into villains by their past worshippers. There will be suspicion even when they are toasting to your health and kissing your cheek."

"I pushed the broth aside and opened the dilapidated bag to spy the wonder that had been the desire of a civilization for thousands of years. I pulled out a white metallic cube. It weighed two maybe three pounds and was polished smooth on all sides except one. On that side were microscopic, nearly invisible etchings. I inspected all sides of the object, my hands felt the smoothness of the five sides and the minute engravings on the sixth and my lips touch the metallic coolness. The surprise I had been expecting was too common, too simple; I had expected more. How could bringing back this polished lump of metal make me a hero?"

"The young man sat down in the sand facing me. His eyes were closed and in a whispery tone he was humming or chanting. When the humming stopped his eyes whipped open and then he spoke tenderly, but in a conspiratorial nature, "Ulysses, when you are ready, I will get you back to your adopted home quickly and safely. When you return, you will be hailed as a hero." Turning his head from side to side he said, "Ulysses, hero status usually does not last very long and in many cases the worshipped hero becomes a burden or a perceived threat. But, if you and I were to make a pact, a friendly agreement, an amicabilis concordia, I can't promise you hero status, but my friend, I can promise a long, long life of wealth, good health and happiness for you and your Penny Fleur."

"I still can remember him on his knees, his arms spread before him and his palms facing up in a pleading manner. He had a mildly embarrassed look when he said that he would give me all that he had mentioned if I just performed four tasks for him. That infectious smile graced his lips when he said, 'Just four tasks, Hercules had twelve tasks, twelve labors and I promise you that you won't have to kill lions or fight bulls or clean stables.' I didn't understand anything that he had said; I just could not stop thinking of Fleur."

"I stood and told him I was ready to go back to Fleur and that after we discussed our future, I would consider his offer. He quickly stood, wordlessly brushed the sand off of his tailored slacks and then escorted me to a small golden door. When he opened the door a large shiny black stallion cautiously walked to the stranger. The light from the opened door made parts of his black hide flicker violet and electric blue then back to black. This beautiful charger was going to be my transportation home. Before helping me onto the animal, my new friend wrapped his arms around me and spoke into my ear. He said he would always be my friend, my protector. Together we were destined to create chaos and to disrupt the constant harmony of the universe. The tight warm hug was an embraced that I had always yearned for from my Father. After I was mounted on the horse, I asked him if he was the Adversary. He walked away with a cocky swagger then turned to face me and with a trace of bitterness in his voice he grumbled, 'When you are different, others become angry. When you diligently perform your job to almost perfection, others become jealous. They invent malicious stories and blame me for everyone's misfortunes. These malignant, spiteful stories are used to malign my character and to spew vicious name calling. Yes Ulysses, I am called the Adversary, the Genie, Mephistopheles, Scratch, the Beast, Prince of Darkness, Beelzebub, Diablo, the Serpent, and the Venom of God.'"

"There was a lost look in his eyes and his voice had risen in heated anger. He shook his fist at me and yelled, "I don't mean to be a self-glorifier, but do you want more. How about the King of Hell, the Antichrist, Lucifer, the Tempter, Satan, or the Devil. There are hundreds of insults, but you my friend, will only ever call me Mr. Jimmie."

Hugo had stopped taking notes and writing questions for future clarifications. He couldn't take his eyes off of the storyteller. Elijah's face was veiled in defeat but his voice had hardened into anger. His eyes were closed but his nostrils flared each time a word was spoken.

"Dinner has been served and is waiting for my two favorite handsome men."

A fear induced electric shock raced down Hugo's spine causing an involuntary shiver. The beautiful Quinn had once again magically appeared. Hugo raised his hand to quiet her. "Wait, let Elijah finish this thought."

Hugo was not prepared for the barrage. Her words were swift, edged and angry. "Hugo! You are a guest, not a paying customer with the audacity to order me around like a wage earner."

At least that's what Hugo thought she had said. Her anger released Quinn's strange accent making her words sound harsh and sinister.

Elijah quickly walked to her side, kissed her on the cheek and said, "Woman you have always been a blessing."

Thoughts during a Late-Night Drive Home

When Hugo turned off of Sweet Faith Street onto Highway 24, he pulled onto the shoulder of the highway. He had to calm his racing mind; the past eight hours had been filled with a variety of intense emotions. It had been a moonless late winter/early spring night of crisp air and bright stars, when Quinn and Patrick had escorted him to his car. Quinn had held on to him for warmth as they briskly walked to the car. Under thousands of bright sparkling stars, they stood for a moment to listen to the melancholy music coming from a yellow light, masked by a clump of trees on a hillside. Before he had gotten into the car Quinn had given him a long tight hug and then quickly kissed his left cheek. It was her last words that kept a smile on his face and his usually well-ordered thoughts in a state of chaos.

"Hugo, with excited anticipation, I look forward to your next visit. I'll give that handsome right cheek a proper kiss when you come back to me."

When he drove the car back onto the highway, his eyes saw the lights of other cars, but his thoughts were on Quinn's beautiful face. He had been in relationships with attractive women but never a woman with Quinn's sensual beauty. Sometimes her face had a special light. Her smile could be affectionate and sunny. On other occasions her face was that of an aristocrat with an alert determined gaze and always her hands and arms moved with elegant grace. Excited anticipation, were the two words that kept ringing in his ear.

The dinner had been savory as usual. Elijah had eaten very little and for most of the meal he sat erect with his eyes closed. Before the dessert was served, he excused himself; said he was tired and was going to bed early. A few minutes after he had left the room Quinn interrupted Hugo's small talk and in her blunt manner, announced that Elijah would be dead in two or three weeks. When he'd asked what was wrong with Elijah. The answer had been brusque and emotionless. She poured the custard over the fresh berries and said that Elijah was tired and the fire in his soul was now only cool embers of regret. Wordlessly they sat at the table eating their dessert and sipping port wine. When it was time to clear the table of dishes, Quinn insisted that Hugo have more wine while she carried the dishes to the kitchen. Once she had stepped out of the dining room Hugo felt someone rush out of the darkness towards him. Startled he quickly stood and turned towards the antagonist; but there was only darkness and shadows. He saw no one, but could feel a presence very near and he smelled sweet pipe tobacco. The day had been pleasant until that eerie moment.

Excitement Anticipation Monday

Hugo arrived early to work on Monday morning. He hadn't slept well that night nor had he slept well that week. He hadn't been able to silence his thoughts. He had spent the past week listening to his taped interviews, reading his notes and deciphering the large number of notes that Elijah had given him. He wrote the story, then rewrote it, then made significant changes and rewrote it again and again. He had learned to love writing. It had recently become a passion to craft each sentence and to build those sentences into a written observation. He loved his work and he loved Mondays. Monday, most workman's day of dread, had become the day Hugo yearned for its arrival.

As coworkers, fellow reporters and office staff did the sluggish Monday morning shuffle, they each stopped to congratulate Hugo on his piece in the Sunday paper. Mr. Ellington, who had edited his piece stopped by to heap praise and to inform everyone that my story had been printed in the forty-nine domestic newspapers, eight international newspapers and mentioned on the four television stations owned by the B&M Corporation.

The drive to Flat Hill had been a high-speed race. He couldn't contain his excitement and speed limits were a needless hindrance. When he finally turned onto Sweet Faith Street, he tried deep breathing to calm his anticipation. He drove down the driveway at one zero eight, grabbed his gear and as he trotted down the walkway, he noticed that all the leaves had been raked, the flower beds tilled waiting for spring flowers, and the driveway and walkway were neatly edged. He stopped for a moment to admire the manicured lawn and to watch the squirrels sitting upright with their paws together watching him. The front door was open as usual, but the dark blue wooden screen door barred the uninvited and the politest of intruders. The usually silent Patrick was waiting at the door barking and whining. Hugo walked in and tried to pet Patrick, but the dog stepped towards the kitchen.

"Hey boy, you happy to see me or are you're trying to get me to follow you?"

Patrick continued to bark and whine, but Hugo stopped following him when the room came into focus. The usually large dark room lined with antique furniture was filled with sunlight and bare of furniture. Cloaked in shadows the dark room had appeared enormous. The room had been a grand illusion. Now the light-filled bare room was poor-man small. It took seconds for Hugo to walk from the bare room to the kitchen, a journey that took many minutes when Quinn had been the guide. Even the once cluttered kitchen was mostly bare. There were a few scattered dishes and two opened wooden chests packed with pots, pans and dishes. His excitement turned into uneasy dread. The world he'd gotten to know was gone. The final shock was when he walked into the green glass enclosed room. Nearly every inch of the room had been crammed with junk and treasures. The room was now spotless and barren. Under a single green pastel shaded lamp, where the majestic carved desk once stood was a small garden table with Elijah's blue red-rimmed coffee cup and saucer perilously close to the table top's edge. On one side of the small table was Hugo's faded red velvet chair and on the other side of the table sat Patrick next to an occupied wheelchair.

"Hugo, come and sit my friend."

Hugo walked to the wheelchair and was saddened by what he saw. The regal man with an old-world formality that he had first met weeks ago, was now a shrunken gray man. His thick black hair was now just a few wisps of gray. The frail wrinkled man in the wheelchair looked at Hugo through milky brown watery eyes. Elijah's signature smile of satisfaction was the only recognizable feature of the man Hugo once knew.

"Elijah, I knew you were sick but I didn't realize."

"Sit Hugo, make yourself comfortable. Yes, I'm at the end. Everyone, everything, even a rock, has a beginning so they must have an ending. In the beginning you accumulate possessions, experiences and memories. In the end, if you are lucky, your precious possessions are given away, taken, or destroyed and you are only left with memories, if you are fortunate. I have been fortunate. I have many memories, a faithful dog by my side, a beautiful woman taking care of me and the acquaintance of an undiscovered literary genius."

Elijah stopped speaking so that he could swallow and take a long deep breath. His voice was weak and a rattle could be heard every time he took a shallow breath.

"I read your story in yesterday's paper and then I had Quinn read it to me last night and again this morning. Hugo, you have a gift, the ability to paint a picture in someone's mind using only words. I know you have wondered why this crazy story is so important to me. In my lifetime I have not heard of a whirlpool of blackness swallowing trees, earth and people. But I know it has happened many times in the past and I am sure it will happen again. I will never again see my Penny Fleur. But if someone that has read your story or if future generations read your legendary tale and that someone is eaten by the Portal and survives. I want that someone to be able to tell Fleur that every morning of my long life my first thoughts were of her and every night my last thoughts have been about the only woman I have ever loved. Everything I have done since I last saw her was for love."

Elijah closed his eyes and struggled with his breath. Quinn usually just appeared out of thin air but today he could hear her rapid footsteps.

"Hugo forgive me for not greeting you at the door."

Quinn's face wore a scowl, an accusatory finger pointed at Patrick and then she barked, "Patrick! Shame on you Patrick; why didn't you let me know Hugo had arrived? When it's time for your dinner remember how rude you were to me."

The dog ignored the finger and slowly looked away from Quinn but his tail was rapidly speaking.

Quinn passed her hand through Elijah's few remaining hairs, kissed his forehead and gently asked, "Can I get you anything, water or coffee? Can I help you to the toilet?"

Elijah reached for her hand so that he could kiss it and then in a barely audible murmur, "Bring us coffee, those legal papers and my notes."

A silly grin spread across Hugo's face; he was mesmerized by the vision of Quinn. Her blonde hair was pulled back in a loose messy ponytail. She wore an ankle length smock with finger-width dark green and gray stripes and pleated at the waist. The opened smock covered a canary yellow, long, slinky dress.

As Hugo's vision of beauty walked away, she said, "Hugo, I'll bring you something sweet to eat with your coffee." She stopped and stared at Hugo. "You should stop that grinning. Making foolish faces is not very manly."

When Quinn disappeared into the kitchen Hugo let out a rush of air. His angelic beauty had deflated him. On the last visit she had slapped his face hard enough to knock spit out of his mouth and now on this visit she was swinging for his manhood. But he still loved her, yes, he loved her.

Hugo could hear a weak laugh from Elijah and then a long phlegm clearing cough. After the mucus was swallowed Elijah chuckled some more and then slowly spoke to Hugo.

"Hugo, she's beautiful, smart, a great lover, and a hard worker, a wonderful manager of a home, a heavenly cook, loving, and warmhearted. Living with Quinn is stress free, because she does the worrying for both of you. She is very protective, which is good and bad. She can be obsessive about details and sometimes cool and cautious. Her faults are few, but Hugo, be wary of Quinn."

Both men watched as Quinn pushed her kitchen cart towards them. "Elijah, I couldn't find room in the chest for this cart, so I think I'll just leave it for the next inhabitants." When she got to the small table, Quinn put the milk and sugar on the table and then poured coffee into Elijah's blue coffee cup. "Elijah, I have a custard tart and two slices of chocolate bread pudding. Can you eat something sweet?"

"No, just coffee, give both of the desserts to Hugo, he likes dessert."

Quinn poured coffee for Hugo, placed the two desserts in front of him, laughed and said, "I think Hugo likes anything on a plate."

Hugo tried not to smile when he answered. "I've enjoyed everything that you've cooked. Why are you packing? Is everyone leaving?"

Quinn took the papers and binder off of the cart so she could use it as chair. Once seated, she turned to Hugo and gave him a warm friendly smile.

"Hugo you ask too many questions. Elijah has something important to tell you; eat and listen."

Hugo could hear sadness in her words. He could see in her blue eyes that the smile was not the camouflage she was hoping for.

Elijah motioned for Quinn to give Hugo the papers. "Give him the legal documents. Open up the folder, it's a bunch of legal mumbo jumbo, but it's legal and binding."

Hugo pulled from the folder some papers. The first page was from B&M Corporation, the corporation that owned fifty-seven newspapers including The City Advocate, and his name was typed in several paragraphs.

"What is this?"

"Quinn my mind is tired, and heavy. Please speak for me."

Quinn adjusted herself on the cart so that she faced Hugo, sucked on her bottom lip and then in a deeply accented melancholic voice began to speak.

"Elijah knows that one of your wishes is to write a novel. He and his associate have negotiated with the B&M Corporation that all work you have contributed to the City Advocate are yours to do with as you please. The City Advocate series and all notes given to you are legally yours. You have the rights to the story of Elijah and if you'd compile it all into a novel, all compensation, all royalties are yours without any restrictions."

Quinn stood and handed Hugo a one-inch thick binder of notes. "This is the last of Elijah's notes. He recalled and I typed. This information is for you. You can use it to write your series, write a novel or to stoke a fire to keep you warm. You now own the story of Elijah. But not the end of Elijah; if fortune shines on me, I will have him for a while longer. Now let him tell you a little more about his friend Mr. Jimmie. We will have a very early dinner. I'm sure you won't mind since you are always starving. Elijah, speak a little while and then rest. You must conserve your energy." Quinn walked over to Elijah and once again kissed his forehead, turned and briskly walked out of the green glass enclosed room. Hugo could see that her beautiful face was twisted with grief.

Hugo put the binder in his lap, untied the leather straps, opened it and was looking at the neatly stacked typed pages when Elijah hoarsely spoke. "If you are ready, I'd want to tell you about the events after I acquired the Key. The Good Samaritan that had given me the Key said that one of his names was Satan. Everyone knew that the

Devil was red with horns, pointed tail and had a pitchfork of fire. This good man that had taken care of me was dressed as a gentleman. The black charger that I rode covered the distance of a months' long journey in a relatively short period of time. When that beautiful animal delivered me at The Wall the shiny metallic bridge was waiting for my crossing. After crossing the raging black river and dismounting my four-legged supersonic transportation I was met by a solitary Dreamer. Within minutes there were thousands and thousands of Dreamers surrounding me. The confused multitudes were gawking, pointing, whispering. I yelled that I had the Key; but not a soul came near me and then she was there. My Fleur, my Penny Fleur was standing before me. The tears started flowing before I could wrap my arms around her. By the time I felt her arms wrap around me and her lips kiss my neck, I was sobbing. I couldn't speak. Fleur was my only friend, the only person I loved. She was my life and a life without her was not worth living. It wasn't long before many Traditionalists arrived to whisk us away. My return with the Key had an immediate effect on both Kingdoms. Within weeks of my return basic assumptions and ways of thinking began to evolve. The two Kingdom's centuries-old framework of society began to change. I was a hero; the Feast of Ulysses was to be an anniversary holiday. I was given a palace in the Land of the Dreamers. Fleur and I were loved. But…yes, Mr. Jimmie had been correct when he said that hero status is usually short-lived. There were many that were angry because of the rapid changes causing confusion in their lives. There were others that were suspicious. How had I acquired the Key? What pledges had I given the Adversary? Maybe I was the Adversary in disguise."

Elijah coughed to clear his throat. His breathing was raspy and shallow. When he attempted a deep breath the gurgle of fluids could be heard in his chest.

"Can I get you something to drink? Should I call for Quinn?"

Elijah waved his hand back and forth, "No, I'll just speak for a few minutes and then I'll have to rest. The suspicious ones were convinced that I was a tool of the Devil. No harm came to Fleur and me. Our needs were satisfied, but we were imprisoned in our beautiful palace. No contact with anyone was allowed. At first Fleur and I were satisfied, we had each other. But as time flowed by, I felt insulted; I grew angry. I had completed the task. Thousands had died seeking the Key and I had come close to death. I gave them their holy prize and I received imprisonment. I grew furious when I'd see Fleur staring beyond the palace walls thinking of her family. Imprisonment and separation from her kin were her penalties for loving me. I didn't want vengeance; I wanted freedom. Then one day the sun was not visible. The swirling black and gray clouds were moving at an unusually fast pace. The menacing veil of darkness was a barrier to all sunlight. Fleur and I had spent most of the morning in our day bed looking skyward at the boiling clouds. I left Fleur on the bed watching the dark sky cinema and went into the palace to fix our breakfast. I smelled him before I saw him. As soon as I opened the door, I could smell an aroma of sweet pipe tobacco and when I walked into the kitchen, there was Mr. Jimmie."

Elijah was struggling with his words but he didn't stop speaking, he had to continue. "There was my friend in his perfectly tailored black suit and polished boots. He had a different chapeau that was too small and not a good match for the impeccable outfit. Mr. Jimmy was standing in my kitchen telling me about his new habit of pipe smoking. His happy delighted smile lightened my heavy heart. He knew about my situation and asked if I was prepared to be his employee. The young man told me he was a master in the arts of deception, but he promised there was no insincerity in his offer of employment. He would teach me to employ the silver tongue of flattery, to be an enabler, to be the creator of traps of deceit. He would be the teacher and I the student. I would perform four benign tasks that would change the course of history. Mr. Jimmy said I would have to work for him for many, many years; but when the four tasks were completed, Fleur and I would be reunited. We would be young and beautiful and live a long, long healthy, wealthy and free life. I agreed to the pact and the next day Fleur and I were separated for the second time. That day was worse than death; I can't talk about it. I didn't realize it was going to be the last time I saw my beautiful Fleur. I told Mr. Jimmy that I wasn't entering the agreement for wealth. I was going to complete the task for a long life of love with Fleur. After all these years I can still see the visceral reaction of his face and how he spoke in the iciest of tones. He told me he was there and had heard Adam's screams of despair and horror when he realized he'd lost paradise for love."

Confusion

Hugo, draped in a blanket paced back and forth on his small balcony. He was waiting for the first light of day to give him strength. Most of his life he'd risen early to greet the Morning Star, a source of strength and peace for him. Since he had started on the assignment to write Elijah's story, his life had changed and the morning sun, for a few weeks, had been unimportant to him. He hadn't slept since he'd last seen Elijah and Quinn. He'd been reading notes and writing and more writing. There were long periods of brooding over Quinn and the loss of Elijah. He had given deep thought about each moment of that day; but it was the dinner that kept swirling around in his confused mind.

Elijah had passed on dinner; instead he chose to lie on a day-bed set up for him near the thick dark forest that surrounded three sides of the estate. Quinn cried softly as she bundled him in blankets and tucked pillows around him to keep him upright. He said he wanted to watch the shadows in the forest grow longer until they merged and became impenetrable and all that could be seen was unexplored darkness. His last words to Hugo were about death. He wondered aloud; what would he be faced with at the moment of death. Would it be unexplored darkness, something his mind could not yet comprehend or worse—nothing? Quinn had motioned to him to follow her and when he turned back to see Elijah for the last time, he and Patrick were staring into the unknown.

Dinner was served on the small garden table in the bare green glass enclosed room. Quinn had changed for dinner and was wearing tight faded blue jeans, tan huarache sandals and a white peasant blouse. Her hair was still in a loose ponytail but her usual fragrance had changed. Usually there was just a hint of fragrance, but at dinner she wore the aroma of a chef. The dinner, as usual, was savory. Fresh baked baguettes with a thick reddish-brown seafood bisque for dipping. The main dish was roasted chicken and braised small potatoes. Desert was warm powdered beignets and café au lait. A beautiful woman, a great meal, and a wonderful conversation made for a perfect evening. Then after dessert everything changed. Quinn's vibrant smile hardened; she grew serious. Her sudden sad haunted appearance alarmed Hugo. But he wasn't prepared for her words. She told him that Elijah would be dead before next Sunday's edition of his remarkable story. She said that he was in the stage of dying when most men and women judge themselves and either confessed or were unapologetic or weeping with regret. Then she leaned over the small table to kiss Hugo's right cheek and then his lips. When her lips touched his, a peaceful foreign feeling flowed through his body. He wished he'd been able to record her next words. He'd tried to recall and write the exact words. He tried to make sense of what she had said but the words kept racing through his thoughts. Hugo walked to his kitchen table to read her last words for the hundredth time.

"Hugo, you are a beautiful, good and innocent man. Elijah always called you an honorable man. He said you were a man that could be trusted to do his best. When I think of you and I think of you often my emotions soar. I want the best for you, only the best, that's why I'm asking you never to come back to this house again. There are affairs here that you would not understand. You have come to the edge of a different world; a world I don't want you to become intimate with. I will say again, Hugo I want only the best for you. You have most of Elijah's notes and I will mail you the rest and the promised comedy club hero interview. You are a great writer. Please remember that you do not need any help from anyone or anything. I need to check on Elijah; please finish your coffee, then take the notes and leave. I will tell Elijah and Patrick that you said goodbye. I will miss you; but I am doing this for your welfare." Before leaving she leaned over the table and kissed his lips again.

He turned to look out the balcony door and saw that the sun had risen and he knew it would not give him the peace and strength that he needed. He sat at the kitchen table, lit another cigarette and decided to read through his rough draft one more time before making revisions. Over the past forty-eight hours he had read most of Elijah's notes and had compiled the major events. The first draft was told in the first person; but he wasn't sure if that's how the final draft would be told. He often read his first draft aloud to picture how the reader might perceive the story. Faintly audible was <u>Lament</u>, by cellist Rufus Cappadocia. Quinn had said that it was an appropriate musical composition for the sadness in her heart. He knocked the ash from his cigarette and started to read.

"I estimate that I was eighteen or nineteen years old when I made a pact with the Devil. Naïve, innocent, ignorant, simple minded and blinded by love were all accurate descriptions of me. I had convinced myself that Mr. Jimmie was a good man that wanted to help me. Fleur was skeptical and was clearly shaken; but swore that she would support me in Heaven or Hell. For a brief time, I feared that I might have fallen into a trap; but when I asked Mr. Jimmie if our relationship was for eternity. He assured me that everything that had a beginning, Earth, the Sun, the stars, laws, philosophies, thoughts, lusty sex and even relationships had an ending. I didn't have a Daniel Webster or family and friends to protect me. All I had, my only possession, was my love for Fleur.

"When we left my palace, we rode in a driverless enclosed golden carriage pulled by four pairs of muscular, shiny black, draft horses.

The streets were lined with the curious and the storytellers. We returned to his lair for what he called a feast to celebrate our friendship. The cavernous room crowded with massive stone and marble columns was in shadows, lit by a tiny flickering yellow flame in a far corner and specks of blue, green and red lights scattered throughout the immense chamber. It was a colorful darkness with movement in the shadows. A tremendous amount of food and drink was served to me by beautiful, scantily clad women with the unblinking eyes of serpents. I ate very little; his speech, his beauty, his vast knowledge was hypnotic. I was an audience of one; a student in awe of his mentor."

"When he finally finished his one-man spectacle, he stood staring at me with a satisfied smile. He ripped off his silly chapeau and threw it in the sand revealing his wavy brushed-back black hair. He sat in the chair across from me and told me that he and I were going to make history together. His smile disappeared when he told me that my first lesson would be extremely simple, but very important. He said that my world was full of idiots, morons, fools, boneheads, numbskulls and fuck ups and each could be guided to do my bidding. He told me to never forget a man's name even if he's a dimwit. He threw a handful of grapes at me and started to giggle. Never criticize, speak ill of no man; people remember the hurt for years and sometimes forever. Heck, God himself, does not propose to judge man or woman until the end of their days. Why should you or I judge? He said that he had been judged and knew the hurt. His smile returned and his wild eyebrows copied the direction of his lips when he told me to show appreciation. Show appreciation to the person for being a friend, for her help, for his kind thoughts, for their genius. Make them feel important, freely give compliments, but try not to flatter, because even some simpletons can perceive the trap. Mr. Jimmie pointed to me and said that those few statements were lesson number one. Life could be simple and the world was full of fools willing to help you because you remembered their names, you gave them such sweet compliments and you didn't reprimand or blame them for their gross ignorance. He kissed my forehead and said there would be other lessons, and when I slept that night I should dream of home.

Home

"When I woke, I was lying on the side of a little-used dirt road. It didn't take long for me to realize that I was somewhere near my parent's home. As I jogged along the road everything looked familiar and everything looked different. It was confusing because I felt like I was home but everything had changed. The road led me to a small town in which everyone spoke to me in English. When I found someone that spoke French, I asked a hundred questions. He said I was in the town of Beaubassin in Nova Scotia, Canada, a colony of Great Britain and it was the year 1790. The French speaker said that it was during the French and Indian War that the British started deporting the French residents of L'Acadie. They exiled many to their southern coastal colonies, which recently won their independence from Britain. It had been so long ago the old man could not remember if the residents of Beaubassin had been deported to England or France. I was stunned into silence. I had left my parents' home in the year 1723. I was standing near that home seventy years later; everything had changed and I was still a boy. I walked away in silence, my chest heaving in pain until I released a raw savage scream. I had been deceived; I had lost my paradise. I became crazed. I waited. I was demented. I wanted to kill Mr. Jimmie."

"I waited for weeks, for months and the Serpent never came to me. I decided to travel to Boston to search for my mother's family, the Bullocks. I found no relatives in Boston but I did learn to rob, steal and kill when I needed money. I hated everyone and everything. I crossed the ocean and brought my hate to France. I unsuccessfully searched for descendants of Beaubassin. Then in about 1792 I joined some brigands called Chauffeurs. The French Revolution had caused chaos and the Chauffeurs took advantage of the anarchy. We became skilled at pillaging, kidnapping for ransom, robbery and murder. It was a time of bitter misery for all. Because of a money-hungry Judas I was betrayed, captured, imprisoned and sentenced to a visit with Madame Guillotine. The French had not yet grown bored with mass executions. It was the night before my execution and I was sitting in fiendish squalor. I was starving, exhausted, filthy and cold. I was defeated; my mind and soul were in such raging pain that I welcomed the morning execution. In the depths of despair and regret, a voice could be heard in the gloom. It was Mr. Jimmy staring between the bars of the cell at me. I spit at him from my sitting position, cursed him and then scooped up slop from the cell floor and threw it at the impeccably dressed villain. He dodged the contemptuous spit but he couldn't avoid the flying slop. The wicked scoundrel pointed his finger at me and started to snarl."

"Ulysses are you crazy! Look at you! You were given a choice. You could have enjoyed your freedom. But look at you, you chose to be an angry victim, a pathetic martyr. I thought we were friends and now you blame me for your bad choices. Maybe I was wrong about your moral architecture. Ulysses, you have a choice, you can love and enjoy life and flow with the events or you can be an angry defeatist that surrenders if instant satisfaction is not granted to you. Worse, like a spoiled child, you blame, curse and hurt others. You can stay in this cesspool and wallow in your adolescent self-pity and end it all tomorrow morning before a cheering crowd or you can step out of that unlocked cell and choose a destiny. If you choose to walk out of this dungeon the road runs east and west. A short walk eastward will bring you to the river and easy access to your new loyal friends. I will be westward, having a smoke in Rouge Square."

"I chose to walk westward."

Hugo put down the typed pages and began to pace from the kitchen table to the balcony; a path he had constantly traveled the last two days. His thoughts and emotions had been swirling and confusing, but now he had a moment of clarity. During that brief moment when his mind had stilled, he made a decision. He would make just a few revisions to the first draft, get some needed rest and then drive to Flat Hill to read the unfinished story to Elijah and Quinn. He knew Elijah was going to die soon and he wanted to be with him at the end and he just couldn't walk away from Quinn. He felt a sense of relief. He had a plan; he had some order and now his mind could concentrate. He would write the rest of the day and make a few rewrites, get some needed sleep and drive to Flat Hill around midday."

He poured some scotch into his coffee cup, and raised it in a silent salute to Elijah. He took a sip of the scotch, lit another cigarette and began reading in earnest with an editor's eye.

The First Task

"Yes, like a fool, like a beaten and confused dog that still loves his master, I walked westward. He talked endlessly. He spoke about his philosophies, the proper way to pack tobacco in a pipe; he imparted lessons and eventually my first task. Two lessons that I can still remember and that he constantly stressed were simple and genuine. Everyone, almost always, is given choices. Anyone can easily review their life and see that their current situations are the result of past choices. Choose wisely because some choices have a momentary effect, but other choices can be a lifelong companion. I've tried to live my life according to that dualist philosophy. Weight the choices according to their consequences', both favorably and unfavorably, make a choice and move on. The next lesson was one that I've tried to etch onto my face. Smile, smile and act like you are genuinely glad to see others. Think of things to be thankful for and smile. Yes, I had a life coach and a demon friend."

"He said if I utilized his lessons my first task should be a frolic, the most pleasant, but potentially the most dangerous. Sophia Belteau owned the Mason Le Sucre and Patisserie located on a cobbled lane off of rue de Rivoli near the Tuileries gardens. A lengthy walk from Rouge Square, and where she was waiting for me. Mr. Jimmy had convinced her to hire me to work for her popular establishment. Neither the rich nor the poor can resist the addiction of sugar. She sold sugar plums, lemon drops, sour drops, peppermints and rock candy to the poor. Candied fruit, sugared nuts and other sweetmeats, liquorice and gummy fruit- flavored molded candies were a little more expensive. Marzipan bonbons with their shiny frosting and decorative gilding in gold leaf, macarons, mille-feuille the layered puff pastry and crème and anything with scarce chocolate was affordable by only the wealthy. I wasn't hired to be a baker or a candy maker. I was hired to shovel horseshit. You could tell how successful a business was by the amount of manure out front. The wealthy came on horseback or in horse drawn carriages and my new job was to cart away the manure. He told me that part of my first task was to convince Sophia Belteau to marry a shit-shoveler. He assured me that if I employed his lessons and gave compliments, exhibited appreciation, never criticized and gave her adoring smiles that I would soon be Mr. Belteau."

"My first encounter with Sophia Belteau was one of mostly silence and stares. She was pretty with a tulip shaped face. From the neck on down, things seemed to go askew. Her pretty face was held up by a thick muscular neck and from that point downward things got bigger. She was plumpish and in eighteenth century France that was a sign of good health."

"Mr. Jimmie was correct. I applied his lessons to my daily life and within six months I was working in the pastry kitchen and married to Sophia. She was a kind and wonderful woman and I spent hours caressing her abundance of flesh. But at all times, the poor woman was a substitute; Fleur was always in my dreams."

"Supplies of sugar and cocoa could be disrupted because of the English coastal blockade or by bands of thieves. Sophia's business never lacked supplies because her agents were always successful delivering the stock. Many businesses had to close their doors because of a lack of the necessary commodities to create their products. We were open for business every day and expanded into shaping marzipan into figures of warriors, saints, castles and anything else necessary to create an edible showpiece for the banquets of the wealthy. As a result of our wonderful products we became the official supplier of sweets to the powerful in the city of Paris. We were known throughout the city as the Masters of Sweets. Because of this popularity we were often hired by the future emperor and empress of the French Empire. Napoleon Bonaparte and his mistress, Josephine often entertained small intimate groups of friends and we catered the sweets, the table showpieces and sometimes our savory meat pies. Mr. Jimmie arrived at the candy store very early one sunny morning to buy sweets and to inform me that Napoleon and Josephine were going to be my first task. Napoleon and Josephine had been married in the early spring and two days after matrimony, Napoleon was appointed to command the Army of Italy and was away fighting battles. My friend, my associate, my master counseled, cajoled and finally commanded that I use his wise words of advice, his instructions, his lessons to befriend, to be a confidant, to seduce Josephine. In addition to his prior lessons, he stressed that I become a good listener. The ideal listener asks questions and encourages others to speak about themselves. Find out what interest them and talk of that topic and not about oneself. Before he exited the store, my customer informed me that he would be back in about four months and he expected me to be Josephine's lover. He gave me four months to convince the future empress of France to commit adultery."

"It didn't take four months and I was not the only sinner in her bed. When Mr. Jimmie returned, I was given a specific night that I must entice and lure Mrs. Bonaparte into a night of sex. On that designated date, Josephine was eager to be guilty of fornication. An evening of flirting turned into a night of indulging mindless animalistic needs. The heated evening affair plunged from swollen-supple, enlarged-limp, puffed-flaccid, and then exhausted and content. I glanced across the room and he was standing in the doorway. Napoleon's hair was windblown; he was wearing a heavy, knee length, dark blue cape and his mouth was twisted to reveal complete revulsion, his eyes met mine and they were boiling with contempt. He turned and walked away. I dressed quickly and ignored Josephine's questions. That night I couldn't sleep because I expected to be executed in the morning."

"The next morning, I walked down from our upstairs apartment into the store and there was Mr. Jimmy standing at the candy counter smoking his pipe and drinking a cup of black coffee. He was dressed as usual in his tailored black suit but his silly little derby had been replaced by a ridiculous wide brim straw hat. He greeted me with a smile and words of congratulations. He complimented me and said that I had been an excellent student. I was disgusted with myself and told him that I had hurt a fine man. Napoleon had always been respectful and kind to me. I had enticed a woman into infidelity and probably destroyed her marriage. But as usual he was able to convince me otherwise when he gave me compliments and explained the reason for the first task."

"Ulysses you have done a service for Mr. Bonaparte. You and I have freed him. He no longer is chained to an emotion. He is free to follow his destiny. He will never again do something frivolous for love. Yes, today he walks with a heavy heart but the Wheel of Fortune is turning for the General. He doesn't need any petty distractions and if he wisely reads the Wheel's predictions, he will accomplish much, his heart will be full and he will be loved by his people. Napoleon's feelings for Josephine can never be the same after finding a candy maker in her bed."

"My mentor informed me that we would not meet again for a very long time. He walked around the counter, put the smoldering pipe into the pocket of his coat, hugged me and held my head to his chest.

My friend spoke softly to me and suggested that I incorporate his wise lessons into my daily existence. He gave a parting code of social behavior. I should always show genuine interest in others. He repeated the words genuine interest. He said that I should always make others feel important and that I display interest in their well-being. Before departing he whispered into my ear: "Most importantly, enjoy your life, be a seeker, be curious, relish the small as well as the big, and celebrate every precious day."

"I lived with Sophia Belteau for twenty-four years. When she died in her forty-eighth year, I willed the candy store to our three living children and continued my journey exploring the world and dreaming of Fleur."

The Second Task
Hugo got up from the kitchen table and walked over to his pantry to find a quick snack to satisfy his gnawing hunger. He had been energized but was now craving food. He tossed a bag of popcorn into the microwave and then unwrapped his last two candy bars. While savoring the chocolate crisp bars, he went over his mental map of the story. He knew he could shorten the wording of the first task and he would completely leave out Mr. Jimmie's departing advice. He would include a sentence or two about Ulysses's travels and experiences between the first and second task so that there would be a smooth flow to the story. Hugo knew that this Sunday's edition had to end with at least ninety percent of the story being completed. The series ended in the following Sunday's edition and he had to include the fourth task and the Hero's interview about the comedy club incident. He hadn't received the dictated notes concerning the incident and he wasn't sure how lengthy the interview or the notes for the next task would be. Hugo put his popcorn into an old plastic bowl, sat at the kitchen table and began reading Ulysses's second task. "I traveled the world for nearly one hundred years and barely aged. I discarded the name

Ulysses and every few decades I changed my name and took on a new identity. By 1909 I was living in London as Michelangelo Oliver; most people called me Micki. I lived in a small apartment on the second floor of a crowded tenement house located on the corner of Willet Lane and Guilford Street. It was a short walk from the tenement house to my place of employment, the British Museum. During my century-long odyssey, I discovered that I had a talent for quickly learning to speak, read and write a variety of languages. Because of this ability I was hired as a linguist, but most of my time was spent translating German, French, Italian and Greek text into English."

"It was on one of my regular early morning hikes to reach the Museum that I passed a figure that awakened a sense of familiarity and then I froze. I could barely turn my neck to aim my eyes at Mr. Jimmie. It had been almost a hundred years since I'd last seen him. I had thought; the Devil had forgotten about me. He was leaning against a red and green advertisement painted on a gray brick wall. A hundred years had passed and he still looked vaguely the same. That lanky physique was clothed, as usual, in a woolen tailored black suit with ruby cuff links peeking out of the sleeve. The chapeau was gone and his brushed back curly black hair was a little longer. The light gray eyes still seized your attention and his expressive eyebrows now had a companion. He had grown a thin mustache that curved upwards at the ends. When he spoke, the dance of the three was entertaining. He still had that jaunty, carefree attitude and when he spoke his rich honeyed voice was soothing."

"Hello Micki, it's so wonderful to see you again. You're looking content and fit."

"He blabbed; he rambled endlessly, but I heard very little. I can't recall most of what he said. My stunned and dazed brain pushed aside the mind fog when my associate mentioned my second task. I had two weeks to leave London and resettle in Sarajevo, a city in the Austro-Hungarian Empire that had a large Serbian population. Aleksandra Dobra, the proprietor of the Dobra Hotel, a small, clean, modern hotel was expecting me. I was to learn the Serbian language and become a member of the Serbian Orthodox Church. My ability, my talent with languages made it easy to secure an instructor's position at the Sarajevo Merchant School, as an English language tutor for the older boys."

"I changed my name to Ivan Abramovic. Aleksandra Dobra provided me with a room at the Dobra Hotel in exchange for help cleaning and repairing the Hotel. My task was to convince students aged sixteen and seventeen the need for a United Serbia free from Austrian tyranny. Teaching English was only a cloak to conceal my true purpose. I was to feed these students the opiate of the poor: blame and rage."

"My mentor suggested that I use all of his simple, superb pearls of wisdom to complete my task. He added another simple lesson. He said that the best way to influence people is to talk in terms of what they want. Always see the world from their point of view. It makes it easier to find weaknesses. His parting advice was that there is only life and death; so, enjoy life, enjoy each large and small task, because what is the alternative."

"It was simple to influence teenagers. Soon my passive apprentices were angry radicals willing to die for the nationalistic cause. I had easily turned innocent cubs into violent extremists."

"On June 28, 1914, three of my former pupils were involved with others in an assassination conspiracy. One of my favorite prodigies, Gavrilo, murdered the Archduke Franz Ferdinand, the heir to the Austro-Hungarian throne and his wife the Duchess Sophie. The assassination created a diplomatic crisis that triggered The Great War, now called World War I. I had created murderers and worse; their actions contributed to the death of millions and unbearable hardships for millions more. I had not fired a weapon, nor raised a hand to strike, yet because of me the world was in violent turmoil. I was sick with guilt and grief."

"Months before the end of the war I was walking pass one of the few cafes still open in Sarajevo and I saw the Mischief-maker sitting at a table waving me over. He was dressed in his usual stylish uniform and a silly black beret was perched on top of his thick hair. The pencil thin mustache was gone but the eyebrows were cocked for action. He always seemed genuinely excited to see me and eager to tell me about his appreciation of our dynamic partnership. But I was still grieving and ashamed of what my actions had helped create. When I sat at the table I looked into his gray eyes and childishly called him the Angel of Death. His reaction was one of disgust. Angrily he said that he was not Azrael nor was he Gabriel, Michael or Uriel, but he had considered adding an el to his name."

"As soon as I returned to the Hotel, I jotted down the following words my mentor used to praise me."

"Ivan for some men life is being a supplicant to a god or an idea, for others it is a constant drama, then there is the depressing life of tragedy and there are those that fight a life-long war of anger. But the Johns and the Janes like you are the achievers, the doers that become history makers. Ivan, don't pass a verdict and then condemn yourself. I think that will be done for you in due time. You must, my friend, not get stuck or waste energy fighting emotional conflicts. You must flow with life; enjoy the moment. Life has been given to you and that is all there is."

"When I walked away from my master, I felt light hearted, free of the guilt. He told me that to prepare for my next task Aleksandra and I had to move to Munich, Germany as soon as the war was over. We were to take possession of an abandoned boarding house, repair the building and rent rooms to the needy. He could never leave me without a lesson on social behavior or I should say manipulation. He said that if I wanted to change someone's mind, I should think of a simple question concerning the subject that the person has to answer yes. Then ask a slightly more complicated "yes" question. Slowly build your case question by question."

The Third Task

Hugo leaned back in his kitchen chair. He was exhausted after editing and rewriting the wording for the Second Task. Elijah's bundle of notes was getting smaller but there was still plenty to read and rewrite. He called Elijah's number to explain his plans. He was hoping Quinn would answer, but instead, a recording said that the number had been disconnected. The recording was troubling, but he had no time to waste. Hugo walked over to the kitchen sink and washed his face. He dried off, lit another cigarette and sat down to read Elijah's account of the Third Task.

"Aleksandra and I moved to Munich as soon as the war was over. We changed our names to Konrad and Adalwolfa Frank. Adalwolfa had become my friend, my confidant and an occasional lover. We posed as husband and wife-The Franks."

"We bought the abandoned boarding house and repaired it. The residence was clean, sturdy and always sufficiently warm. The upper two floors had sixteen rooms and two bathrooms for rent. The boarding house never had an official name, but we always called it The Adalwolfa Zuhause."

"My Third Task was to house, befriend and influence a certain war veteran. The young veteran was depressed, confused, lost and bitterly angry about the humiliation of Germany by the terms of The Treaty of Versailles. It was hard to gain his confidence. He was a loner, peaking over a social wall, wary of perceived intruders. He was interested in politics, so together we attended the political rallies and meetings of a radical mob called The German Workers' Party. The bitter veteran was impressed with the leaders of the Party, Herr Aton Drexler and Herr Dietrich Eckart. Their anti-Semitic, anti-Marxist, nationalistic views aroused his emotions and awakened a passion for politics and power."

"Every morning when the young man ate his breakfast in the boarding house's dining room, I sat with him and discussed his work in the Party. I tried to shape his opinions, but it was difficult, because the war veteran didn't care if you were genuinely glad to see him or if you gave him compliments. The Devil's simple wisdom was useless against an enthusiastic, fixated mind. I was invisible to the aloof young man; but when Adalwolfa entered the room her sensuous beauty turned a man that was icy and indifferent into a giggly teenager. When she sat at our table, he stole glances and listened to every word. That's when we poured poison into his ears. We would talk about how the communist were ruining the country and the Jews were worse. Sometimes the morning conversations turned to the Slavic people or gypsies or the Jews and how they were a stain on mankind. We found fault with the German government; we debated racial purity and the beauty of the Nordic tribes. Each breakfast conference ended with a simple question that required a yes for an answer."

"Soon he started to rise in the Party's hierarchy. Then there was a setback when he was arrested and imprisoned for an amateur attempt to overthrow the government. After prison he continued to rent a room at the boarding house. At one of our daily breakfast discussions the rising politician proudly presented a book to Adalwolfa. He explained that he had written the book, which interpreted his guiding principles, while in prison. After I had read the book, I knew that my third task was nearly complete. I was to poison the mind and nurture the ego of this man and I had succeeded. The book was a publication filled with hatred, vitriol and moronic nonsense. Every morning we continued to feed Adolf's hatred and nourished his ego. We viewed him as basically harmless, just full of bombast. To our utter surprise from 1929 to 1933 Adolf's political career had a meteoric rise to power. On a June night in 1934, a night historians call the Night of the Long Knives, the beast assassinated all of his rivals. We understood that we had created a monster, but underestimated the carnage he would create. We did know that if we lost control of the beast, we could become his victims. Two months after that shocking June night, Adalwolfa and I left Germany to settle in Flat Hill. We needed to change identities and decided that it would be fun to create names for each other. She gave me a choice between Blue King or Elijah Cayenne. I gave her the name Quinn Sunshine. Adalwolfa was furious."

The Fourth Task

Hugo was exhausted; he felt feverish. He knew his body was rebelling from the lack of sleep and food. He wasn't going to rewrite his version of the Third Task. He had made extensive editorial instructions in the margins of Elijah's notes. Hugo needed rest; his plans were to rise early, drive to Flat Hill and read to Elijah and Quinn excerpts that would be in Sunday's paper. But the story was only a pretense for Hugo's real motive. He planned to take a vacation or an extended leave of absence or maybe quit the paper so that he could stay at the house on Sweet Faith Street and help Quinn take care of Elijah. When he finally tried to get some rest, the words Quinn Sunshine kept buzzing his brain.

After six hours of restful sleep Hugo had greeted the Morning Star as she rose over the eastern horizon. He had survived the fearsome morning melee on the Interstate and was now speeding up the last hill before Sweet Faith Street. He slowed the car and swerved onto Sweet Faith, and as the road descended the hill the early spring sunshine streamed through thin sparse clouds announcing a triumphant morning. The valley was glowing with a mellow yellow sunlight and Hugo took that as a sign of good luck. He turned onto the drive at 108 and what he saw caused a mental tremor, confusion.

The light gray stone house with the green metal roof was now painted white with a red tile roof. The manicured lawn had splotches of early spring greenery. The once dormant flower beds were brimming with flowers. Hugo slowly exited the car and surveyed the changes made in the past three days. The walkway to the front door was lined with bright pink, stormy blue, flinching violet and sunny yellow colored tall-stemmed flowers thickly bunched together. He haltingly treaded down the walkway. When he had reached the front doorway, he looked back down the path. The flowers were staring at him. His thoughts were racing and his emotions were working his stomach and heart. Hugo smiled when he realized just the sight of Quinn would be calming. He reached for the golden door knocker, but it was gone. The dark blue wooden screened door had been replaced with an aluminum and glass door.

A stranger pushed open the metal and glass door. The young doorman, grinned a smile of recognition and said, "Hugo! Quinn said you would return."

The stranger didn't introduce himself; instead, he turned to some unseen person to joyfully announce that Hugo had returned. A diminutive woman with mahogany colored hair in a windblown Einsteinian style appeared at the door.

"Good Morning Mr. Richard, we've been hoping you would visit." The pretty young woman stepped through the doorway to greet Hugo. She extended her hand to him and said, "I'm sorry, I should have said Mr. Ree Chard. My name is Ooona' Schmidt." The two syllables of her first name were long and slow, her last name hit you like a hatchet. She turned to the young man standing safely behind the metal and glass door and spoke gently, "Patrick, bring me Elijah and Quinn's notes and the garden blanket."

Hugo blurted, "Patrick? Where's Quinn?"

Ooona' took the notes and blanket from the smiling young man and commanded Hugo. "Follow Me."

Obediently, robotically Hugo followed the green-eyed woman down a path that led from the house into the dark oak forest. Soon the path led from the cool dark woods to a sunny bright glade. In the center of the glade was a circle of planted trees flush with early spring greenery. Everything was green and gold, including the long, belted shirt dress that Ooona' was wearing. The tiny woman spread the blanket in the middle of the circle of trees and again commanded

Hugo. "Sit." The woman's emerald green eyes were looking up at the sky searching for something. She sat on the blanket, faced Hugo and growled, "I know you have lots of questions. So, I'll get right to the point. Elijah died the morning after your last visit. Early that fateful morning, an ancient, feeble woman appeared at the door of Elijah's home. The woman at the door was Fleur. Mr. Jimmy had released her. After hours of disbelief, joy, and grief, Elijah asked Quinn to spread this blanket at this spot. Quinn carefully squeezed the reunited lovers into Elijah's wheelchair and pushed the couple to this blanket. She served them French toast and coffee. The couple reminisced, cried, laughed, hugged tightly and stared into each other's eyes. Around noon Quinn checked on the couple to see if they needed lunch. She found the aged sweethearts lying on this blanket with their faces almost touching. They were both smiling, looking into each other's eyes. They were both dead."

Ooona' took a deep breath, slowed her narrative and began to speak tenderly.

"I was summoned that day. Quinn, Patrick and myself cleaned and dressed the bodies. Elijah had already given Quinn instructions for his burial. He wanted his body to be carried to a glade, similar to this one, but much deeper into the forest. At the western edge of the glade is a large flat stone, maybe four feet in height. That's where he wanted his body laid in permanent rest. He had said that he wanted his body to experience the morning sunrise until his bones turned to ash. We covered the rock with blankets, thick quilts and pillows. We laid the bodies on the bed that we had created and covered them in silks and furs."

Ooona' held up the binder and said, "In this binder is the last of Elijah's notes. He does not mention Fleur's arrival because he had finished dictating his narrative the night before his death. After the notes is his promised version of the events that occurred that night inside the comedy club. The last page in this binder is a letter from Quinn. Quinn insisted that you read the pages in the order that you find them. Please take your time reading everything. Later I will send Patrick with tea and a light brunch. I know you have many questions. You will find most of the answers in these pages."

Hugo watched as the tiny wild-haired woman rose and marched down the path disappearing into the dark forest. He felt helplessly tired and confused. Where was Quinn?

The fresh light of spring broke through the young foliage and errant shafts of sunshine dappled the shade. Hugo stared at the spots of light that floated around the leather binder waiting for him on the blanket. He took off his shoes, folded his legs into a comfortable position, opened the binder and began to read.

"Hello my friend, when you read this summary with the nearly infinite notes, I suppose I will have stepped into the great mystery.

I want to thank you for writing my story. You often asked why it was so important to me to have my saga told. Well, I finally realized that I would never see Fleur again. The dark portals to Fleur's world had never reappeared in my lifetime; but I knew that they had sucked life off of our world in the past and they would return sometime in the future. If, the story of my life is told as an epic struggle for love and it becomes legendary, to be repeated for generations and familiar to future travelers to Fleur's world; then Fleur and members of her community will hear of my undying love. The tale of my life will be the only way I can touch her."

"There was no fourth task. Each task eventually resulted in suffering on a massive scale. I had participated in these endeavors in a mindless pursuit of a personal need. After the resulting horrors of the third task, I knew I could not continue. I never again wanted to be the spark that caused vast carnage."

"For the fourth task, Mr. Jimmy wanted me to befriend, guide and influence a tyrant that had threatened to use nuclear weapons. I could not do it and I was aware of the consequences of a broken contract. I said no, but the King of Hades gave me numerous chances to change my mind. He said he was sad, felt dismal and heavyhearted to be losing a good friend and associate. But a contract could not be broken or renegotiated and so he would really miss me. I asked him what would happen after death. He took off his black felt fedora, releasing his long black hair to fall about his face, and then spoke in a quiet earnest voice."

"I've always tried to be honest with you and answer all of your questions. I like providing answers."

His gaze shifted from my face to a distant beyond me. He slowly shook his head from side to side and said, "But death, I'm not sure. I am sure that when every man or woman is born onto this world, they are not created for immortality. I know that every human mind eventually gets impossibly fatigue and will want to abandon the journey to sleep. Does the mind ever reawaken to a new world or is there just darkness or worse just a fading memory in the minds of others. The question of: what is in back of death can only be answered when experienced."

His gaze shifted to my eyes and in a loud pleading voice he yelled, "Hell Ulysses, I'm not sure why I exist. I can say with total honesty that I have been given a job or a burden and I have worked diligently to be the best workman in all of creation."

"Hugo, the demon looked scared and confused, not unlike his victims. When he yelled the name of my youth; it was like a slap of awakening. I was centuries old and I have known the Prince of Darkness for most of my life. I have been a slave and now I am impossibly fatigued. I already miss talking to you. Telling you my story has made me remember things that I had forgotten. Telling my life story has set me free. I have had a relentless appetite for reading great novels for the last few centuries and your work captivates me like no other. I've read your work when you were in college, also, your earlier work at newspapers, magazines, news feeds and that unpolished script for a television series and I was always left with a vivid visual. You have a preternatural talent with words. Saying thank you on paper is only written words. If our faith or our dreams are correct then I will be there at the Smoldering Door to Hell or at the Pearly Gates to greet you, my friend."

At 108 Sweet Faith Street all events flowed with precision and accordingly as soon as he had finished reading Elijah's letter of farewell the young man from the house walked out of the forest carrying a tray and a tea kettle. Hugo could hear the young man chattering as he walked up the path. "Ooona wanted me to check if you needed anything and she sent some tea and cookies. I am to check on your comfort. Do you need anything? Hugo it's so good to see you."

Hugo studied the young man's face and said, "Do I know you?"

"It's me, Patrick the dog."

Hugo continued studying the young man's face and smiled, "Is this one of Quinn's psycho dramas? She's going to tease and toy with me before we meet for some lavish meal."

"No, no, Ooona' warned me not to blab my story. No, Quinn is gone. No, I'm Patrick the dog. Please Hugo; Elijah and Quinn are gone; they were all I had; and I need to talk to someone. Ooona didn't know Elijah and Quinn; plus,she's domineering and irritated by questions."

Hugo laughed, pointed his finger at Patrick and said, "You're a good actor. Do you know what Quinn is preparing for dinner?"

The young man placed the tray and tea kettle on the garden blanket, knelt in front of Hugo and spread his hands to plead, "Please Hugo, believe me, Quinn is gone. Like you, I loved her and now I feel lost. You knew her for a few weeks. She has fed and taken care of me for over eighty years. Like Elijah, I willingly chose servitude. When I was a young man, I made many silly mistakes in my life. One day the problems grew unbearable and I fled into the woods to escape. After hours of wandering aimlessly in the dark woods I met a well-dressed stranger with sparkling ruby cufflinks that was eager to listen to me moan about my difficulties and to help find a solution. He said to call him Constantine. At first my guard was up, because I sensed a wicked pervert; but soon Constantine made me feel confident, secure.... complicit. He knelt with his arms hanging lifeless, but his palms were facing me suggesting honesty and openness. He promised to help me completely escape my problems if I became a loyal protector for one of his friends for a period of time. He promised that once I fulfilled the obligations of my contract, I would be free to pursue a new life as an extremely wealthy young man."

"Once again I am a young man. I inherited an enormous sum of money from Elijah. Constantine's promises have all been fulfilled; I just didn't realize it would take over eighty years."

"After we had laid the bodies of Elijah and Fleur on that stone in the woods, I went to my pile of rags in the kitchen for a quick nap before Quinn started cooking lunch. Quinn came to me in my dreams to say goodbye. When I awoke, I was once again a young man, but just as lost as I was eighty years ago. Elijah never knew that there was a human mind behind those dog eyes; but Quinn the master sleuth knew that I had been captured by the Devil. Constantine is Mr. Jimmy."

"Hugo, have some tea. I have to return to the house, if I stay too long, I will risk an hour-long lecture from Ooona'."

Hugo looked down at the cup that Patrick was filling with tea. He saw the chipped bright blue red-rimmed coffee cup and saucer.

"That's Elijah's cup."

"Yes, Elijah wanted you to inherit two things from him, a valueless centuries old coffee cup and the story of his life. I must go; Ooona' will be waiting with questions. She will stay with me for a few months to tutor me on how to access my wealth and how to blend into my new world. After Ooona' is no longer my guiding mother, could I visit you at your home if I need help and to relive the memories of Elijah and Quinn."

Hugo nodded his head yes and the young man rose and trotted into the forest. He picked up and cradled the blue cup. The warmth of the cup traveled from his hands to his heart and mind. He stared into the cup and felt calm, reflective. His eyes saw brown tea, but his mind saw a smiling Quinn.

Hugo sipped the tea and flipped through the countless pages of notes. He stopped turning pages when he got to the one titled THE INTERVIEW. Part of the original agreement was once a shorten version of his life had been printed in the City Advocate over a number of weeks, Elijah would then grant an exclusive interview about the night that he prevented a tragedy. He had risked his life to save others from a catastrophe. Hugo smiled as he read the four thin paragraphs.

The Interview

Other than long walks in the woods, most of my winter had been spent in my home debating a decision I had made. It was late winter and driving was not pleasant, but The Comedy Club had a Cajun comic that specialized in telling Boudreaux and Thibodaux jokes and I always enjoyed his comedy. His clothes were always damp and his hair dripped from stress sweat, even before he walked under the bright stage lights. It was his voice that revealed the fear. The more laughs he received for his jokes the steadier his voice became, the hair dripped less. He was hilarious; he always made me laugh.

I rarely over-eat or drink alcohol to excess or overmedicate; but the comedian was special and a reason to over celebrate. I was drunk and had smoked some weed. I was sitting at a front table near the stage waiting for the show to begin when the gunman jumped out of the men's room wearing a Bill Clinton mask and fired his weapon into the air. My heart was beating so loudly that I didn't hear what the idiot zombie shouted, but I knew he couldn't see me.

Yes, at times I am invisible. My father never saw me; I've been in the middle of battles as an unseen spectator when butchery was occurring all around me. I've been to parties of three and the next day I am the only one whose name and face can't be recalled. But let there be a problem and everyone's averted stares shout guilty and everyone remembers my name.

The confused or heartbroken or misunderstood angry maniac never saw me coming. I jumped on his back, we toppled over onto the floor and I held him for a few seconds, then others pinned him to the floor until police arrived. I was hailed a hero and could have given a good hero interview and then forgotten the next day. But I needed more than a temporary elevated status. I needed to tell a story.

Hugo's grin expressed the laughter in his thoughts. He knew that for Elijah the hero interview was only currency to pay for a need. His only thoughts were to get his story told. He often wondered why Mr. Doucet, usually a very conservative publisher, agreed to Elijah's demands. There was always a puzzling hint of fear and dread in Mr. Doucet's voice each time we discussed the Elijah section in the Sunday edition.

Hugo slowly turned over the last words of Elijah and there was one page left. It was pastel green with a border of fingered watercolor red smudges. The words were printed in black ink with precise and uniform dimensions. At the top of the page in large perfectly crafted letters were the words, My Goodbye. Hugo took a deep breath and as he read the letter, he could hear Quinn's Germanic staccato cadence.

My Goodbye
Hugo we only met on four different occasions but each encounter was fun and exciting. I've met men that would envy a dog for its social abilities. Men like you are few, a scarce breed in a world that has become too brusque, too common. I will miss your bashful smile and boyish charm. Your intelligence is evident and your ability to express your thoughts verbally and on paper is remarkable. Handsome, intelligent, charming and creative! You are blessed. Don't dwell in problems; live for the challenges of life.

Beware Hugo, evil is everywhere and it is unrelenting. The wicked can be a lifelong foe. You do have a choice. I forbid you to ever speak to Mr. Jimmy or any of his associates.

I am and always will be only a memory for you and that's how it should be.

Love,
Idonia Uoolva Elizabeth Roth

He was disappointed; he had fantasized about words of undying love. Her exasperating brief message touched him as a note of motherly advice. He thought, "If I could have just one more meeting, I could convince her to love me." He kept thinking that she couldn't be gone; she needed to give him one more chance. Quinn liked to use teasing as a form of erotic torture. He'd experienced her meanness before; she'd soon appear with a sly smile.

Then a sudden chill raced through his body; he sensed the familiar smell of smoke from sweet pipe tobacco. He was surprised to see a well-dressed man sitting on an old paint-starved wooden park bench at the near edge of the glade smoking a pipe. Hugo stood to get a better view of the stranger. The man was wearing a black suit and perched on his head was a short brimmed black pork pie hat. When the stranger's hand reached for the pipe Hugo saw the ruby red cufflinks.

The bottom of his stomach fluttered with spasms of nervous anxiety, his face was black with tension and his voice trembled when he said, "Mr. Jimmy?"

The stranger slowly, meekly rose from the bench. With a flourish he removed his trendy hat and took a miniature bow. His long black hair hung loosely framing a handsome, friendly face. He took a tentative step closer to Hugo and said.

"Are you my next Adam?"

Two Years Later

Hugo's internal clock woke him. He sat on the side of the bed putting on some shorts so that he would be modestly clothed when he walked out on his balcony. He rose as he did every morning and looked at the other side of the bed to see his beautiful wife. Each morning as he gazed at her night-wild blonde hair veiling her pretty face he knew he'd made the right decision.

He walked out on his balcony to await the morning star. When he had built the house, he included an eastward facing balcony so that each morning he could watch the sun rise from the ocean.

Each morning before the first light and after he'd done a few yoga stretches he said a prayer of thanks to whoever listens to prayers. Often when he said the prayer, he held the successful novel that had changed his life. After giving thanks he looked down at the novel and silently read the title.

For Love

Moochie

He arrived on a cool, rainy March night, He wasn't sure of his plight.
Standing next to the gate, in the rain, all night,
He nor I realized that our lives would be intertwined so tight.
Free food and a place to sleep,
Why should I give him a name to keep?
But, as we got to know each other, we knew he had a home, a place to sleep.
Stuck with the name Moochie, a name to keep.
Tired and depressed, not a good day at work,
Open the gate, he sees me, he's excited, ready to drain away the hurt.
Every day is Christmas, I am his Santa.
The only present he ever wants is me.

Together in a Church

(Late Afternoon Roman Sunlight and Shadows The Smell of Old Times)
Old legs aren't meant for walking. Hardy workman they were, friends once taken for granted, but now complain when asked to do too much. Jack knew he had to sit. He had kept up with the group for the last four days. In fact, he and Emelye had done more than most. They had gone on both the day and the evening tours for the last three days and nights. But now his legs were hurting and the dull heavy ache had turned to a screaming fire. Jack bent over to whisper in Emelye's ear, "My legs are hurting a little bit so I'm going to take a seat; you go with the group." Emelye gave a loving sympathetic smile and watched as her old warrior walked crookedly to a pew.

Jack flopped his bottom onto the hard, wooden seat and then took a deep relaxing breath. The group had been to at least five huge churches or basilicas. Each church was amazing. Anyone of the churches would have been a centerpiece of a community back home. Rome had a magnificent House of Worship on every block. Each Roman church looked like a celestial castle that was both spiritual and golden and, in some ways, forbidding. Jack looked up at the ceiling of the nave to marvel at the workmanship, the artistry. He didn't need to be with the group or to hear the history lesson from Michella, their tour guide, to appreciate the beauty and the history of this time-worn building. Whenever Jack went into old historical buildings, he always tried to visualize what the place and people would have looked like two hundred or five hundred years ago. There would be no lights, only window allowed sunshine, probably candles, smoke and the smell of unwashed bodies. If it was the winter season, a heavy scent of dirty unwashed-for-weeks hair. The ceiling smudged from smoke. The walls sweating and the floor slippery. He liked to fantasize about being there, a visitor with no responsibility other than to observe. Jack was deep into another century when out of the corner of his eye he saw Darwin join him in his pew and unfortunately close enough to alert the socially intelligent that a conversation was coming. Damn!

Darwin's eyes had that faraway dead look, but he beamed a comfortably brash smile. Out the side of his mouth Darwin loudly whispered, "I don't know about you bro, but I got enough of churches. How about an afternoon in a pub and most importantly a ride back to the hotel?" Darwin let out a friendly chuckle but his dead eyes were searching for a reply.

Jack smiled and said, "A pub would be nice but I like these old churches. Sometimes I can feel the history walking by me."

Darwin's chuckle stopped at the back of his throat; he leaned closer and, in a tone, just above a whisper he grunted, "That either sounds creepy or LSD influenced." Darwin rearranged his large frame on the hard, wooden seat into a more comfortable position now that he had broken the barrier that exists between strangers. Looking straight ahead both men could see Michella, waving her flag draped baton as she walked and rattled her rehearsed lesson to the historically deficit group. Darwin interlaced his fat fingers and rested his large hands on his basketball sized stomach. He cleared his throat and said, "What cha think about Michella the Nazi? She looks like a little brick with hands and feet jutting out."

It was Jack's turn to chuckle, "I think she's kind of cute. She's good at her job, confident in her abilities, proud of her city and can control the group with a steady voice and eyes that speak loudly. I like how she takes charge and gives commands. Those laced-up knee-high leathers suit her personality."

Darwin tilted his white moss-covered boulder head toward Jack and out the side of his mouth he truly tried to whisper, "I bet her husband catches hell. You know she's a ball buster."

They both watched Michella and the group with their heads tilted skyward as she pointed to different aspects of the church's dome. A thought, a picture came to Jack of a pack of geese all looking skyward trying to commit suicide by drowning during a rainstorm. He laughed at his ridiculous thoughts and turned to face Darwin, "Yeah you right. It would be fun for a while, but not the whole endless journey of a marriage." Michella and the group disappeared down some steps located near the altar.

Darwin ears and vocal cords finally came into agreement on the intensity level of a whisper. A huge sly grin bared his teeth when he whispered, "You know the first time I felt enlightened in a church was during a Sunday mass when I was a teenager. Two pews in front of me sat this beauty. All through the Mass I couldn't concentrate on anything but her shapely behind, her small waist and her long silky auburn hair. When she went to accept communion, I waited for her to return to her seat. When she came into view I gasped. My father turned to see if I was O.K. I never thought two sides could be so different. There are always two sides to the story. There is a Yin and a Yang for everything."

Jack was happily surprised that Darwin could think. He turned his head to face Darwin and softly replied, "My first enlightenment in the House of Jesus wasn't as profound as yours. It was all negative because in my youthful ignorance I misinterpreted a situation. When I was ten, eleven, twelve years old I went to accept communion almost every Sunday in front of the congregation. At that age, what was probably a congregation of two hundred people seemed more like two thousand sets of eyes. When I received communion and then turned left or right to walk back to my seat, I could feel every one of those eyes staring at me. They stared at me in adoration. They fawned on me because of my attractiveness, I was solid, respectful. They watched my every step.

I was a good kid; I kept my gaze lowered. It would have been disrespectful to look an adult in the eye. I always felt like I was in the spotlight. I could feel the heat from the spotlight. How could it have been different? My family loved me. They always kept their eyes on me. They were proud of me. Then when I was about thirteen, I decided to rebel. I was going to look into the spotlight. I was going to boldly meet the gaze of the congregation. When they saw my confidence, they would know that I was now a man."

Sunlight burst through one of the upper stain glass windows and a shaft of light illuminated a massive statue on the far side of the church. Darwin and Jack sat silently and looked at the stone man whose solemn expression cast an accusatory glare in their direction. Always looking for signs from heaven, Jack wondered who was looking at him. Within seconds a cloud abruptly stole back the light.

Darwin's gaze turned from the statue to Jack and asked, "So what happened, they threw popcorn at you?"

The church returned to its somber shades. Jack kept his eyes on the statue and resumed his story. "The music that is always played in science fiction movies when a mystery is found or solved was drumming in my ears when I got up to go for communion. A deep bass crescendo, its volume built, it was overpowering, I could feel its vibration, then a split second of silence, I received communion, and then I turned to walk to my destiny and the deafening boom exploded in my mind as I looked up. All I saw was the tops of heads or people with closed eyes looking at the church's ceiling. Not one set of eyes were transfixed on me. I was stunned, shocked, something was wrong. Each Sunday I became more frustrated when I walked invisibly back to my seat. That's when I had my epiphany. I knew then that I was not special. The world did not revolve around me. I was just like an insignificant ant drifting in the wind of the swirling chaos that we call life. I was so naïve. It was months before I realized that everyone had just gone through a ritual and they were all kneeling and bargaining with God; something I was supposed to be doing. But it was too late.

Once I had tasted insignificance and darkness those two brothers have become my traveling companions for my journey."

Darwin slowly turned his huge head to face Jack. His eyes lacked any expression, but the smile was still there. "Man, you were a dumb kid. Sex must have really confused you. Hey you think our group left us. I still don't see them."

Embarrassed that he had told such a personal story to a new acquaintance his eyes went from the statute to his balled-up fist lying in his lap. He knew Darwin was right. A dumb kid and not much wiser as an adult. "Don't worry. Emelye wouldn't let the bus leave us." Jack focused his gaze on the altar and with a sigh said, "They're probably walking around the grotto where some pope or Renaissance artist is buried. They'll be up soon."

When Darwin laughed, it rolled up from his stomach and came out as a muted snort. Darwin snorted and smiled, "You don't know Priscilla. She probably paid the bus driver to leave me here. Leave me and then hope I get lost forever. We got one of those love-hate relations. Hey, in the airport, did I see you wearing a ball cap with a Vietnam Vet patch? You were in Nam?"

Again, Jack looked down at his hands. He didn't feel like explaining again that he had not been a warrior, only an office worker. "Yeah, Long Binh, 506 Field Depot, company clerk assigned to the Directorate for Data Processing in seventy-one."

Darwin turned his large torso so that it was facing the same direction as his big head. In an attempted whisper Darwin grunted, "You kidding me. I was at the 506 with the 31st Quarter Master Company as a forklift operator and anything else they needed. I was there seventy-one and seventy-two. Hell, we played cards, got drunk, and got high with a lot of the clean shirts. I told Priscilla that you looked vaguely familiar. Heck, I can remember one of the clean shirts raped me in a poker game and when I had nothing left to lose, I knocked his ass out."

A momentary darkness appeared to remind Jack of the feeling of losing consciousness. His eyes bolted from examining hands to being a seeker of recognition. When he was sure of the identity he said, "That was my ass that you sucker punched."

Satisfied, Darwin lowered his scrutiny, his lifeless eyes looking inward into memory. "I thought it was you. I recognized your voice and then you started to come into focus. Hey, I'm sorry. I was sorry as soon as I saw you lying unconscious on the floor. Man, I never played anyone that was that good in poker. It was like you knew what cards we were holding. I know. I was a sore looser; but I kept thinking you had to be cheating. No one wipes out the able."

A smile of remembrance spread into a grin; it was Jacks turn to look into the past. "Yeah, I was on fire that night. I was in a zone. I had a feeling of supernatural abilities. It was like it was my destiny to win and win big. Someone, something wanted me to win. I've lost a lot of money trying to recapture that zone, that feeling. I definitely wasn't expecting a sucker punch."

Turning his hulk forward so that he could search the front of the church for the group, Darwin grumbled, "All I can say is that I'm sorry. I'll buy you a drink. Why did everybody call you Duke?"

Jack scanned the front of the church to help in the search for the missing tour group. "Because my name is John Wayne."

Darwin spoke into his hand, "Oh my God! Your parents screwed you as soon as they named you. How could any kid live up to that name? No wonder you were such a screwed-up kid.

Jack's smile of reflection grew wistful. "You learn to live with a name. You were forgiven long ago. Life has thrown more vicious sucker punches and each one led to something good. It's like you said. There're always two sides. There is always a Yin for a Yang. I've always studied the collision of events and their aftermath. That night I won a lot of money; that was good. But that led to a sucker punch which was bad. But that led to a medical discharge because of a broken jaw and headaches. I was glad to get out of Nam, so that was good. Then I drifted for two years. I had no direction. So that was bad. Then I took all the money I had won and invested it. Those investments made me huge amounts of money and of course that was good."

Darwin unfolded his huge hands and his right hand slowly drifted toward Jack with the palm facing outward to signal for him to stop speaking. "Stop Jack, you talking crazy like Priscilla. Don't try to torture me. Speaking of the witch; let me check to see if she texted me."

His eyes measuring the massive marble column, Jack smiled to himself. He knew that his thoughts, his philosophies had a tendency to torture many listeners. His tongue had never been able to match his mind. "Is it easier to communicate with Priscilla through text?"

Darwin put on a pair of bent reading glasses and then squinted his eyes to focus on his phone. "Nothing, no text, she's officially silent. No, we don't communicate much. She'll send a text to notify me that she is having a good time and glad that I am not there. She always had a hard time saying that she loved me. Mean teasing is her way of showing affection. I know it's weird but it's a family trait. About that poker game, I never realized one punch would create a riot. I didn't feel the tension, the racial hate. I didn't know I was going to light the wick for an explosion. You said you were given a medical. We were all officially discharged from the military. No one was given a dishonorable discharge. No one was arrested; not even for the killing of that black kid. The war was coming to an end and so the military set free thirty-one young men. I've often thought about that night. It was a life-changer for me. A sucker punch was so wrong and there you were either dead or unconscious lying on the floor. Then total pandemonium; it's a wonder that more people weren't killed. We were alcohol and drug addled. It was a crazy, angry, confusing time and now here we are together in a church; an appropriate place to unburden myself of a sin. Hey is that our group?"

As soon as Michella reentered the basilica her eyes were searching. Two of her flock was missing and her eyes were searchlights scanning every crevice of the church.

"Look at that little Nazi," Darwin turned to smile at Jack, "She's looking for us."

When Michella spotted Darwin and Jack she continued her rehearsed lecture but kept her blazing eyes focused on her prey.

Jack could barely hear Darwin say, "Oh-oh! She wants to castrate us."

As she walked up the church's center aisle with her flock following close behind, she kept her eyes focused on her two strays. She knew words may only anger, so she communicated her displeasure with her practiced visual scolding. When Michella saw that her two strays recognized her annoyance, she lowered her gaze and gave a small smile of forgiveness. When she was even with the pew that sheltered the strays, she looked straight ahead and in a deep sultry voice gave the command, "Andiamo!"

Pig Bones

The Cast

Light chatter filled WJ's multicolored rustic kitchen. He had invited six friends and family members to dinner. He frequently held dinner parties in his modest house that featured his eclectic taste and fondness for junk. There were unfinished projects in nearly every room which gave the house an air of casual messiness. The mob of cats and Bullet the ancient mutt held claim to certain pieces of furniture and were not shy about showing their frustrations when you invaded their territory. The meal at WJ's house was usually sumptuous and savory, the conversation was always smart, fun and sprinkled with many jokes. But, until the cocktails broke down social defenses everyone was on hyper alert for WJ's eventual intrigues. He had the charm to convince people to step out of their comfort zone. His get-rich-quick schemes and his personal and financial adventures were always to be viewed through a protective veil of suspicion.

WJ's older cousin, Alida, was helping him with the final preparations of the feast, or as he liked to think, they were preparing– the bait. Alida was nearly ten years older than her cousin, widowed for three years and always excited to be near him. She knew her cousin had many faults, but he was blessed with an abundance of good looks and country-boy charm. That charm was the honey that attracted both men and women. On these fun occasions Alida's handsome cousin made her feel special and took her out of her memories.

Mr. Leander Faucheaux had already staked out his territory at the dining table. Mr. Faucheaux was old and pissed at the world.

He was working on his third self-made martini. Soon his anger would be a weapon at the dinner table. When his anger erupted into a vein-popping boiling crescendo, just a few reassuring sympathetic words from WJ was enough to soothe the raging man.

Sitting on the other side of the table was Hollis, Leander's divorced neighbor. He had told Leander on the drive to the dinner party that he couldn't stay very long after the meal due to his need to wake at four in the morning. He hoped WJ would quickly lay out his current project. He needed to rest. The twelve-hour work days were killing him. He always held out desperate hope that one of WJ's ideas would make a lot of money. He couldn't work harder, lottery tickets weren't working, gambling had been a bad idea and his only hope to escape his current slavery was WJ.

Standing in the middle of the kitchen was Candice in open-mouth awe of WJ. Candice, a gorgeous woman from northern Alabama, had a beautiful southern accent that made you want to listen. When she spoke, everyone smiled and attempted some of her words in an exaggerated southern accent. Her words were contagious. From the moment she'd first seen WJ, he became her mission and he had been basking in the glory.

Sitting on Bullet's pillow was Fig the Hunchback. His upper back towered over his head, magnetically attracting eyes. He was giving Bullet a neck massage. The old dog had found a willing masseuse and was now drifting into a dream world slumber. Fig couldn't stop grinning; sitting on WJ's kitchen floor was high drama in his dull friendless world.

The far corner of the kitchen was shaded in shadow and in that gray area was Miss Nancy sitting in a lawn rocker sipping a rum and coke. She was quietly inspecting the other guest. Nancy had been a widow for decades and for most of that period voluntarily deprived of a man's friendship. Whenever WJ called for a dinner invitation, her impatience caused the days to slow and the minutes to lazily creep along. When she knelt at night to give thanks, she began her evening song by saying, "I've weathered the challenges you've given me. Thank you for WJ's friendship, a worthy reward. "

The Proposal

WJ ladled and piled huge portions on each dish and Alida placed the plates around the beaten and scarred wooden table set for seven diners. The guest didn't wait for a signal, they all made haste to the table. WJ was satisfied; everything he'd cooked had come out perfect. The baked sliced pork sausage and sweet potato casserole was savory. The red beans were the perfect consistency and the rice for once was fluffy and a little salty. The aroma of warm garlic bread always pleased the senses and he thought that his second try at Opelousas Baked Chicken was a success. He passed bottles of red wine to his guest and was about to say *bon appetite* when he heard Leander already giving one of his sermons.

"For four decades I was a public servant employed by the United States Postal Service. I was a servant and I was expected to shut up and serve. If I paid a yearly sum of money, I could keep my house and if I shut my mouth, I could keep my job. But it's even worse today. The self-appointed sophisticates and their outrage mobs have convinced many to lead a deathless Inquisition. "1984" is here and the powerful have persuaded many to prey upon their own. The powerful no longer need the tools of the government to suppress. They have traitors that are leashing the people. If you peel back the veils of legitimacy and expose the methods of the powerful, you are swiftly labeled a conspiracy theorist, a UFO nut. When the American aristocracy and their surrogates have no answers, they brand you a vigilante conspiring to harm the innocent. You can no longer exchange ideas without risking your reputation."

WJ knew he had to stop Mr. Faucheaux before he boiled over into cursing and swearing.

"Leander, we all agree with you brother, but fussing and anger ain't gonna do us any good. We've got to enjoy small pleasures that lighten the struggle."

Hollis had been shoveling food like a starving man. He stopped his gorge fest for a brief moment to respond to WJ.

"I think it's the media. Most of what you watch, read and hear is controlled by global conglomerates. Information for the masses created by a few in league with certain captains of capitalism and academic thinkers that are social engineering a generation. The outcome, positive or negative, I have no idea. But like everyone else I feel controlled and fear that an unforeseen "Reichstag Fire" will negatively influence our lives. The common man experiences the struggles; the powerful create them and then fashions false hope."

WJ held out his hands to halt Hollis's speech.

"I didn't cook my ass off all afternoon to sit here and listen to Marx and Engels debate the social ills of capitalism. Stop this bleak discussion; I want you to eat, drink wine, let's have a fun evening."

Nancy had a habit of air writing or pointing with her fork when she spoke. Her fork was pointed at WJ when she said, "WJ this sweet potato casserole is divine. I gotta get this recipe. This chicken is wonderful."

Everyone grunted their approval. Nancy waved her fork, like a conductor's baton, then haltingly said, "If you don't want us to talk about our problems; does this mean you're about to explain your newest proposal."

"What proposal?"

Alida giggled and fawned ignorance. "Whaaaaat proposal?"

Candy's sparkling, smiling lips straightened and her eyebrows rose to display curiosity and confusion, "What proposal? What ya'll talkin about?"

Fig tapped his fork on the dark blue plate, "I hope it doesn't require money; because my property taxes are due in two months and I desperately need to start saving for that expense."

Candy stared straight at WJ, assumed a look of genuine concern and asked, "What are they talking about?"

WJ thought Candy's reaction was annoyingly theatrical; he smiled at her and said, "That's for later. Right now, I want you to enjoy my cooking, enjoy everyone's company, and have fun."

Leander spoke in a volume like most near-deaf men—loud and usually blunt. "I hope we make some money this time; my doctor bills are killing me. Got anymore picks like Amazon?"

Alida turned to Leander and said, "That was a nice little profit. That pulled Frank and I out of a financial hole."

Fig nodded in agreement, "Yeah a big hole for me."

Candy questioned Fig. "You talkin about the stock, right?"

Fig continued to nod his head. "Yes, in 03 he convinced us and a few others to each invest at least a thousand dollars in Amazon stock. A few sold their investment when it doubled or tripled. But most held on to their stocks since WJ wasn't selling his shares. Ten years later our investment was sixteen times more valuable at over three hundred dollars a share. Then one day, without explanation, WJ sold all his shares. Thinking the worst; we all rushed to sell our shares. He'd cashed out to pay for a climbing trip to Mount Kilimanjaro for himself and three of his female friends."

Candy's head jolted around to face WJ. "Three female friends, darling you might be too much for me."

Looking at Fig in mock anger and shaking his head, WJ grumbled, "You had to add that part."

Tapping his finger on the table top to get Candy's attention Fig continued, "Listen, Candy, after the racketeers, the brokers and the government extorted their toll we each had ten desperately needed grand."

Candy had put down her fork and was no longer interested in the food. "So ya'll a stock picking club?"

Leander yelled, "Hell no we ain't no damn club. I lost five hundred dollars on some scheme about zirconia diamonds".

Hollis stopped chewing to agree. "Yeah, I never understood that project."

Nancy's mouth was full of food when she croaked, "I lost several hundred dollars to World Wide Fucking Bingo."

Candy's hands were poised asking for answers, she laughed and said, "You actually invested in bingo?"

Hollis had cleaned his plate and turned to answer Candy's question. Now that his stomach was full, he became conscious of Candy's beauty and it was obvious he was ready to be her Sir Lancelot, "Actually, I really thought that World Wide Bingo was going to be our ticket to an easier life. We each...."

"Excuse me dear," Candy put her hand up to silence Hollis and turned to WJ, "Honey could you put these persistently rude cats in another room."

Leander shouted, "Just call the damn dog-catcher."

Nancy jabbed her fork at Leander, "Don't shout you'll wake Bullet."

Everyone turned to see the old dog sleeping on his pillow.

WJ used his plate of uneaten food to lure the cats into another room. Candy turned to Hollis and said, "Now you were saying."

Hollis cleared his throat to speak, then took a sip of his wine and again clear his throat. "Well like I was saying, I really was in favor of our investment in World Wide Bingo. It was an over-the-counter stock, a penny stock. We bought thousands of shares. The company was to sell tickets at convenience stores, much like lottery tickets are sold today. Winners would be announced during halftime at NBA games and eventually NFL games. I saw a great potential, then the morality police swooped in and said that gambling and sports were not a good mix. The company went bankrupt."

Leander's fist crashed on the table top, "The bastard greedy governments wanted to control the whole racket. Within a couple of years they were promoting gambling and creating lotteries throughout the country."

Alida laughed, "But we have fun and we occasionally make a small profit. It was lots of work, but the fried chicken delivery during the Holidays put a few hundred dollars in my pocket and I think we still have a chance to make a hefty profit from the web domain names we purchased."

WJ returned from jailing his cats, sat in the chair with a thud and said, "I just let go the BushCruz16 domain name. Unfortunately, that won't happen."

Fig rested his head on the back of the chair and muttered, "We've made more than we loss; but not much more." Candy, Hollis, and Miss Nancy were seated across from Fig and they were too distracted to hear anything that he said. When he rested his head on the chair back, his hump was squeezed and rose even higher. The hump looked like a character in a horror movie.

WJ wore a defeated grimace when he growled, "I'm gonna tell you about the proposal in a few minutes but first I have to tell you that next time we meet, there won't be a cooked meal. Hot dogs, mustard, stale buns and maybe a beer or a soda will be your next meal in this house."

A collective groan could be heard from everyone. Then shouts of: "We loved the meal." "You're a great cook." "Best meal I had all week."

Leander's voice could be heard booming over all the chatter. "Stop being such a sour puss; let's get to work. What's the next mission?"

WJ looked at every one and said, "Yeah, I'm sorry. I just hoped there would be lots of laughter and jokes at the table. The coffee is made. Let's enjoy a cup while I explain, as Leander just said, the next mission. Let's get down to business. Candy, would you and Alida serve the coffee. I'll slice and serve the cake."

When cake and coffee was placed in front of Hollis his eyes widened. He had struck gold. He loved WJ's warm cakes buttered with milk chocolate and dusted with crushed pecans. It was always warm and sweet.

WJ took his seat at the head of the table, took a sip of his coffee and said, "Great coffee, I have to compliment the cook. OK guys, let me give you some history or some background on our next profit-making adventure. Three weeks ago, I was in Austin for the Southeast and something or other music festival. Without the help of my usual accomplice, Fig my wingman, I met a Miss Hellen Green from Los Angeles. She was reporter for a TV station. She did investigative pieces, feel-good stories, and stories that educated the public, blah blah, blah blah. Basically, anything that caught her eye. My thoughts started racing; how could a reporter help me, help us, my friends."

Fig lifted his hand and his index finger was curled into a question mark, "Why didn't I go that weekend?"

WJ's eyes flashed anger at being disrupted. He bluntly growled, "You weren't invited."

Candy guzzled the last of her wine, snatched the bottle from in front of Hollis and in a volume to match Leander said to Fig, "So you WJ's wingman." Candy poured a full glass of wine and challenged Fig, "I can't picture you as a wingman. I'm intrigued."

That sounded like an invitation to brag about his adventures with WJ.

"One night in Miami, WJ parked himself at the far end of a bar in an establishment that was ways above my social strata."

"Crap" WJ pushed himself out of his chair and stared at everyone at the table. He took a deep breath and swallowed his burst of emotion. This was business; passion and emotions could wait. "OK, get your yakety-yak out of the way before we get to work."

Candy stared at WJ and a forced straight lip smile threatened him, "I need this story. I need some insight."

WJ walked to the crowded counter to get more coffee. He turned on some music and Patty Smith's weary and heartbroken voice grabbed the attention of some of the guest.

Nancy didn't recognize the voice but she was sure the song being sung was sixties soul about different dances and it had an infectious beat. Soon Nancy, Leander and Alida were bobbing their heads to the beat of the music. Nancy's fork and head were keeping the same beat when she looked at Fig and said, "I hope this is not another man-whore story."

Candy's head stretched a little further out so she could see around the spoon-licking Hollis. Her eyes fasten onto Nancy and said, "Miss Nancy, I am going to hear this story."

Everyone smiled; they loved hearing Candy's emotional southern belle accent. Leander thought he'd prefer listening to her recite the contents of her grocery list than to listen to the packaged content of television. Media had become an addiction for society; an addiction that everyone was told they needed. Leander knew with the ever-increasing bills, something had to go and TV and the internet were an easy choice.

Candy took a large gulp from her half empty wine glass and gave Fig an order, "Continue!"

WJ sat down at the kitchen table with his second cup of coffee and said, "Yeah Fig, continue with your gossip."

Candy folded her arms hugging her body just below her breast and slowly said to WJ with a tinge of acid in her voice, "WJ, kindly refrain from comments. My friend Fig was telling me a story."

Hollis cleared his throat, "Fig, is this going to take long because I have to get up very early in the morning."

Fig sheepishly looked at the other guest, but avoided the eyes of WJ. He kept his gaze focused on Candy as he continued his story.

"I was instructed to exit a taxi a block away from the genteel enterprise. I was wearing a dark suit, shiny black shoes and a chauffeur's driving hat. The hat was perched on my hump. I walked past the maître d', waitresses, waiters and probably security, mumbling that I was a driver, jingling the keys as I burst into the candlelit haven. I weaved through the tables with a destination for the far end of the bar. All chatter ceased; all eyes fixated on a cap wearing hump. I was illuminated by at least one hundred pairs of eyes. I brought that spotlight to WJ. When he spoke to me, he spoke as a man blind to humps. I was instructed to return in an hour."

"When I returned in an hour, WJ was sitting at a table of nouveau aristocrats, paying particular attention to a pretty middle-aged woman. He ordered me a soda and had me wait in his shadow. I heard when he used the word, choo chooma'."

Candy blurted, "Choo choo ma?"

"No, it's pronounced choo, then chooma' as one word. Accent on the ma."

Candy snapped, "What does it mean? What language are we talking? Who speaks this language?"

Fig tried to give a quick definition of the word, "It's a word that adapts to the situation; it's like the word----."

WJ quickly barked, "It means nothing. Sometimes Fig and I can be a little silly."

Alida's smile had evaporated; she looked irritated. "You seem proud to have helped WJ lure this woman to his bed. You sound like a worshipping shadow."

"No! No! And hell no," roared a visibly upset WJ. "Remember poor Ouida Babin whose little boy has that rare cancer. No help down here, but there is an experimental treatment at a hospital in Cleveland. Insurance companies don't pay for experimental treatments. The burden was crushing Ouida. Debbie Guidry is the name of that woman. I told her about Ouida's life, her beautiful young son and her dilemma. Mrs. Guidry is financially able to help. She created a fund to help with medical expenses. Her first deposit was fifteen thousand dollars with a promise of the same amount in three months. I thought that was choo chooma'. Everything was beautiful. Everything can be beautiful."

Alida stammered, "Oh WJ, I'm so sorry; you too Fig. Sometimes I can be a bitch." Alida leaned towards WJ and gave a light kiss to his cheek. She turned to Fig and gave him a cheek to cheek touch.

"I'm sorry; I guess I was getting jealous listening to your adventures."

Candy stood to give WJ a hug and a lip kiss, "I knew you were a good man."

WJ was basking in the glow of admiration. But, only loud mouth Leander could crush the beautiful moment.

"After WJ gives his proposal, we can have a few more cocktails and I'll tell how WJ and I almost got killed three times on our profitable drug smuggling adventure."

Candy stiffened and her voice went deep, serious and devoid of all southern charm, "You ah dam drug dealer?"

"Dammit Leander! Candy don't listen to him, he's in the early stages of dementia."

Hollis waved his hand like a student requesting permission to speak.

WJ yelled, "What is it Hollis?"

"I'm really enjoying the conversation and the food was the best I had all week; but I have to wake up at four o'clock in the morning. Leander rode over with me and we are going to be leaving soon. I want to be part of the next job and I'd like to hear some of your plans.

WJ took a deep breath and then said, "Yes, let's do this. Stop with all the foolishness. It's time to get down to business. Nancy! You, Candy and Alida clear off the table, get us each a cup of coffee and then I'll start."

Nancy partially rose from her chair and said, "Why all the women have to serve?"

WJ slapped the table and snapped, "Sit down Nancy. I'll help; I don't have time for your feminist foolishness."

Nancy was notorious for having the last word. "I got enough damn bosses."

WJ pointed his finger at Nancy and snarled, "You better stop it girl or I'm gonna go over there and give you a spanking."

Needing the last word, Nancy sarcastically said, "I dare you. I'll give your ass a whippin."

Sounding like a Confederate general, Candy poked WJ and said, "You will not touch that woman."

Leander, always quick with sarcasm shouted, "Candy is jealous. That's what she was hoping for tonight."

Candy's face scrunched up in anger, her eyes were glaring at Leander when she shouted, "Shut up you old purrfick."

Everyone laughed, even Candy, at her amateurish attempt to show anger.

After coffee was served WJ began his proposal talking softly and cautiously. The guest each held a coffee cup and leaned towards WJ like starving dogs waiting for their food bowl.

"Ya'll this adventure is not gonna cost anyone a dime. But you will have to work and be a little creative. You may have to be a little untruthful, but you won't be hurting anyone. Most of all we gonna need team work. We're a team. We need to help and support each other and stop all this damn bickering."

"As I was saying earlier, I was in Austin three weeks ago and I met a Miss Helen Green, a reporter for a Los Angeles TV station. The night before I had finished reading a novel about a ruined society that depended on miracles from holy relics. That concept was still fizzing in my head when I met Miss Green. I used the plot of the novel to guide the conversation with a few changes. I told her I was the owner of a holy relic that has been in my family's possession for over six hundred years. St. Thomas, a bone from St Thomas."

Leander yelled, "Is there even a St. Thomas?"

Alida skeptically whispered, "She's got to be dumb if she believed that bull."

"Yeah, I checked; there are about a hundred Thomases. We can choose which one later."

Candy's corner of the table was the color of fire. Her red dress, red lips, sparkling eyes, ivory skin and straw-colored hair created a chaos of color and light. Around the rest of the table it was grayer, worn, tired and when Candy spoke the guest turned to her, to see, not to listen. "So far, your proposal sounds stupid. It sounds to me that you are just lying to another woman."

Nancy threw her hands in the air and wailed, "Shut up! Please let him finish."

Candy gripped the table to confront Nancy. "My dear Miss Nancy, don't you tell me to shut up."

A snarling Leander snapped, "Shut the fuck up; I want to hear the rest of the dam proposal."

Candy drew back and asked WJ. "Where did you find this insane old fossil?"

WJ ignored the carping and continued the presentation of his plan. "Leander…. this is the core of the proposal. I told her the relic has always been selectively used by my family to help individuals in need. That caught her attention. I revealed to her that it had been used eight times since my inheritance. Six of the requests or the fulfillments of a need were a success. My family has handed down various theories of why the success rate is not one hundred percent."

"Next week she'll be exploring New Orleans for four days. On one of those days she wants to come down here and do a story about the relic. A former co-worker from California is living in the city and she hopes to hire him to do the camera work."

Each guest looked puzzled; but Alida was the first to voice doubt, "But where is the relic? What is it? Why do you need us? Where's the money angle?"

"Great questions!" WJ used his hands to put emphasis on each word of his answers. "I've got a few ideas about the relic. I'll take care of the relic and everything else. Your job is to come up with a convincing story of how the relic has helped you."

It was Nancy's turn to ask for details. "This reporter is going to film our stories. Our stories are to be about how the relic has saved or changed our lives. So, you want us to create the stories. But where is the money? How are we going to profit from this task and can someone turn off that damn music?"

WJ rose quickly from his chair to turn off the music and in a soft conspiratorial tone he said, "That's it! She will film your stories. Your stories will explain the power of the relic. I'll take care of everything else. I'll get us a holy relic. I'll also have a story to tell. When my turn comes, I'll tell the camera that I am the last relic keeper of my family. I have no children and will not have any in the future and so I want another family to experience the wonders of the mysterious. I will sell the family treasure and share the proceeds with family and friends. No one needs to know that you are my friends and family."

Leander's deaf ears heard every word of WJ's softly told narrative. He whispered, "Beautiful."

Candy's elbows were planted on the stained tabletop. Her hands were covering her eyes when she lamented, "But it is all lies. It's all lies."

WJ turned to face Candy; his voice had a heartbroken tone, a sadness that the other guest immediately recognized. That tone was a tool that they had seen him use before.

"Candy, I'm sorry, I misjudged you. I thought you were like the rest of the team; tired of struggling financially and spiritually. Tired of being told that you are the lucky, the privileged working class. We're tired of paying higher taxes and knowing the money is being spent to help others while we struggle to keep up. Tired of seeing our parents, our aunts and uncles work and struggle their whole lives. We all have a desire that someday, we will figure out where our American Dream is hiding. We've listened to lies our whole lives, while we watch others get rich. This task may not be a big money-maker. We can only try. In this house, even a hundred bucks would help."

Candy's elbows were still firmly planted on the tabletop. Her hands were vigorously rubbing her eyes. When she stopped massaging her eyes, her lips hardened before shouting, "Fuck it! I'm in!"

Nancy always got goose bumps when WJ spoke for the dispossessed. He was her rebel leader. He created adventures. When she heard Candy speak, she instantly sprang from her chair, raised her fist in defiance and shouted, "I'm with you Cappytain."

All the guest clapped, yelled something and nodded in agreement. Leander was nodding his head and a big grin graced his old face. He could use the extra money; but WJ gave him something more valuable. He made life interesting. His hoarse and gritty voice broke through all of the chatter, "WJ I'll stand with you and if we get knocked down, I'll stand with you again."

WJ nodded his head and voicelessly mouthed thanks to everyone. Hollis was checking his watch. Fig was misty eyed and deep in thought giving thanks. Alida sat silently admiring her handsome cousin.

WJ stood up and held up his hands to silence everyone. Everyone noticed the glint of mischief in his eyes. "OK, here's your marching orders. Miss Green will be here next Thursday afternoon. That gives everyone six days to formulate a story and email me a copy or at least an outline. I can maybe give you some advice to revise and refine your miracle. I chose you guys because of your intelligence and creativity. Candy said that we are lying. Well, I expect well crafted, heartwarming, mysterious lies. Don't put any sugar on these lies, make them meaty."

Hollis was the first to push back from the table to leave. He walked up to WJ and offered a handshake. "I no longer have the internet. It was an unaffordable luxury. I'll type my plans and bring you a copy."

Leander had thought he'd enjoy a few more cocktails but Hollis was his ride. He barked at WJ, "I got some ideas. I'll write'em down and bring them tomorrow. Later dude."

Fig stretched out his arm to fist bump WJ. "Later gator."

Alida gave WJ a hug and whispered in his ear before she disappeared into the darkness.

Nancy lightly held WJ's face with both hands and kissed his lips. "I'm excited," she looked back at the table where Candy was still sitting, "be careful of that bitch; love ya."

WJ watched the departing headlights, waved, then closed and locked the door.

The Trap

The team of two performed a kitchen ballet swirling in the oven heat. The moaning bass range of a cello filled the warm kitchen with an urgent seriousness. The spectator of one, Bullet, was awake and intrigued with the dance of the chefs. WJ was concocting the gumbo and Alida was crafting the potato salad and baking the first batch of brie filled bread. WJ and Alida were preparing their bait. Two dozen oysters had been shucked and were chilling in their half shell on the bottom shelf of the fridge. Together the chefs had prepared a dozen crust less, diagonally sliced chicken salad sandwiches. The sandwiches were piled on a platter and placed in the middle of the stained and scarred kitchen table. WJ had already taken four dozen sugar cookies out of the oven. Two dozen were gone. The flower girls, Annie Zeringue and Betsy Aucoin, had come earlier to get their cookies. The flower girls were two mentally handicapped adults that lived with their parents. They had attended a flower arranging class and had duped WJ and a few other gullible people to pay sixty dollars each month for a bouquet of flowers. The girls kept the previous month's bouquet to recycle the faded silk flowers. WJ's monthly payment included two dozen cookies. Each month Alida inspected the new bouquet resting in the etched brass vase and always grew irritated with the shoddy arrangement.

"You should tell the girls to put more flowers in their arrangements."

WJ looked up from his gumbo masterpiece and laughed. "I can't do that. The girls are so excited and proud of their artwork."

"That's what they call it, artwork? You got three faded flowers and a bunch of greenery. They're taking advantage of you."

WJ backed away from his culinary artwork and in a matter-of-fact tone said, "Well fortunately for me most women take advantage of my kindness. The gumbo is finished; I'm gonna take a quick shower so I don't smell like roux."

"You make a roux for your gumbo?"

WJ sipped from the wine bottle, "You gotta make a roux for a good gumbo."

Alida took the wine bottle from WJ and took a sip. "I brought a change of clothes. I think I'll shower also."

WJ shoved a spoonful of potato salad into his mouth and muttered, "You go first."

"I thought I'd scrub your back," smiled Alida

WJ darted from around the counter and grabbed Alida's arm, "Let's go girl."

WJ walked into the kitchen towel drying his head. He was wearing his favorite faded rusty colored baggy corduroy shorts and his new gold and purple LSU polo shirt. He spied Fig sitting on Bullet's pillow sharing a chicken salad sandwich with the patient beggar. "You better not let Alida see you feeding her sandwiches to Bullet."

"Why are you dressed so casual?"

Before WJ could answer the question, Alida walked into the kitchen wearing a black satin dress with raised velvet flowers of various colors decorating the eye-catching party attire.

WJ regarded his cousin's beauty, "Alida, that dress looks great. You add the pizzazz to it. After this is all over, we gonna all go out and dance. That's a dancing dress. A warning if you dance with Fig. He's a bit of a show-off."

Alida glanced at Bullet and saw him alert and licking his lips. "Why is Bullet licking his lips? Fig I hope you didn't feed him some of the sandwiches. We didn't make that many."

WJ came to the thief's rescue. "Hello Candy."

Candy walked through the seldom locked kitchen door wearing tight white jeans and a pink blouse. "I hope I'm not late."

WJ wolfishly grinned at Candy. "Perfect timing, you look great or should I say sensational. The first team is here. Leander, Hollis and Nancy will get here in about an hour. I wanted Leander to come later so he wouldn't have time to get worked up and start shouting. Everything is ready, I just need to light a few candles in the living room. I think that's a good place to have the interviews. Miss Green should be here within the quarter hour. Alida, you go first. Then Fig you do your song and dance. After you interview, stay in the room for the rest of the interviews. That way you can slip out and get me if something goes wrong. If Leander arrives early, let him go next. Let's do him before he starts with the cocktails. The trap has been set. Any questions?"

"The relic, the saint, you need to explain that part. I need to see it," whispered a nervous Candy.

WJ walked into the kitchen pantry and came out with an old worn wooden pencil box.

"I've been having this box since first grade. It was a gift from Aunt Menola for making excellent grades."

WJ opened the old box and took out a vial or a test tube containing a brown liquid and corked at one end. "The bones you see in this vial were the forefinger of St. Thomas the Apostle. Over six hundred years ago, my ancestor, Tarlton of Sardinia, was sent by Pope Gregory to investigate the ancient stories of St. Thomas's death and burial in India. Tarlton found the stories to be true. St. Thomas was an important saint to the Christians of India, but they gave the bones of St Thomas's right forefinger as a gift for the Pope. Unfortunately, Uncle Tarlton died in India and so his possessions were sent to his wife that lived in France. This holy relic was mixed in with the rest of his gear. For centuries the oldest child in the family inherited this secret relic and was expected to use it for the family's common good."

"What is it really?" Candy blurted.

WJ looked at his watch and knew his prey would arrive very soon so he gave an abbreviated recipe for making a holy relic. "I bought some pickled pork and ox tail. I baked the meat until it easily peeled from the bone. I took the small bones from the ends of the tails and put them in the vial with some lightly brewed tea, a little bit of cocoa and some shaved bits of cork. I whittled a cork to fit the opening, buried the vial in the garden for a few days, rubbed some truffle oil on the cork and presto a holy relic. It looks old, the bones can be partially seen and it smells exotically earthy."

The Interview

Miss Helen and Dave, her cameraman and friend were prompt. The reporter and Dave had arrived at midafternoon and before the introductions had been complete, informed WJ and the others that they could only stay for about two hours. They had tickets to a Jazz performance. A number of New Orleans Dixie-Land Jazz bands were having a benefit performance in the French Quarter in the gated square in front of the Cathedral. She said she thought the name of the square was the Robert E. Lee Square. They both felt fortunate to have tickets.

Candy and Alida appraised the reporter and were delighted. They had been expecting a California sophisticate with an air of superiority. Miss Green's face was severe with a manly jawline. The women were pleased to see the Californian was wearing an ill-fitting gray jersey dress with an empire waist to hide her obvious high body mass index.

"We have some raw oysters on the half shell and some beer or sangria to wash them down," Alida offered to the guest.

The reporter's nose and lips expressed revulsion, "I can't put oysters in my mouth. They feel like cold snot."

"Oh, what a shame," Alida turned to the cameraman and asked, "How about you Dave?"

Dave had an easy smile and stoned eyes. "I've been living in New Arlins for about a year and I have yet to master oysters."

Alida smiled sympathetically, "We have some freshly made chicken salad sandwiches."

Both Helen and Dave bobbled their heads and answered, "We both don't do mayo."

"Maybe some wine?"

Helen shook her head no and said, "I never have alcohol when I'm working. But I wouldn't mind a cup of coffee."

WJ knew it was time to change the flow of the dialogue, "Helen, while Alida gets the coffee, let's all go into the living room. I thought that room would be best suited for the interviews."

Everyone exchanged small talk while waiting for the coffee.

Fig was always happy and relaxed when he was in WJ's living room. He loved the lighting. A dim pinkish light in one corner. A faint yellowish glow between two large beat-up quilted chairs illuminated another corner. The addition of candle light made everyone's eyes sparkle. Moving shadows created by the candlelight disappeared into the shadows created by the dark colored wood-paneled walls. Everyone loved the huge burgundy clam shell couch. This room was heaven when the music hovered at decibels lower than conversations so that WJ and his wildly eclectic group of friends could tell their stories and laugh. In that room he always felt like an equal.

Alida entered the living room carrying a tray with five cups of coffee, milk and sugar.

"I've poured coffee for each of you. Helen before you leave you must try some of WJ's gumbo. A visit to Louisiana would be a major disappointment for many people if they couldn't have some of his yummy gumbo."

"Thanks, we'll stop a little early so I can try some. I like gumbo."

Alida slipped out of her new shoes and curled up on the huge burgundy couch. Her gaze travelled around her favorite room. She had always felt safe in this room, part of a special community. She could feel Frank's spirit watching. He would have loved to be part of WJ's latest adventure. The first time she brought her husband to meet WJ, it was in this room that Frank fell victim to WJ's charm and wild adventurous thoughts. After a few drinks, WJ had convinced Frank that the best lubricant to use on the human body was vaginal fluids. He had focused his serious penetrating gaze on Frank and concocted a story about his chemist friend creating artificial vaginal fluid in his laboratory. He and his chemist friend were going to mass produce the fluid, bottle it and market it as vaginal saliva. He assured Frank that the manufactured fluid was a slippery sexual lubricant and moisture retaining body lotion. Men, women, couples and habitual masturbators would be eager customers. He and his chemist friend were selling shares of their unnamed company. Ten thousand dollars would buy an eighth of the company. The next morning Frank had still been contemplating the offer. They had laughed for weeks after she'd gently explained WJ's games. The following Christmas, WJ gifted Frank a small bottle of clear lotion with a typed label. In bold print the words Vaginal Saliva were typed on the label. Below the bold type was printed: sexual lubricant for couples.

Miss Green's commanding voice stifled all conversation and fond memories, "Dave we may need a little more lighting. Set up your light in the direction of that beautiful couch. I think that's where I'll conduct the interviews. Who will be first?"

Alida was ready to tell her life story. She wanted the world to know that she had been married for twenty-five years to a wonderful man and the mother of two fine sons. When both sons had finished graduate school; her husband, Frank, retired. She and Frank had looked forward to traveling, relaxing in each other's arms. She pictured them cuddled together taking afternoon naps. But God had other plans; Frank was dead six months after retiring.

"Alida we'll start with you on camera, talk about the miracle for about two or three minutes, Dave will get a shot of the relic then he'll refocus on you as you wrap it up. We'll interview three or four of you guys and select the best two to put on the program. We'll have about a fifteen-minute segment that includes multiple commercials so everything has to be brief. Look at the camera when you're speaking. It's OK to turn and talk to me but always return to the camera." Helen looked past Alida and yelled, "Somebody tell WJ to kill the music. We're not making a movie. You look great; that's a beautiful dress and I love your short and sassy blonde hair. Remember, be brief. Introduce yourself when you are ready."

Alida could feel her heart beating faster. Her preparation had been three type pages. She hadn't expected to be told to condense her story. She cleared her throat and looked deep into the lens.

"My name is Alida Davis. My husband's name was Frank. A month after he retired, he started losing his balance and then one day he lost vision in his left eye. The doctors said that he had glioblastoma multiforme, an aggressive brain cancer. They said that if they'd been able to treat Frank at an earlier stage, he would have had a life expectancy of six to eighteen months. Because his cancer was at such an advanced stage, he had two to four weeks to live. We were numb; our souls had been crushed. The boys came home, we locked the doors and mindlessly paced. Then one day WJ showed up at the house and invited us to his home. When we got to his house, this room was filled with friends and family. In every room there were colleagues and old friends. There were acquaintances with sleeping bags on the porches. WJ had fed them all and now they had a job to perform. We all closed our eyes and said silent prayers, occasionally someone would break out in song or prayer and we all followed along. We talked and laughed all night. It was a glorious night."

"Was the relic nearby?"

"Yes, it was here in this room. We prayed and partied from sunset to sunrise. Four days later Frank walked into his doctor's office a different man. The doctors were amazed. The cancer had stopped progressing and actually died back in some areas." Alida's voice began to tremble; she could feel tears in her eyes. "It was a miracle. It wasn't a cure; but it gave my family six more months with the rock of our family."

"Alida I'm so sorry for your loss. You did good. When we edit this piece, I'll add a lead into your story and then concluding remarks. You did good; who's next?"

Alida hadn't expected to become so emotional. She needed to get to the bathroom for a quiet cry and to wipe away the sniffles. Everything she said was true except for the relic. She thought to herself, "Please God it was just one small innocent lie."

Fig held up his five pages of notes and said, "I don't think I'll need this." He had so much he wanted the world to know.

Helen smiled as the hunchback pulled himself onto the huge couch and squirmed into a comfortable position. Fig could hear Candy's gentle voice from across the room. He thought her beautiful voice sounded like a dream. She was scolding him for putting his shoes on the couch.

"How did you get the name Fig," said Helen to the smiling hunchback.

My parents, brothers and sisters were embarrassed of me and so when visitors came to our home, I was told to go sit under the fig tree to drive away the birds. In the winter months, when there wasn't even a leaf on the tree, I did my assigned duty. After years of banishment, my family would just yell fig and point to the back door and I would trudge off to my only companion, a fig tree.

Helen's smile bent into a frown and said, "Oh Fig, that's so sad. My heart hurts for you."

Fig could feel a commotion in his chest. He hadn't expected this woman to have empathy for him.

"OK Fig, you heard my directions to Alida. Keep it brief; look at the camera when you are speaking and when Dave films the relic turn to me. Take a deep breath and when you are ready introduce yourself."

Fig had talked to a tree for much of his life so it felt normal to be speaking to a camera lens. "My name is Fig Malbrough and I'm here today to tell you about the magical powers of the St. Thomas Relic. My life began thirteen years ago on a cool rainy night. My car had broken down and I had no phone because it had been stolen two weeks earlier and I couldn't afford to replace it. I was on the side of the road, wet and miserable when a Mercedes Benz, severely dented, but polished to a sparkle, pulled out of the line of cars and drove up to me. When the window came down a voice came out of the darken car shouting that I better get my butt out of the rain. I apologized for soaking his car seat and WJ looked at me and said not to worry, the seat was just a thing. He brought me to his house, gave me dry clothes and fed me corn soup and bread. Some of his friends came over and we sat in this room and talked. They were interested in my hunchback and asked questions. I told them about the severe pain in my back and chest and at times of extreme pain I could only have a liquid diet. I held the Holy Relic as we spoke. I passed my hands over it, I petted it, and I kissed it. That night I slept here on this couch cuddled next to it. That night my whole life changed." Fig couldn't hold back his emotions. His hands covered his face and he started sobbing. "I still have a little pain but my life is a million times better than it was before that night." He couldn't hold back his emotions. It was a cry of gratitude that was pouring from the Hunchback.

"Dave stop filming. Helen placed her hand on Figs shoulder and said, "I'm so sorry Fig." Candy could be heard weeping in the shadows.

Before more sympathies could be shared with Fig, loud voices could be heard in the kitchen. Then the living room door slowly creeped open and a portion of WJ's face appeared. "Hey, you finished with Fig, because I got three more criminals." He opened the door further so that Leander, Hollis and Nancy could enter the living room. An open door was an invitation for the three cats to ride in like a wild wind. They inspected their furniture and the big orange cat, Tiger, was irritated with Helen. WJ scooped up the three balls of squirming fur, made the introductions and noticed Fig's solemn face.

"I'll get these bad guys out of here. Fig, you come with me and Alida. You look like you need a drink. Helen, Leander will be next because he can't stay long."

Leander could be heard muttering to Hollis, "Am I going somewhere?"

WJ closed the door and hoped for the best. He put the three terrorists into another room, got a wet wash cloth for Fig to wipe his face. Fig was petting his friend, Bullet, while WJ was fixing him a drink when they suddenly heard yelling in the living room.

WJ rushed to the living room and swung the door open. He heard Helen calmly asking Leander to leave the room. WJ muttered, "What's happening?"

Helen calmly and impassively said, "Darling I've asked this gentleman to leave the room. He's a name caller. He called me a stupid donkey."

"I also told her that she is ass supreme of the universe," yelled Leander.

Helen was shaking her head and answered, "Yes, that to."

WJ knew that the weak part of his plan might be Leander. Leander had always been reliable; but the past year everyone noted a change. He had become listless on occasions and at other times extremely combative. Everyone knew from Hollis the Gossip that his wife was insistent on moving up north to be near their daughter. At his age, Leander was not interested in change, he only wanted peace. He often railed about the word change. He would always yell that when a boss told you to embrace change; it was always the bastard's interpretation of change. His change usually caused inconvenience for you and more money in his pocket. When a boss said if you don't change, you become static and you begin to rot. It's his way of saying you are fired if you don't change to suit my needs.

WJ looked down at his old friend and smiled. "Leander go fix yourself a cocktail. I'll tell your story. I know all the details and I can show the x-rays that you brought."

Leander grumbled from the couch to the door and could be heard yelling in the kitchen.

WJ closed the door, sat across from Helen, beamed his lady-killer smile and gently said, "I can tell his story. I know everything about Leander and I got an x-ray showing a tumor near his spine and then another that shows the disappearance of the tumor after praying over the Holy Relic."

Helen shook her head no, "I don't need his story. I'm just gonna interview Nancy and that should be enough footage. This is just going to be a small segment of a larger story. The fifteen-minute segment will include your story and three commercials. We're always filming, then editing the piece and then canning it until it's needed for a larger story. We're working a story on the strange customs and habits of the citizens that live within a hundred miles of the north rim of the Gulf of Mexico and I think your story could be part of this larger story. After Nancy, we should have forty-five minutes before we must leave. We can then relax and enjoy some gumbo. I'm looking forward to the experience of eating real Cajun gumbo. Now go and take care of Leander; something is really bothering him."

WJ walked into the kitchen thinking his team's best story had just crashed and burned.

"I'm sorry WJ. She's a nice girl but I tripped over a couple of her words and I just exploded."

Leander was sitting at his corner of the kitchen table hunched over his cocktail. WJ walked behind Leander and hugged him and spoke tenderly, "That's OK old friend. I often think of our past adventures and my biggest wish is that you and I and the members of this team and our close circle of friends have many adventures in front of us."

Helen walked into the kitchen and saw the table was set for her experience. This experience would be one more thing to add to her brag list. Nancy was the last to exit the living room. She was smiling; she felt a sense of relief. She had always wanted to tell someone about the day she first met WJ. She was usually conflicted, but today, she told Helen and the camera lens everything she had wanted to shout from a mountain top.

It was a regular Saturday morning. She could only shop for groceries on the weekend because her work schedule didn't leave much time for shopping. The employed masses invaded the grocery store by nine every Saturday morning. To avoid the crowd, Nancy usually did her shopping when the store's doors opened at six. There were very few shoppers that early and to accomplish her Saturday morning ritual errand, she wore baggy comfortable unstylish clothes, no make-up, and her hair in a mess.

She was feeling and smelling the summer melons when she heard the voice and then in her ever-decreasing field of vision she saw the handsome face.

"I bought some last week and we loved them all. Those yellow and cream-colored melons were everyone's favorite."

He never stopped talking. The couple slowly strolled up and down the aisles enjoying their early morning encounter. They went to separate lines to check out and he continued the conversation. WJ gave her his recipe for oven broiled oysters while waiting for checkout. Talking in the grocery store at six was usually in hushed tones so when WJ invited her to dinner while standing at their respective counters everyone heard and waited for her response.

The dinner had been wonderful, but contact with the constantly changing cast of friendly and interesting characters had been life changing. WJ's living room and kitchen became her home for most of the weekend. A friendly dog, unruly cats, people beautiful and ugly became her holy relics.

Six weeks later, her doctors told her they must have been misdiagnosing her for the past two years because her incurable condition, retinitis pigmentosa, was gone.

Nancy sat at the table in her usual spot across from her friend Leander. She couldn't control the silly grin.

Gumbo

WJ had hoped to sit Helen away from Leander, but reacted too slowly. Helen sat in the chair at the end of the table with Leander to her left and Nancy on her right. She had lodged herself between the two crazies. He knew that combination could be trouble. The usual routine was for WJ to ladle the gumbo and Alida would serve; but emergencies change routines. Alida ladled the gumbo and WJ served. He brought the first two bowls to Helen and Nancy.

"Gumbo for our friend Helen and a bowl for Miss Nancy."

"Why do you always call her Miss…. Miss Nancy?"

WJ turned to Helen and saw her normal rigid, marble-hard face. Her thin lips were drawn back poised for attack. He put on his surprise mask and winked at Nancy. "Miss Nancy is a Southern Belle and should be treated as such."

"Southern belle, hell, usually when he says Miss Nancy, he wants something. Miss Nancy do me a favor; Miss Nancy get me a cup of coffee; Miss Nancy I'll be away for a week, could you take care of Bullet and the Monsters," blabbed Nancy as she strained to see if WJ was listening.

WJ brought two more bowls to the table and alertly saw Leander say something to Helen. Keeping his eye on Leander, WJ announced to his guest that he had potato salad and Alida was slicing her fresh baked brie filled bread. He rushed back to bring Leander's bowl of gumbo, hoping to catch what poison he was spewing on Helen. He missed the first part of the old man's story but he did hear the following.

"I bought into all the peace shit in the sixties and seventies. I listen to all the gentle bullshit from Taylor, Stevens and fucking Simon. I listen to all those bastards. But I can tell you now; it's the tigers in the room that got everything. They sell you peace and conformity and then they take everything from you."

Helen was vigorously shaking her head yes. "Yes, I very much agree. You have to be prepared to fight for what you want. Others will gladly stand on your shoulders and crush your ego to accomplish their goals."

WJ laid the last two bowls of gumbo on the table and Alida followed with her tray of potato salad and bread. When everyone was seated, he poured a glass of red wine for Alida and one for himself then passed the bottle down the right side of the table. He gave Dave a bottle and said, "Dave pour a glass of wine for Candy and one for you and then pass it down the table. Oh, and Helen, don't leave the bottle near Nancy. She's got a serious problem."

Nancy smiled; she loved his attention. WJ raised his glass of wine and said, "Bon Appetit!"

There were many oohs and aahs and quiet compliments until Helen broke the trance.

"WJ this has got to be the best soup I've ever eaten."

WJ didn't hear any of the compliments because he was seated next to a gumbo sucker. He could feel his tension level rise each time Dave noisily sucked gumbo off of his spoon.

"My legs are cramping; I need to stand. I'll eat at the counter," as he tactfully retreated from the California savage.

Helen gave WJ more compliments and said she needed to get his recipe. He had started to talk about crafting a good gumbo when he noticed Helen asking Fig what he had just said.

"I was asking Leander when was his court date."

Helen turned to face Leander, a Walt Whitman look alike, and said, "I knew when I first laid eyes on you that you were an outlaw. What kind of trouble are you in?"

Leander put his spoon into his bowl and said to WJ, "As usual the gumbo is excellent bon ami." He turned to face Helen and muttered, "It's really silly. An old man's problem. I usually sleep three or four hours and then I'm wide awake. If I walk around the house or watch TV, I wake my dear wife. My solution has been to dress, then drive to a nice well-lit neighborhood about three miles from my home. I park the car, then walk the quiet streets and admire the beautiful homes. In the past the police and the paid security service have stopped and questioned me. They have repeatedly insisted that I limit my nightly forays to my side of town. I always explain to them that I'd probably be killed or at least robbed if I walked the streets of my neighborhood at night."

"So! They arrested you for walking in an affluent community," Helen angrily asked.

"No! No! One night I stopped to admire a house. The owner couldn't sleep, peeked out of her window and saw me standing on the sidewalk staring at her house. She called the police and I was arrested for creating a disturbance."

"They can't do that; you have the right to walk on any public street or sidewalk," Helen angrily growled.

Nancy stabbed the air with her spoon and said, "Leander, if I ever look out of my window at two in the morning and I see you staring at my house; I'm calling the police."

Everyone laughed at Nancy's teasing.

"Where do you walk now?" asked Candy.

"Same neighborhood," laughed Leander. I still get hassled; but I enjoy the nightly mini confrontations."

Candy asked Helen if she liked living in California. Helen gladly listed the positives and negatives of living on the West Coast.

"Do you live near a beach? Do you surf?" asked Candy.

Nancy quickly blurted out her answer to the question. "We can't surf in Louisiana. The oil companies wouldn't allow it."

Again, everyone laughed at Nancy the comedian. WJ was relieved that the dinner conversation was going well. His main concern was the interviews and Helen's unwillingness to film his story and his desire to sell the Holy Relic.

The Lucky Star

WJ had spent most of the morning sitting in the shade on his screened, side porch, working on his dwindling finances. He knew if he couldn't think of a plan to fill his treasury, he would soon be a public defender once again. He had hated that job; but he had hated all other employment in the legal profession. The big prestigious firms were too regimented and too firm oriented. It was frowned upon to take a month-long travel experience or to stay home for a week to just read, write and watch movies. At the Public Defender's Office, he could stay away for months and still be welcomed back. At the Public Defender's Office, the pay was so poor most lawyers never consider the meagerly subsidized position. The clientele for a public defender were usually from the Land of the UnNormal. Some of the clients were truly hard-working poor in need of help. But many others were raging maniacs that didn't care about themselves, others or the law.

He was still subtracting future bills from his budget when he noticed in the stack of yesterday's unread mail a red, white and blue priority mail envelope. He pulled the thick letter from the stack and saw a California return address. He ripped it open and pulled a letter and DVD from the parcel. The letter was from Helen telling her Louisiana friends hello and thanking WJ for a charming afternoon. She explained that the interviews had been packaged into a documentary highlighting superstition in the Deep South. The program had been shown on an independent California television station. She had downloaded the documentary to a DVD so that her southern friends could view their cinematic debut.

WJ stood and took a deep breath. He marveled at how emotions could be so dark and heavy and then the next moment soaring and glowing. He shoved his carefully calculated budget, unpaid bills and the rest of yesterday's mail into the drawer of his old faded green porch desk. Bullet was dreaming on his outdoor pillow and never woke when he opened the porch's screened door to release the three monsters to wreak havoc on the neighborhood.

It had been six months since he'd last seen Helen. The Holidays had come and gone and Spring was beginning to green the earth, but he had never given up hope. He knew that some jobs could be accomplished quickly with a minimum of work. But other jobs took patience. Some jobs had to slowly unfold and give its unforeseen choices. He passed his fingers through his thick scruffy black hair and thought to himself that Lady Fortunata had not abandoned him. He knew that sometimes you had to wait for the Lucky Star to shine.

He decided to take a stroll through the neighborhood so that he could think. He woke Bullet from his canine dream and leashed him so that he could get his daily exercise. The old dog gave his usual sitting opposition to exercise but knew that resistance was futile.

The Premier

For weeks there had been a battle between the young warm eager Spring and the old cold hard Winter. Mr. Winter was winning the battle on the night of the Premier. The night was chilly and buzzing with excitement. All the men wore dressy sport coats; Fig and Hollis were both wearing badly tied ties. But the women's sense of style exceled in comparison.

Nancy wore a checkered green and white dress, black belted at the waist and flared outward from the hips. A billowy dress that was in fashion during another decade. Her dress looked dated but her face radiated a soft brightness, like young peaceful daylight.

Alida, as usual, was classic in attire. She was a middle-class struggler; always dressed like Old World wealth.

Candy's beauty was electric. For the Premier, she wore the old reliable for most women, a simple black dress.

No one possessed a red carpet, so WJ had covered the front walkway with blue towels. Everyone did the blue carpet stroll in front of thousands of imagined photographers. The movie stars were feeling festive; cocktails were flowing and the grand buffet had been WJ's threatened meal, hot dogs.

The pre-Premier cocktail party had been fun; even wide-eyed Bullet could feel the surging pulse. When the lights came on in WJ's living room after viewing the documentary the mood had changed to darkness, anger and embarrassment. The investigative or educational journalism of the film was sixty minutes of mockery and ridicule of the customs and superstitions of the various cultures of Old Dixie. Thankfully only Fig's interview had been included in the film. The voice-over didn't insinuate disdain. It bluntly used Fig as a caricature of southern ignorance. The documentary stated that the people of Fig's tribe would rather recite prayers over a holy relic, which were decaying human bones, instead of using educated Twenty-First century methods to solve their problems.

Everyone was voicing their anger when WJ walked back into the living room with a cup of coffee. He could hear Nancy screaming that she'd love to stick her foot up the bitch's ass.

"There's hot coffee in the kitchen," said WJ as he sat next to Alida on the couch.

"You not angry," yelled Nancy.

"Fig shifted his gaze from everyone's manic behavior to WJ his friend, his brother, his door into a different world. It was always reassuring to see his rugged face displaying a relaxed demeanor; but the glint of mischief in WJ's brown eyes captured everyone's attention. His friend always had a knack for recasting disasters.

"The film was terrible and offensive," said WJ as he sipped his coffee. "Fig, I'm sorry for the way the pigs insulted you. If I ever see Helen again, I will tell her how hurtful she has been to us. For the last one hundred and fifty years it's been considered sophisticated comedy to ridicule and satire the people of the South. We should laugh at the opinions of self-perceived superiors. But the sole purpose of Helen was to get some free publicity for the sale of our Holy Relic."

"I'd like to go to California so I could stick my fist down the bitch's throat," cursed Candy.

WJ spoke tactfully, "We can't let negative words hurt us. We needed publicity and she at least mentioned the Relic. I'm disappointed that she didn't mention our desire to sell it."

"How can negative publicity help us if no one knows that the Relic is for sale," asked Alida

The three sassy cats sensed a change in the energy level. They charged into the living room and after racing around the room they head bumped legs offering sympathy and a back in need of a petting.

WJ didn't trust the three Monsters. He kept a watchful eye on the pranksters as he spoke.

"This revolting film is just a start. We needed some publicity and we got it in the form of a West Coast film. Now when we bargain with potential buyers, we can reference the documentary."

"But who or where are these potential buyers," asked Hollis.

WJ deeply inhaled, then rounded his lips to let out a long cleansing exhale. "Finding potential buyers is our job. We're all intelligent people. Capable of using educated Twenty-First century methods to solve our problems. Let's not let this silly film define us. Maybe we can pitch the documentary to Louisiana media outlets and convince them to play the film."

"Hell no!" screamed Nancy. "I don't want anyone to know I had anything to do with that crap."

"That's fine, but we need to collect a list of ideas. We can take a week or two to formulate a plan. For the next two weeks give me your ideas, your thoughts, your opinions, both negative and positive. I'll compile everything, then we can meet and go through the list of ideas to decide on our best options. This is just the beginning. Be positive; positive thoughts attract positive consequences. Let's have fun with this project and who knows soon we may all be wearing silk."

Fig stared in admiration of his friend. How could someone like WJ have so much charisma and he had none. He marveled at how WJ spoke with such authority to the correctness of his opinions. You would have thought he was God.

WJ looked at each of his friends. He respected and loved each one. He valued everyone's thoughts and views, but he sought the opinion of only one.

"Whatcha think Leander?"

Prayers

WJ and his team created a long list of possibilities to exchange the Holy Relic for money. The girls had worked together to advertise the Relic on every online auction and retail site. WJ and Leander had written a short story praising the powers of the miracle producer and had submitted it to numerous newspapers. Hollis and Fig convinced a Baton Rouge television station to film a ninety second segment for its morning news.

There had been a few sale prospects, but only a church in Kentucky had shown a real interest. The church had offered eight hundred dollars, which was seven hundred more dollars than the next bidder. The gang had agreed that eight hundred dollars was better than nothing.

This morning, after taking Bullet on his forced exercise routine he would call the Kentucky church to finalize the sale and then later that day he would visit the Public Defender's office to offer his services. This project had been a dud. Most of his schemes over the years had been flops. But he had always enjoyed the teamwork and comradeship, the sense of a new beginning, a new endeavor, a new adventure and a few had been real winners.

WJ and Bullet's morning routine was a spectacle of protest and cheerleading. Bullet protesting and WJ coaxing and cheering the old dog for putting one paw in front of the other. Progress was slow and the pair never got very far down the road; but WJ's motive was to get the old fossil to move his sack of bones. This morning when they started their struggle the sky had been cloudless and blue, everything was wearing jewels of sparkling dew, the sunshine was still friendly and the shadows were still deep. By the time they returned the sky had become bruised with many black and blue threatening clouds. He was looking skyward at the mean-looking clouds when he heard his name.

"Mr. WJ?" asked a whispery voice.

WJ looked down and saw Bullet busily sampling a little girl's scent. The surprise had been swift. He was unable to mask his shock. The emaciated, hairless, ghostly white and grey little girl looked to be recently from the grave. The waif's black ringed eyes grabbed WJ's attention. Her determined, but exhausted stare froze him into immobility. She spoke again.

"Are you the Mr. WJ with the Holy Relic?"

The thing was speaking to him and he could only grunt out a single word. "Yes."

The ghostly apparition spoke again. "My name is Autumn Rose from Paradise, Nevada. I've been very sick and I was hoping to be able to hold your Holy Relic while I prayed for relief. We spoke to Miss Helen; she gave us your name."

Horror was sapping his senses. Once again WJ could only croak out one word. "Yes."

The little otherworldly creature at the perimeter of life shuffled to a white rental parked on WJ's side street yelling, "Mommy he said yes!"

WJ's eyes followed the little girl as she excitedly struggled towards the car, but he felt a presence. He turned to his right and saw a man speaking.

"Hello, my name is Samuel Rose. I'm Autumn's father. Thank you for doing this. We have about seventy-five people waiting at the airport for a phone call. Friends and relatives would like to hold a prayer vigil."

WJ looked in horror at the man that was offering a hand to shake. His voice croaked when he said, "No! God no no! It's just some pig bones. We were just trying to make some money."

Samuel put the offered hand into his pocket and said, "Yeah, we figured it was a scam, but how do you tell your little girl no, when there's nothing else. I just want to make her last days happy. She asked to do this. She's never complained, never asked why was life so terrible for her. But she did ask to come here."

Many years earlier, while standing before a jury explaining his client's position WJ had experienced the same loss of control. Burst of thoughts were exploding in his mind but none were connecting. The cerebral turmoil caused momentary loss of mental mastery then and now. His only option was to retreat inward; but on this occasion, he would utilize his learned breathing techniques to quiet his paralyzing confusion.

WJ closed his eyes and inhaled through his nose, filling and expanding his lungs with air. He held the air in his lungs for a few seconds and then forcefully expelled the life sustaining oxygen through his pursed lips. His mind was focused on refilling his lungs once again, he held the air for a few seconds then he softly expelled the air through puckered lips. He continued focusing on his breath until he could feel his mind slay the panic.

When he felt strong enough, WJ opened his eyes, and saw a look of concern on the faces of the mother and father as well as a smiling puzzled expression on the face of the frail grey, white and yellow little girl. WJ reached down to hold the little girl's hand and turned to walk with her down the footpath to the porch. He thought how he had leashed on one hand, death slowly eating life and in the other hand, death eager to feast. WJ bent down to whisper in Autumn's ear, "Think about what you want to achieve, then create it in your mind and will it. If you have a powerful hunger or passion and discipline, there are no limits to what can be achieved." WJ opened the screened door so that Autumn could enter his sanctuary. She carefully negotiated the three steps and WJ continued in a whisper. "We usually think in secret, but today and tonight everyone will need to project their thoughts and desires."

Prayers Pt. II

WJ recruited the gang to help him herd the influx of guests. He had bought twenty-five pizzas to feed the masses and Hollis and Fig purchased cases of bottled water and soft drinks, plus extra toilet paper. Leander's specialty was cooking a large kettle of jambalaya to assist in the feeding of the dinner guest. Alida, Candy and Nancy found space for everyone. Autumn's friends and relatives filled every room of WJ's modest house. The overflow of guests was guided to the front veranda and the side porch. Some of Autumn's friends brought sleeping bags to camp on the lawn, but the stormy sky had threatened rain all day.

It was minutes before sunset and everyone had been instructed to pray, in their own way, until sunrise. Members of the Rose family had been assigned to lead thirty to sixty-minute prayer sessions. At all times, there would be a prayer leader walking through the house leading the vigil.

Autumn was sitting on the floor in the living room holding the Holy Relic and seated next to her was WJ. He bent over to gently speak to Autumn, "Focus on your goal, envision what you want and go and get it. Tonight, you need to be fierce and unrelenting." While WJ was talking to Autumn, the first prayer leader told the group that the sun had set and the vigil would begin. The sun had been hidden all day by storm clouds, so sunset had only been an estimate and the thunder began to explode.

For the first few hours WJ prayed fiercely and unrelenting. But eventually his mind began to wander and memories weaken his focus, his resolve. Memories of the last time he prayed with such intentions invaded his thoughts. A life-time ago, doctors told the scared couple that her prognosis was not good. After five months of horror, science and health experts had failed the couple; and, there was no other place to turn other than religion. He'd prayed, he begged and pleaded, he bargained and he'd screamed in anger. Silence and an absence of miracles destroyed WJ's shaky faith. He had never been very religious, but when his wife died, he condemned it as a fraud. He hadn't told Autumn to pray to God. No, he told her to picture in her mind what she needed and then create it. He was still searching and maybe God was not above; maybe he was within everyone. We all possess a miracle, a powerful conscious brain and maybe, just maybe, that's where God can be found. Tonight, his hypothesis would be tested, with over a hundred minds fighting to defeat the tireless Grim Reaper.

Throughout the night WJ etched a picture in his mind of a healthy and happy Autumn. He also prayed profusely and once again begged for a life. Every time he checked the wooden disc clock on the living room wall, he wondered if it was working properly. Time had become impossibly slow. At around three in the morning, he decided to rest his burning mind for a few minutes; but when he looked again at the clock it was straight up and down, lined up with the Roman numerals twelve and six. The time startled him; he'd thought he had closed his eyes for only a minute. It was near sunrise and since the thunder had stopped hours ago, probably a cloud-free morning sky.

WJ sat up and looked down at Autumn. Her Mother was curled up next to her, holding Autumn's hands which were still clutching the Holy Relic. Autumn was sleeping but her Mother was still whispering prayers. He rose and stepped over bodies scattered everywhere. When he silently entered the kitchen, a pile of fur on the countertop morphed into a three-headed furry hydra. The cats were still angry about strangers invading their home. Bullet was in canine heaven. He was on his pillow, in a deep sleep, and surrounded by friendly people. WJ whispered Bullet's name three times. Slowly the old dog's head rose but his eyes remained shut. He planted his feet between sleeping bodies, bent over and lifted his ancient friend. His plans were to release the three monsters and he and Bullet could mingle in the backyard bushes and take a pee. He opened the side porch's screened door and the three neighborhood bullies whizzed out the cracked door like furry bullets. He was negotiating the three steps when he heard a voice say, "Good Morning!"

His occupied and tired eyes had been looking down at the thinning hair on Bullet's back. His eyes shifted to track the voice and when his eyes focused on the side street, he saw hundreds of people crowding the tree shaded roadway. Everyone was looking at him and more voices broke the silent morning with the greetings of "Good Morning." "Good Morning WJ." "Good Morning neighbor."

Still holding Bullet, WJ walked towards the crowd to inquire why they were standing on his street minutes before sunrise. He entered the crowd of friends, neighbors, acquaintances and strangers; hugging, kissing, shaking hands and listening to everyone's explanations.

It seems that a few neighbors heard about the vigil and they called other neighbors and those neighbors called others. Eventually the crowd of mercy and sympathy met and planned their contribution. They divided into four teams of grace. The first team would fill St. Joseph Church at sunset and for four hours they would pray and meditate on the health of a little girl they'd never met. A second team of prayers would replace the first team after their four hours of spiritual communion were completed and then four hours later a third team would continue the vigil until sunrise. The fourth team was in charge of setting up tables on the banquette. Each table was laden with food for WJ's guest. Other members of the fourth team were waiting with trucks and vans to take any member of the vigil to neighborhood homes to shower and toilet needs. At the first sunlight, people slowly trickled out of WJ's home and then a rapid evacuation occurred when food was mentioned. The vigil keepers mingled with his neighbors and the hugging, kissing, crying and eating began. The last to exit the house was Autumn, the star of the event.

When Autumn's mother opened the screened door for her to exit, Bullet was waiting on the top step and slowly waddled back into the comforts of the house. The little fragile girl held her mother's hand and in the other hand was the Holy Relic. The laughter and mumbling of the crowd stopped and everyone turned to look at the little girl. Someone started clapping and then the crowd started clapping their hands and greeting her with, "Good Morning!" WJ studied the child as she strolled towards the crowd. She looked less deathly white and yellow. Her eyes were less sunken and the darkness surrounding her eyes was gone. That evening she had struggled to walk and now she had a steady gait. WJ smiled to himself and thought, "The power of prayer, a miracle or maybe just his tired eager imagination."

The Hound Dog

By noon all of the vigil keepers had loaded their rental cars and drove back to the airport. There had been lots of hugs and invitations to come back to the Good Coast. By midafternoon the neighbors had cleaned WJ's lawn, removed the tables and were starting to drift back home. The gang had all stayed to help WJ clean the dishes, straighten furniture and to put the house back into its familiar chaos.

"I say it's a miracle!" yelled Nancy as she swept the side porch.

"She did look and act different." voiced Alida as she washed dishes.

"Maybe it was her body surging the last of its energy for one final event," grumbled Leander as he arranged the bottles in the liquor cabinet.

Candy dried a dish and smiled as she handed it to WJ. "I think you're a miracle. These people, in this community, did all this for Autumn and for you. I've never known anyone that was so loved by so many. Mister, you're a miracle. I can't stop smiling, but I feel like crying."

"You can just call me Mr. Miracles," laughed WJ as he placed the dried dishes into his over-crowded wall cabinet.

"Mr. Miracles!" screamed Hollis and Fig moving furniture in the living room. Their exhaustion had lowered their defenses and they both broke out into hilarious drunken giggling.

It was Leander's turn to speak again. He poured a jigger of whisky into a rocks glass. After his tongue, had swam in the whiskey for a second or two, he swallowed and spoke. "Maybe it was just the zeitgeist of the moment."

"Leander!" snapped Nancy, "Zeitgeist?"

Leander the teacher, the philosopher, the opinionated old man continued his thoughts. "The people that came to this house, came with love and regard. The spirit was irresistible. It was perfect. It spread to others. It made everyone feel good, even and I dare say even, if it didn't do any good for Autumn. It did a world of good for everyone else. That peaceful contented feeling infected us. The last thirty or forty hours should be one of the highlights of our lives."

Leander stopped speaking to concentrate on pouring whiskey into his waiting glass. The whole gang was now in the kitchen listening to their friend, the sage. Leander swallow the whiskey, sat in his customary station at the kitchen table, and continue his explanation of the past two days.

"As I was saying, we can call the last few hours a miracle or just a communion of good people. But one thing you can be sure of; if not for us, the people in this room, this event, this miracle, this communion would never have happened. If a miracle occurred; we were its creator. With that said, I say thank you to each and every one of you."

As often happened, after one of Leander's sermons, everyone was speechless, smiling and thinking about the words that made them feel thankful. Hollis broke the silence; offering anyone a ride home. He had to get some rest; he would be at work soon. Leander and Fig left with Hollis. Alida and Nancy decided to walk home since they lived only a few blocks away. WJ closed the door, turned to Candy and said, "How about a warm shower?"

After the shower, WJ followed Candy into his guest bedroom. Candy was wearing one of his tight V-neck shirts, thin silver chain-link bracelets and nothing else. He was gonna have to write in his journal describing the scenes in the shower that kept zipping and zooming in his mind. He didn't ever want to forget what had just happened. She knew he was still aroused; boxer shorts couldn't conceal his erect begging cock.

Together they dragged the lumpy feather mattress onto the porch. Because it was probably one of the last nights of very little tropical humidity; they had decided to sleep on the side screened porch and listen to the night. Candy covered the mattress with torn, faded, green satin sheets and pillows. WJ put two wine glasses and a bottle next to the mattress. He lit a candle, thought for a minute and then blew it out.

When Candy settled onto the mattress, she was naked. WJ laid next to her and kissed her. The first kisses were gentle. They kept their eyes open, studying each other. When Candy closed her eyes, WJ passed his hand through her thick damp hair and gently kissed her ear. The smell of her perfume pulled him to her neck. He kissed her neck, then his tongue barely touched skin as it wandered further down. He sucked up the soft flesh of her neck and caught the skin in a tender bite. He did it again, but crueler, and Candy's hips floated in imperceptible waves. WJ crushed his cock against Candy's leg. He had to slow his desire for savage fucking.

She could feel his breath on her neck as it came in warm blast with an urgency. He looked at her face, the eyes closed, the brow knitted into concentration, her lips smiling because she knew he was looking at her. He passed his chest over her breasts lightly grazing her nipples. Her hard, pale pink nipples looked like flower buds. He grabbed a nipple between his teeth, but didn't bite. He massaged it with his teeth and lips. Candy murmured a low guttural moan. He sucked on her other nipple, using his tongue and lips to caress. His nose traced a path to her navel and he scraped his teeth on her velvet soft flesh. His nose sank into her groomed pussy hair. At first, he smelled a perfumed fragrance, but when his nose traveled further down between her legs, he could smell her skin, he could smell a woman. His breathing became wild and his cock was straining to be set free. He pulled off his boxers, grabbed Candy's hands and pulled them between her legs.

He held on to her hands and stammered, "Show me where you want to be kissed."

Candy ripped her hands away from WJ and in a breathless rushed tone said, "Anywhere!"

He kissed and traced his tongue along her warm swollen lips. Candy's hips were floating in rougher waters; rhythmically up and down, up and down. His tongue parted her pussy lips. He licked upward and the rhythm of her hips slowed to concentrate on the bliss. He sucked on the moist flesh. WJ could hear Candy's breathing and her hips were moving with an urgency. He didn't hear what she'd whispered but he felt her hands in his hair pulling him upward and, in a voice, thick with lust, commanded, "Up!" She arched her back and her hips rose searching for his cock. He steadied her hips and guided her search. When his cock entered her, she slowly pushed her hips down, rose again and shoved her hips further down. For a brief moment, she felt euphoric, then frenzied and the song she sang went:

"Uh. Uh. Uh. Uh. Uh. Uh. Uh. Uh…. Uh…. Uh…. Uh. Uh. Uh. Uh. Uh. Uh…. Uh…. Uh….Oh. Ooooooh. Oh yeaaaah. Mmmm."

WJ could no longer hear her because in a burst of violence and in a barbaric grunt he sang:

"Oomph. Oomph. Oomph. Oomph. Oomph. Mmmm." And in a rapid guttural baritone, "Oomph. Oomph. Oomph. Oomph. Oomph. Oomph. Ahh yeah. Ooooh yeah.

Within seconds the wild warrior morphed into a harmless, sedated man basking in after-sex euphoria. He rolled off his conquest and cuddled her to his chest. After a few moments, she rolled on to her stomach and looked out into the night. "Is that the cats?"

"Yes, when they are inside, they want to go outside. But when they are outside, they want to come inside."

In a rapid whisper, "WJ look at the pale blue house up the street there's a woman in the window staring at us."

"Yeah, that's miss Gloria Champagne. She's our neighborhood voyeur. She's not a spying peeping-tom. She's a full out blaring gawker. I think it's more exciting for her when she knows that you know she is watching you."

"Eeew, what a pervert!"

WJ rested on his elbow so that he could look at Candy's ass. She had a round bottom wrapped in luminous skin with a pale pink and white glow. His cock had awakened from his temporary stupor.

"Do you know her?"

WJ diverted his eyes from Candy's bottom and looked into the darkness. "Yeah I know her. I like her. She's a smart lady. She just satisfies her sexual arousal in a different way. I guess."

"She visits here? Please no."

"No, she never comes out of her house. Sometimes when I bake cookies for the flower girls; I'll bake an extra dozen for her. While they're still warm, I'll bring her the dozen minus one or two. She always enthusiastically invites me in for coffee and then visually inspects my body and without one wit of guilt stares at my crouch. Kind of like I'm staring at your luscious butt."

The biologically controlled robot pushed himself up to get control of Candy's ass. Candy rolled on her side and with a mischievous smile said, "Nope! Not yet! I want to stare at your crouch like your neighborhood pervert. You obviously enjoy that perversion."

"Hey, really, she's a good person, just different. I can't condemn most. I was always taught to try each day to make life a little bit better for others."

Candy gave a sarcastic laugh and said, "So that's what we're doing here. Making life a little bit better for your perverted neighbor. WJ, I said you were a miracle man, but I was wrong. You're just a hound dog."

WJ rubbed Candy's arm and said, "Yeah, hound dog. Yeah, I'm more the hound dog type."

Candy stood up and walked to the screened door. She stretched the screened door wide, stepped on the top step and gave the command, "Get your fuzzy butts inside."

The three cats raced across the porch and into the kitchen on the serious mission of finding the reliable food bowl. WJ didn't notice the cats, he was watching Candy expose her naked backside to the world, to his neighbors.

She walked over to the makeshift bed and gently pushed WJ onto his back. She knelt between his legs and inspected his cock. "It looks angry. Dangerous and helpless." Her lips were very close. She blew a warm breeze on his cock and watched it rise like an alien animal. Her lips parted and delicately she touched the tip of his cock's head with her tongue. She watched the animal rise and plead, giving a false sense of helplessness. She licked gently, then she sucked the cock head into her mouth, closed her lips and massage the underside of his penis with her tongue. WJ was groaning and writhing. He was in a sexual fever. She straddled him and he watched as his cock disappeared inside her. Her lips came near his ear and she whispered, "Let's give your friend, Miss Gloria, a show that would cause even a marbled Venus to get wet."

Money

The mild and bright spring had disappeared and summer's jungle heat and humidity made each day laborious. Outside activities were usually steamy affairs that wet the skin. But on that sweltering July night the gang were in WJ's air-conditioned kitchen singing, yelling, dancing, and getting soused.

Autumn had returned to her home in Nevada and her health had puzzled the doctors. Her disease had stopped spreading and was in retreat. The doctors didn't have an answer for the disease's defeat. Autumn's parents were sure that the demise of the disease was the result of the prayer vigil. Autumn told everyone the Holy Relic had cured her. She told the local newspaper that the Holy Relic was capable of miracles. The story about Autumn's medical miracle first spread to the West Coast, then around the world. The first offers to purchase the Holy Relic were in the thousands. The latest offer was almost two million dollars. That's why the gang was celebrating. WJ had ordered three pizzas and when the pies arrived everyone sat in their customary seat at the kitchen table. Hollis and Leander ate like wolves. Fig and the ladies nibbled, but kept their cocktails nearby. The only person neither eating nor drinking was Candy. She had been very subdued the whole evening. She seemed worried about something. She had spent a couple of weeks with her family in Alabama and WJ figured her morose demeanor was probably the result of some family argument.

"Ladies and gentlemen, bitches and bastards, members of the board, shareholders, once again we've shaped a small endeavor into a profitable achievement," yelled a tipsy WJ. "But my fellow travelers, my merry friends this evening we have a decision to make. Mr. Hudson has presented an offer of one million six hundred thousand dollars. Upon the advice of our former tax accountant, Nancy has advised that we divide the offer seven ways and Mr. Hudson has agreed to write seven checks of equal amount. Each one of us would receive two hundred twenty-eight thousand five hundred seventy-one dollars and forty-two cents. According to Nancy, depending on your tax situation and after you willingly allow your Uncle Sam to rape you. You could have a net profit between one hundred ninety to two hundred thousand dollars or maybe a little more."

Everyone sprang from their seats, yelling, spilling drinks and screaming, "Two hundred thousand!"

WJ stumbled back into his chair and waited for his friends to finish their celebratory cheer. "There are other offers and some are for more money. But Mr. Hudson seems to be a safe bet. We could have the money in our bank accounts by the end of the week. We have to do this soon. We all know that when Miss Fortunato smiles on us, it's always been for a very brief moment in time. We need to make a decision this evening."

Candy's head hung low, she rested her forearms on the table and her hands were balled into fist. In a voice, devoid of accent or emotion Candy loudly spoke. "I need to say something."

Candy was looking at her fist when she said, "I need half of all the money. I'm prepared to go to the media and tell them that everything is a lie. I'll tell them there is no St. Thomas, just pig bones."

The sound of a chair being slowly pushed from the table disturbed the stunned silence that had descended on the festivities. Nancy stood up and growled, "I say we kill the bitch, dig a hole in the back bushes and let her rot. This is your fault WJ. I knew the first time she walked through that door wearing her skin-tight white pants advertising her camel toe that she was nothing but trouble. Every time you see the bitch, the seams of her pants are screaming in agony." She pointed a finger at WJ and said, "You let your dick make bad decisions."

Fig was waving his hand for attention, cut into Nancy's accusations and drunkardly blurted, "Nancy you're old-fashion. It's no longer called a camel toe. It's now called a mumbler; I can see your lips moving but I can't hear what they're saying."

"You, filthy monster," yelled a red-faced Candy.

Once again silence rushed in to flood the room. Fig's jaw hung open, his face crimson and his gaze was cast downward. In public, he weathered the stares, the insulting comments and the giggles; but in WJ's house he always felt free. He always felt comfortable. That feeling of a connection with other humans had just been attacked.

WJ broke the silence with pity rather than rage. "Candy if you'd asked for help, I'm sure everyone here would have given you a small portion of their profits. You gonna live with these words the rest of your life. You can't blackmail these people."

Hollis turned to face Candy and in a soft nonthreatening voice said, "Candy, my job is killing me. I'm hoping this money will buy my freedom. The last ten years of my life has been about a job that I hate but need. My life must change and I need that money."

Nancy was staring into the void past Leander's head when she grumbled, "The first thing I'm buying with my share of the money is a pistol."

WJ continued his lawyerly lecture, "Candy, each person will get an equal share and I'll contribute twenty percent of my share to help you."

Nancy glared at WJ and cursed, "Dammit WJ, you're not giving that bitch any money. Sometimes you can be such a dolt, a dam fool."

In a drunken snarl, Leander mumbled, "I'll pitch in five percent."

Nancy shook her head and with a sarcastic laugh said, "Two stupid dick heads."

Candy's burdens forced her head closer to the table which was wetted by tears dripping from her chin. Alida had gotten a dish towel, "Here, wipe your tears." She gently kissed the top of Candy's head and said, "We all make mistakes; we all say things we instantly regret."

WJ grabbed Alida's hand and kissed her palm, "Thank you!"

Leander sensed he had an opportunity to share his philosophy and in a slurred voice, "Money is the great corrupter. It can cast a spell that makes us hungrier, greedy. It can inflame jealousy. It blinds us to our past. Money can be the mother of each of the deadly sins."

"Whoa, not tonight Socrates. We have to get back to business," snapped WJ.

"I'm sorry. I'm so sorry. Fig, please forgive me," cried Candy. She didn't wait for forgiveness. She rose from the table, still sobbing into the kitchen towel, she opened the door and disappeared into the darkness.

Hollis watched as Candy walked to the door. Nancy was right, the seams of her pants were stretched. He thought how great Candy looked when she was coming and when she was leaving.

"Should someone go after her," asked Alida.

"Thank God she left; I won't have to kick her butt. Damn recreant," yelled Nancy.

"Somebody has been reading the dictionary. No, let her dwell on this tonight," WJ spoke gently, "I'll speak to her tomorrow. I'll find out what's troubling her and see if I can help."

"WJ, the Salvation Army," laughed Leander.

WJ put his finger in the air and said, "By the way, our group of seven, Autumn's parents and Mr. Hudson are the only ones that know the Relic contains pig bones. I took a chance and told him that the bones might smell like bacon. He just laughed and said they were obviously holy pig bones."

"Do you mind," WJ pointed to Alida's martini.

"Help yourself," said Alida.

WJ drank the rest of Alida's martini and was chewing on the olive when he said, "As we just witnessed, Lady Luck is already packing her bags for a long holiday. We don't want to dilly dally and find ourselves without a customer. I think I should contact Mr. Hudson Monday morning and finalize the deal. By the end of the week, he'll have the Relic and we'll be spending our money."

He looked at each one of his friends to see if there was any sign of indecision or doubt. When his eyes settled on Leander, his old friend, his confidante, his partner in crime for many years, he asked, "Whatcha think Leander?"

Endings and Beginnings

It had been fifteen weeks since each member of the gang received an equal share from the sale of the Holy Relic. WJ had visited each one, but tonight was the first time the remnants of the gang were going to come together for an evening. The gang sitting around his table would be different on that night. Alida and Nancy would grace his table and, of course, Leander would never miss a free meal and cocktails and a captured ear to hear his solutions for a better world. Candy, Fig and Hollis had decided on journeys of exploration. He was always pleased when friends graduated from his kitchen table.

Candy had moved back to Alabama, very near her parents and was working on a bachelor's degree. She seemed to be enjoying her part-time job at a radio station.

Fig was now the owner of a business. Because of his childhood disfigurement, his parents had apprenticed him to a woodworker during the summer months and during school holidays. The wood worker taught him the seldom-used-art of intarsia. With his share of the money he bought the proper tools, hired some help and has become a local celebrity in home construction. His wooden designs for walls, ceilings and furniture are very popular and expensive. He also started designing and producing wooden cremation urns that were very popular. He joked that he had an undying demand from a dying clientele. A couple of times he had called WJ late at night to say that the night of the prayer vigil, God had smiled on Autumn as well as himself.

Hollis was gone. He had sold his dilapidated house and was now traveling across the country in a small recreational vehicle. He said he was finally free and was already feeling healthier. WJ had received a couple of postcards, signed, "Thank You-WJ-Thank You."

He could hear Alida greeting the guest and fixing cocktails. He was slowly dressing as he reread the words that he had written in his journal last night. He wasn't a consistent journal keeper; but in times when he needed to quietly scream or when there wasn't anyone he could confide in, he would seek help by writing his thoughts. Often his written words helped explain his pain or his rage.

Yesterday morning he received a phone call from Samuel Rose. Mr. Rose had called to thank WJ for his kindness and to tell him his daughter had died from a heart attack. The disease, the treatments and the horror of living so close to death had weaken her heart. The phone call had floored him. Just two days earlier he had buried Bullet in the backyard. His emotions had surged into rage and then melted into self-pity. He wasn't good at expressing his feeling and so once again he turned to his journal. He was now saddened at the words he'd written last night. He had written the first time he'd really prayed it had been to save his wife. He'd prayed with rage and insults which had ended in pleading. His prayers had been a failure. For Autumn his prayers had been devotional. He thanked God for allowing him to know the beauty of Autumn for a few hours and the friendship with Bullet for many years.

The bedroom door opened and Alida peered into the bedroom. "Everyone is here. Are you almost ready?"

"Yeah, just a few more minutes. Did I tell you that dress looks great on you?"

"Yes, twice."

When the door closed, he took off the pullover and put on a white long-sleeved wrinkled oxford. He looked down at his words one last time and thought to himself, "Am I only talking to darkness, a complete void. I wish I could sing hallelujah and know that I was being heard."

When he walked into the kitchen the first to greet him was Nancy. She gave him a kiss on his lips and said, "Bullet lived a good and long life. You did him good. No more sad eyes; I want to see that sparkle again."

No one knew about Autumn. He hadn't had the will, to call and deliver the dark news. The gang was still celebrating their temporary liberation from money problems. Tomorrow he planned on visiting everyone to give them a familiar heartbreak. He'd call Candy and Hollis.

Standing next to Nancy was Ruby Picou. Ruby was an English teacher at the Catholic high school. She was cute and petite and wore her tawny hair, cut into a shag that was popular decades ago. She looked like a young lion. Her thin upper lip appeared to be continually hiding a secret. Her eyes were small, bright, moist and mahogany. She wore her clothes tight like Candy and was a friend of Nancy. Nancy sipped from her rum and coke, her eyes watching WJ's inability to resist appraising unfamiliar flesh.

In her best teacher's voice, she asked, "How old was he?"

"He was with me for fifteen years; but the previous owners of this house left him when they moved. So, I'm not sure of his exact age."

Only Ruby's bottom lip was moving when she said, "He wanted affection from everyone. I remember once at the Café. He went to each table and politely offered a paw to everyone in exchange for a treat."

"Yeah, I miss him. Now I should give more of my attention to the three monsters." He spied Ouida standing alone in the room. The woman always had a look of concern and her eyes were constantly searching, looking for answers.

"Hello Ouida!"

The tall raw-boned woman's face broke into a sense of relief. She wrapped her strong arms around WJ and rubbed his back with large, dry, rough hands. Ouida had always reminded WJ of a strong Cajun woman capable of leading a team of oxen plowing a southern Louisiana lowland prairie. The mumble of the crowd got noticeable lower. Everyone always wondered about WJ and Ouida's friendship. Only Leander's loud rants prevented everyone in the room from hearing their conversation.

"Alida fixed me a shandy. It's good! I've never had a shandy."

"Don't drink too many."

The lanky woman looked directly into WJ's eyes and said, "John sends his love. He's just so exhausted after a day's work and so, he's watching the kids and of course there's a protocol we must follow each night with little Johnny Junior. He said to repeat again, that he is forever in your debt and if there is ever anything you need."

WJ kissed Ouida on the cheek and spoke softly into her ear, "Tell John that ya'll friendship and trust is the only payment I'll really appreciate."

"WJ would you like me to fix you a cocktail?" asked Alida. She was wearing a candy apple red satin dress with occasional tiny splotches of gold and black. WJ's mouth wrinkled into a smile. His cousin, silky, swirling, exotic, her light amber hair swishing on her sateened shoulders was the oldest woman in the room and the most attractive. Her pale icy blue eyes gave commands that he always obeyed.

"Alida you're such a great host and a wonderful bartender. I'll take a martini. If I'm out of gin; I have more in the pantry."

"Hello Eve, I'm glad you came."

The woman standing next to Alida was Eve Leblanc. Two years ago, her husband destroyed their marriage for a much younger woman. She had stoically handled the disloyalty and the embarrassment of not being good enough. But now, the mortgage payment, health and auto insurance payments and the needs of an eight-year-old daughter were destroying her meager finances. It was going to be difficult to get this group to accept Eve, thought WJ. She could be arrogant, opinionated and combative. Her eyes slashed through people, missing nothing that could be useful. Her conversations were usually competitive. The totality of her imperfections made most people flee, but WJ felt himself attracted to the alluring woman with short curly brown hair. Her baggy neon emerald green pants next to Alida's red dress illuminated WJ's kitchen like a flame. She wore a loose white pullover and no bra. Leander would later say that when he first saw her thinly masked nipples, he could feel the air being sucked out of his lungs.

"Did I hear Nancy say your dog died?"

"Yes, a few weeks ago; I miss him."

"What did he die from?"

"Old age."

Her bottom lip gently pushed her upper lip into a pout; an expression imitated by everyone that knew her. WJ tried to stare at Eve's unusual khaki-colored eyes, but the nipples had control of his eyes.

Alida handed WJ his cocktail, "Here you go, one olive-free martini."

"That's a fine dress. Is that the dress you wore when we set Vegas on fire?"

"Yep! I hadn't seen you in a while, so I wanted to brighten your day."

"Don't ever put that dress in the back of the closet. I'm gonna go see what the old wizard is yelling about."

Leander was preaching one of his end-of-the-world sermons to a human mountain. Leander said he spoke loudly because his hearing was poor; but everyone noticed that the number of cocktails determined his loudness. By the fifth martini or rum and coke or straight Irish, or whatever type of booze WJ had in quantity he was usually at the yelling stage. Leander's prey, Mayor Toups, sat motionless as the preacher of history and forecasting shouted at him.

"Mayor there's always been a counterculture. Every society, every generation there's been a counterculture. Sometimes a positive influence on the status quo; but sometimes destructive…vitriolic. In this country, mostly in the East during the early decades of the 1800's, there was a scorn of all things Victorian and a contempt for those that clung to past glories. Others despised the Eastern Elitism and the ever-present societal division grew larger. This division explains the relative ease this country slipped into a civil war. The last great influence by the counterculture was in the Sixties and Seventies. There began a semi successful fight against institutions like the government, schools, churches, marriages that locked everyone into a willing captivity. For a brief moment, there was a brotherhood in American society. But after two failed presidents and a frail economy the Eighties arrived with an economic boom and the resulting excess. Society's divisions began to reopen. The people had tired of social struggle and succumbed to materialism proving that a consumer society can absorb a cultural revolution."

Leander stopped his lesson to take a sip of his alcoholic concoction. He didn't care what his drink tasted like; after a week of sobriety, he just wanted to get drunk. He swallowed the alcohol, pointed his finger at Mayor and yelled.

"A consumer society can absorb a cultural revolution. The problem was that high property taxes to pay for failed social programs forced many to flee the cities. Mostly whites fled to the suburbs, so a division between the races, always large, now grew larger. The Nineties ushered in globalization and technology; both, positive for many, but ruinous and isolating to large segments of this country's population. We've poorly managed globalization and technology and allowed class division to grow. Today's counterculture, during this Age of Perceived Victimization and further social liberation is no longer fighting against institutions. They are fighting against their own countrymen. They are insisting that others kneel to their values and debate is met with hatred and ridicule. Our national shrines are now T.V. and social media. Requiring sacrifices at their alters of great amounts of personal time. Date nights have become screaming protest marches and pizza, while a Gilded Age is again flourishing in the privacy of the wealthy. They've forgotten the lessons of the past."

WJ put his hand on Leander's shoulder to still the old man's lecture. He wrapped his arms around Leander's shoulders and kissed him on the forehead. He had decided that in the morning, Leander would be the first that he'd visit to make known Autumn's death. Many in the community had to be informed.

WJ extended his hand to shake Mayor's hand. "Hey big guy. You learning something from the professor?

At least seven feet tall and covered in enormous slabs of muscle and fat, Mayor usually drew everyone's attention. His head was the size of a boulder covered in black wild and wavy hair. His brow was so protruding that Neanderthals would have stood in awe. Way down hidden in the deep shade was two small electric blue eyes. Everyone else's knees fit under the table. Mayor's knees formed barriers around the edge. It wasn't until his parents enrolled him in school that they found out his name had been misspelled by one letter. His parents still call him Major; to everyone else he's Mayor Toups. Mayor, Alida and WJ were cousins. Their great, great grandfathers were four brothers that arrived in Louisiana the year before Succession. They each forged very different American lives, creating four distinct branches on the evolutionary tree.

Mayor smiled, two piercing blue dots searched WJ and from a voice deep in a cave he said, "I thought you were going to be his agent and bring him on a lecture tour."

The Obligation

"Hey, why don't we gather around the table and discuss why we're here before we eat. I have a nice shrimp stew and rice and a few crawfish pies. I made a German potato salad. We got a green salad and buttered toast courtesy of Alida." Who sat in her usual seat of privilege to WJ's right.

"The beautiful Miss Nancy made her famous white chocolate bread pudding covered in her secret sauce. You really look pretty tonight with that new haircut."

Nancy, sitting as usual at the end of the table across from Leander took a sip from her rum and coke, then pointed a finger at WJ. "When you make enough money to pay all your bills and still have some moola left over, it's easy to be pretty. Remember, I didn't have to give twenty percent of my take to little Miss Candy."

Seated next to Nancy at the foot of the table, the human mountain spoke in a voice echoing from a cave, "WJ has always lived in the Land of Puppies. He always helps strays. There's been a few times he's helped this stray."

Ouida seated to WJ's left rose from her chair to give WJ a quick small kiss to his cheek. "He's definitely helped this stray with money, kindness and emotional support."

Eve seated between Leander and Alida pushed her lips into a smooch and said, "Well I'm not a stray, but I could sure use some help."

"Baby, let me," Nancy started to say when WJ raised his hands into the air and said, "Whoa."

"Nancy, as usual, you've taken us off track. Let's get down to business. We all know each other. I've worked with everyone before, except Eve."

The dulcet beat of the music, which hadn't been noticed because of the conversations and the loud rantings of Leander, was now the background melody for the impresario.

"We're all here to make some money. We're here to start on a new endeavor or adventure. You've all heard me say this before. We're all here because it's an obligation. It's our obligation to make some money to support ourselves and to help our families, our friends, our community. I have two different jobs and we need to choose one. One undertaking would be about two to four months of work that would be safe, kind of boring, relatively legal with a potential of about twenty thousand dollars for each of us. The other job is for a year and it's very illegal. Its very time consuming and maybe dangerous. You'll live for a year with a short fuse burning in the very bottom of your stomach, but a potential for each of us to make seven hundred thousand dollars are more and none for Uncle Sammy. If there is a failure at this job.... it could result in extensive prison time."

Seven hands lifted cocktails to moisten dry mouths. The music got louder, faster, more strings.

Alida called WJ the Great Attractor but this evening he was the counselor presenting the facts to a jury of friends and family.

"Let's start with the safe mundane job."

"I like safe and I don't mind boring," said Ruby timidly.

"It's safe and it's simple. We do a lottery that has prize money for a few people but we keep the majority of the proceeds."

"Is that legal," Alida querulously asked?

Leander barked, "It was illegal. Then the money-hungry government made it legal for itself, but illegal for citizens to compete with its monopoly."

"Leander, that's true. But raffles for charity are legal and governmental rules for them are lacking and shady."

"The laws are shady, because they are open to interpretation. The fucking government's interpretation," growled Leander. "OK!" Let me fill in some details and give you some numbers. Maybe some more info will help answer some of your questions. First, what charity will we be working for?"

WJ reached over to pat Ouida on the shoulder. "Everyone in the community knows the medical expenses for Ouida's family are overwhelming. The raffle would be to raise money for relief from that burden. We sell fifty thousand tickets at five dollars each."

"Fifty thousand tickets," groaned Mayor.

"Shhh.... Shush. Let me finish. Fifty thousand at five dollars is two hundred fifty thousand dollars. We give away forty thousand in prize money. One twenty-thousand-dollar prize, ten one thousand dollar prizes and twenty for five hundred dollars. We deduct ten thousand for expenses, give Ouida forty thousand and we'd still have one hundred sixty thousand to split between the eight of us including Ouida. Twenty thousand tax free and if we can keep the same narrative no one will be suspicious. Our story can be that Ouida got sixty thousand dollars total and we each were paid for our expenses."

"Ooh…, WJ I don't want to go house to house selling raffle tickets," lamented Eve.

"Oh fuck!" snapped Nancy. Pointing a finger at WJ, Nancy snarled, "Everything can be rosy and he always has to bring in a thorn."

A finger the size of a club appeared before Nancy's face and Mayor blurted, "You da thorn."

"Shut up, you big cyclops, I won't bake a cake for your birthday if you get smart with me," threatened Nancy.

The big finger found Nancy's back and gently massaged.

Ruby spoke cautiously, "In three weeks our church has a fair and the week after the volunteer fireman have a fair. I'm sure they'd let us set up booths to sell tickets."

Nancy cackled, "We can set up a booth and Mayor and Eve can sell kisses."

Mayor grinned revealing huge yellow teeth. His big finger began gently poking Nancy's back.

Nancy turned her back to Mayor and said, "Lower, you big galoot."

WJ laughed and said to Mayor, "Do a good job; maybe a massage will silence her sassy tongue."

He looked around the table and said, "There's only one hard part to this job and that's selling the tickets. Ruby just gave two great suggestions. That's why there is eight of us. We all must come up with ideas.

Eve wasn't interested in sparring with Nancy. She took a sip of her cocktail, gave a dismissive smile and asked WJ, "So…., what's the other job?"

WJ had hoped for more discussion; but was prepared to present his briefs on the second endeavor.

"Leander and I recently met with an old associate that we had worked with many years ago. He's starting up his old business and wanted to know if we had a team that was interested in working with him. He's been a fisherman, a shrimper for most of his life. He works out of Bayou Lafourche, has two boats and a small bayou-side shrimp processing company. Times are tough. He's idled one boat and let go a few workers, mostly family. His old business was smuggling. When Leander and I worked for him he would meet a mother ship in the Gulf, transferred the products from the mother ship to his shrimp boats and then motor up Bayou Lafourche disguised as working fishing boats."

"And what were these products," asked Ruby?

"It ranged from Cuban cigars to counterfeit money and purses; but his specialty was smuggling weed."

"Ooooh no, I'm not selling drugs," objected Alida, her jaw line set in opposition.

"Yeah you can count me out. Let's just sell tickets, said Ruby as she squirmed in her seat.

"Let the man finish," snarled Leander. "Ya'll don't even know what he's talking about."

WJ took the last sip of his martini and continued his presentation. "This man, whose name and face you will never know, wants to just smuggle large quantities of weed. The legalization of pot in some states has actually, substantially increased the price of weed. In its mindless greed, state governments have levied such high taxes making black market weed more affordable. There's big money to be made and we will only be couriers. Someone has to distribute the weed, usually to large cities out east and north. How we get the pot from point A to point B won't matter to our employer. Just transport the pot from point A to point B and then safely bring back the money. We work as two teams of four. Each team would lease a truck for moving cargo. Each truck would be loaded with at least a ton of marijuana or sometimes other contraband. Each team member would take shifts driving the truck. A car would be driven by one of the team to trail the truck and to haul supplies. The only stops made would be to refuel. Each team will be paid forty-five thousand dollars with successful completion of the job. Each team member pays his share for fuel and truck rental with a net of about ten thousand dollars per member. Two trips a week, eight each month, for nine months. You do the math. Both trucks working nonstop."

Just as he had done many times in front of a jury; he looked into the eyes of each person seated in front of him, and asked that they close their eyes for a few minutes to picture what he had just said.

"Close your eyes and make a visual list of the pros and cons of each job. Think about how much income do you really need. What are your needs? Is it purely financial or the need for fraternity or the desire for some adventure? Go ahead close your eyes, relax and quietly exam your situation."

Ruby's eyes were tightly shut, her jaw tightened in an expression of concentration. She thought how her student loan payments were financially straggling her and she wanted desperately to financially help her parents. She chewed on the inside of her lip thinking how she had always been Ruby-the-good-girl and where had that got her.

Eve also looked very tense as she considered her needs. She knew seven hundred thousand dollars would easily pay all bills and expenses with plenty left for enjoyments and a little extra to pay someone to kill her fucking ex-husband…. and his bitch.

The profits from the sale of the Holy Relic had paid off his debts and had given Leander a bit of a financial cushion. He didn't really need the money. Working with WJ had never been about the money. It was about being alive.

Mayor's chin rested on his chest balancing his huge head. His eyes were shut but his lips had cracked into smile. He knew he wasn't selling any damn tickets. With his pile of money, he knew he could pay off all of his debts, gift a few people that had helped him and replace his patched roof. His brother had told him about a small castle near the ocean in the city of Caracas. The castle was a house of prostitution, famous around the word for its decadence. He would be able to afford a sinful vacation in Venezuela.

In her self-assured regal manner Alida sat relaxed in her chair and thought how her late father always warned her and Frank to stay away from WJ. He had said that WJ was too unsettled, too much raw dark energy. At her stage in life, most people wanted to be safe and settled and waiting. She was tired of waiting.

Ouida 's face grimaced in emotional pain and conflict. Life had never been easy for her and she wasn't expecting a miracle. If something happened to her she was not sure if John could cope. Dreams of financial security sugared her fears.

Nancy couldn't sit still. She was rocking in her seat and repositioning her fidgety legs. She was excited. She wanted to be a courier; she wanted to break the law. Ever since that fateful day when she'd met WJ in the grocery store, she had slowly, cautiously chopped away at her cocoon of isolation. She was ready to be a butterfly.

WJ looked at the faces of his friends and family and thought how he loved them all. He was allowing thoughts, ideas, emotions to just crash through his mind. He was confident; he felt his heart beat faster. He didn't need to be focused, the time for steel concentration would be later. He looked at Nancy and was amused how she could get so angry with him and a second later, she could be laughing. Mayor had been right. He did live in the Land of Puppies and he always looked for strays. Anyone could buy a purebred, whether it's a dog or a friend. But you just bump into strays. Fate brought you together for a reason and WJ had always felt guiltless for deciding the reason. Everyone had problems and he was willing to listen. He liked introducing strays to his community of friends and to give them protection from their demons.

He stared for a moment at Eve. Her eyes were closed and he thought how her face was an aura of soft innocence; but he knew that behind the calm exterior was a pissed-off dancing cobra. Eve had something to prove. She wanted to prove that her bastard husband had made a mistake leaving her for a tight-ass bimbo. WJ was hoping that Eve would prove to him, her ex-husband's mistake.

The guest seated around his kitchen table began opening their eyes after listening and questioning their thoughts. WJ had learned how to read a jury and he was thinking that he had chosen wisely. He knew before they closed their eyes which job they would choose. For most people, money and especially money in quantity is a seductress. He knew each of his friends and family were easily seduced.

It bothered him, like a small itch, that he couldn't share with them the full details of the next job. The shrimp boat would be a disguise, the cargo truck another and the weed another. Hidden like a needle in a mountain of marijuana would be the true mission. Little by little, bit by bit they would smuggle the cargo, a major disrupter, through layers of protection and security. When the mission was completed, the eight members of the team would be wealthier by the millions and one group of leaders would be as powerful as the President of the United States.

He closely watched Leander. The old man had opened his eyes and was staring at his hand pawing his rocks glass. It all depended on his old friend, his part time mentor and his partner-in-crime. If the old doomsday soothsayer said no, then his team would be selling thousands of tickets.

The other members of the team were curiously watching WJ intently eyeing the old man. They were waiting for their team leader to speak. WJ drained the last of Alida's martini and in Leander's direction he cautiously spoke.

"Whatcha think Leander?"

A Good Sunday

The Family
The Caillouet family could now scratch church off their must to-do list. The brothers had already stripped off their church clothes and were now sitting at the kitchen table jabbering like normal nine and ten-year-old boys. Silva was seated in the bay window with her arms crossed in a defensive position. The constant scowl was there, her anger made the space around her thick with negativity. She had been carefree and fun, then teenage confusion invaded her mind and body and a barrier had been quickly built. Her father, Michael, was worried about his daughter; so far, the barrier had been impenetrable. The mother, Jennifer, carried a stack of plastic cereal bowls and spoons to the table. The brothers had already brought the cereal boxes and milk to the table; they knew the Sunday routine.

Jennifer gave the same speech of resentment every Sunday morning. She had cooked breakfast and dinner for five people for six straight days and it was time somebody else helped with the cooking.

Michael had learned to put his hearing into sound blocking mode. A wife, three kids, parents, three bosses, customers and nearly forty demanding and helpless fellow workers had created the need for a sound filter. He vaguely heard his wife. After fifty job hours, nightly help with the boys' homework, Saturday morning yard work and bringing Michael J. and Gabriel to their Saturday afternoon game, he just wanted one free hour to sit and relax, have a cup of coffee and read the Sunday paper in peace. He knew Jenny was tired. Maybe he'd cook pancakes for lunch. He had finished section A of the paper and as usual he was going to skip the last two pages of editorials, commentaries and the obituaries; but a name caught his eye and hooked his attention.

"Ooh no, Mr. Landry has died." Michael squinted his eyes to bring in focus the small print of the obituary and he said to no one, "They didn't follow his wishes."

Jennifer poured cereal in a blue plastic cereal bowl and absent-mindedly asked, "I guess I'm supposed to ask, 'Who is this person and what were his wishes?'"

He could feel a wave of sadness flow over him, casting him in a flood of nostalgia. People, places and attitudes of his youth were quickly disappearing.

He was Bobby's dad. Bobby was a neighborhood friend that lived two houses from our house. This was the late Sixties and no one had home air conditioning, so we'd sit outside in the coolness of the night until the mosquitoes chased us inside. All the kids in the neighborhood would drift over to Bobby's house because his dad would tell us such fantastic stories. On cool evenings, he'd burn wood in a metal tub resting on bricks. We all sat around in a circle of plastic and aluminum folding chairs. We called those chairs, beach chairs. We could only catch four TV channels and it just wasn't very important back then. It was more fun to be with friends. Often parents came to listen, they'd bring iced pitchers of water and some plastic drinking cups and on cool nights maybe some cocoa."

Michael was deep in thoughts of his past when he heard an unexpected voice.

"What were his wishes," blurted Silva from her fortress?

Silva's words were like cold water stunning him back to reality.

His daughter had not spoken to him for a month. Attempts at conversation always resulted in screaming anger and rude remarks. When Silva was born, he had been forty and he often wondered if he was too old to parent a teenage daughter. His two sons were still in the father-worship stage. He was already dreading their teenage years.

"He said many times he'd hope and wished his family and friends would put his body in the shady area of a cow pasture. His body could feed the worms, bugs and birds and he'd become part of a living animal once again. If that wasn't possible because of the numerous government rules and laws that regulate our lives; he'd settle for cremation. He wanted to go straight from the scene of his death to the crematoria. His ashes could be dumped anywhere except for the obvious places your father's ashes should never be dumped. His family and friends could scatter his ashes in a river, lake or ocean, even a drainage ditch that didn't have too much litter. His ashes could be left in the deep swamp, on a prairie or on a mountain peak; as long as his ashes could mix with the mud. His mantra had been ashes to ashes, dried mud to mud, of the earth to the earth."

Michael J, his oldest son, with the analytical mind, like his mom, asked, "Dad, did this man believe in reincarnation? I think it's the law that all dead people must be embalmed and so the bugs probably wouldn't be interested in eating him for lunch."

Michael laughed when Gabriel, his clone, yelled, "Jay! Worms can't eat people. Pops! What…. umm, what kind of stories did he tell?"

"Sometimes his stories were about ancient Greek gods, warriors and the super heroes of the distant past. He spoke of battles that were fought centuries ago and of more recent historical events. Many of his stories were about the hope, courage and endurance of the men and women that made the high ground and cheniers of an ancient swampy delta their home."

Jennifer and her two sons continued feasting on milk and cereal. Silva stared out of the window searching for potential enemies. Michael finished section A, folded it and put it and the obituaries and Mr. Landry to the side. He was reading the headers of the sports page when Gabriel asked, "Hey Pops, why don't you ever tell us stories?"

Silva yelled from her fortress, "He's always telling us dumb stories."

"Yeah, but I was thinking about adventure stories or maybe some hero stories."

"Yeah Dad! Since you can't cook breakfast, maybe you could entertain us," Jennifer grumbled between spoonsful of cereal.

A smiling Michael J poured his second bowl of cereal and asked, "Do you remember any of Mr. Landry's stories?"

Michael put down the sports page and in a soft reflective voice, he said, "Not in detail; but yeah, I remember many of his stories."

Sitting on her high mountain of judgement, Silva sarcastically shouted, "Please, please, dear old Dad, please tell us a silly story."

Silva's rudeness, her priggish behavior hurt Michael; but his philosophy had always been to combat rudeness with civility. "Let's see. Give me a minute to recall a story."

Michael took a deep breath and closed his eyes. His mind wandered through stories he'd loved during his childhood. His family had been semi poor, but his childhood had been a time of peace and joy, endless possibilities and an eagerly anticipated future. Which story would he choose to bring peace and joy to his family?

The Story (Sunday Morning)

Michael kept his eyes close and spoke cautiously:

"It's a cold drizzly November night in 1917. A sixteen-year-old boy named Josiah sat in the dark on the floor of St. Joseph Church. He and his family were in a dilemma and he had to make a decision, the right decision. His teachers had always told his parents that he was a brilliant student, but his job was to help run the family farm while his father, a rifleman in the U.S. Army fought Germans in Europe. Life for Josiah had settled into a safe routine until last week. On a claustrophobic, overcast, November Monday afternoon Josiah's family received two letters. The first letter his mother opened was an official government notification that his father had been missing in action for the past month. All families of soldiers knew that missing in action meant the army had yet to find a body to bury. The best they could hope for was that his father had been taken prisoner. After reading the government letter his mother became emotionally paralyzed. Her face wore the constant expression of a stunned victim of a tragedy.

His grandfather opened the second letter. The letter was almost as crushing as the first. His father had secured a loan from the community bank. The loan was to give his family funds to draw from while he was away fighting a war. This letter had been sent to all of the financial institution's customers that owed money to the bank. The letter stated that the bank was in financial trouble and anyone that owed money to the bank must pay it back within the next sixty days. The letter continued to explain that money owed and not paid would result in the sheriff confiscating their property. In sixty days, Josiah's family, could be fatherless and homeless."

"Dad, is that the same thing as imminent domain?" asked Michael J.

Gabriel laughed, "Yeah Pops! What's amine main?"

"Will ya'll shut up and let him tell the story," yelled Silva.

"Silva!" Jennifer admonished her rude daughter.

Michael gave his daughter a smile. He was hoping for a dialogue. "It's OK Silva. We're not in a hurry. Gabriel, imminent domain is when the government pays you for your property so they can build a road or something else that would help the whole community. Let's get back to Josiah and his problems."

"Outside it was cold and drizzly, but inside the church it was freezing. Josiah couldn't see them, but he could feel the statues of Mary, Joseph and Jesus staring at him, waiting for him to make a decision. He had two choices. He could quit school and get a job to help financially support his family. He was powerless against the bank and his father's destiny, but he could do his duty to help his mother, grandparents, brothers and sisters. He loved each one and would do anything to help them.

"The second choice could alter his life and his family's future or he could meet Death. Since he had been a small child, his great grandfather and then his grandfather and his two grandmothers had told him stories about the Land of the Rougarou. They had known many that took the journey to the faraway mysterious land and a few had returned. They would point out certain prominent families in the community and swore that their wealth, health and good luck was the result of a successful journey to this Land of Mystery. His Grandparents knew where the road to this distant land began, but they could give no other guidance.

"After a week of studying his options, his mind was screaming with confusion. Josiah had to make a decision and he chose to take the risky journey. He walked out of the icy sanctuary into the cold drizzle. The road to his destination began in the Church's graveyard. Everyone in the community knew of the tomb that he was seeking. It had always existed. The Indian tribes that had populated the area along the bayous said the tomb existed before the white man had arrived in Louisiana. Josiah lit his lantern so he could inspect the tomb. The tomb was constructed of white Alabama marble, weather stained with light yellow and brown splotches and streaked with veins a hue of dark green. A lichen covered heavy brass door guarded the contents of the tomb. Encircling the death home was a fence made of connected black steel javelins. The gate was open, inviting. He raised his lantern to inspect above the door where a family name or ancestral crest should be located. There was no name, no crest, just a carving of a man's face, his mouth etched open in a scream, his eyes wide in fear. The face made his confidence and his will drift away. His fear was controlling him, preventing him from moving. A picture of his family living in rags and working only to survive flashed into his mind. The thoughts of his family put steel in his heart and legs. He walked through the gate and when he reached the tomb door there was no doorknob or latch. He put his shoulder to the door and with all his strength he pushed the door enough to squeeze through the opening.

Before he could take a breath from his exertion, the door closed with a thud. He looked down at his watch. It was five after twelve. How long would his mission take?

"Josiah raised the lantern high so that the light would allow him to survey the inside of the tomb. On the left wall were three shelves carved into the marble wall. Each shelf contained a dusty deteriorating wooden coffin. On the floor below the shelves was a disintegrating coffin and he thought he could see bones. On his right were coffins in different stages of rot stacked on top of each other."

Gabriel leaned towards his father and loudly whispered, "I hope this isn't a ghost story."

"Oh fuck! Can't you just shut up and listen to the story," yelled Silva.

Her mother pointed a finger like a weapon, "Silva, I'm getting tired of your juvenile anger. Someday your silly, little-girl moodiness will be gone but everyone in this family will be scarred by your childish outbursts. Talk to us respectfully, like family members and if that's not possible then just don't speak to us. I rather your silent rudeness."

Michael spoke gently to his teenage daughter.

"Curse words are easy. You don't have to think of a more complex answer or convincing reply. Usually these words are used by people that are too lazy or too stupid to think of more interesting remarks."

"Oh, so now you're calling me stupid," mumbled Silva.

"I know you're not stupid, but people that don't know you might think you're crude and low I.Q."

Michael J. raised his hands in a pleading motion and said, "Let's please get back to the story."

"Yeah, back to the story and Gabriel it's not a ghost story."

"The back wall of the tomb was an ornate lacy iron gate that separated the house of peace from dark oblivion. He opened the gate and plunged his lantern into the darkness. The burning light revealed a much-trodden trail. He cautiously followed the trampled and littered path. The walls and ceiling of the tube of darkness was a continuous swirl, like the inside of a snail shell.

"Josiah walked for hours and everything remained the same except the tube of darkness was gradually being squeezed smaller and the path was becoming steeper. He looked at his watch. He brought it to his ear to hear if it was still ticking. It was working. The second hand was still racing, but something was wrong. The watch's hands were stuck at five after twelve. He knew time wouldn't matter if he didn't find a way out of the darkness. His lantern had burned most of its fuel and soon the blackness would devour him. He started to panic when the lantern light had retreated and was little more than candlelight. His legs and feet began to disappear into the darkness. The flickering light had almost died when he came to a dead-end. The impasse was a five-foot tall, dirty glass window, covered in dusty cobwebs. The filth blurred the dim gray light filtering through the translucent impediment. Josiah attempted to wipe away some of the dust clouding the window. When his hand wiped the glass, it sank and disappeared into the window. He quickly withdrew his hand and inspected it for damage. His hand was ok, so he tried penetrating the glass with his foot and then withdrew it. The dead-end was a doorway allowing him to continue his quest.

He stepped into the glass escaping the frightening darkness and emerged into a midnight illuminated by moonlight. He had stepped onto a stone stairway as wide as a boulevard. It was covered in gray moss; green and yellow algae and a chaos of litter lined its edges. Bones, yes human bones and crumbling gray human skeletons were strewn about the steps. The stone-stepped path continued as far as Josiah could see. He looked over the edge of the stairway and saw serpents of ash-colored fog rushing far below. He slowly walked down the infinite stairway and after he developed a walking rhythm, he increased his speed to a fast trot down the endless path.

He raced down countless flights of stairs and the end was still not in sight. The punishingly boring pathway continually looked the same, except there was less litter and most of the bones had been neatly piled to the side of the stairway. He stopped to survey his surroundings and noticed that his watch's hour and minute hands were swiftly moving in a counter clockwise direction but the second hand was moving in the opposite direction. He looked back to see how far he had hiked. His starting point was no longer visible. He couldn't see the end of the stairway and now he couldn't see the beginning.

He turned to continue his journey. He took a step forward and heard a voice. The only sound he'd heard on the stairway had been his footsteps. His eyes scanned the piles of bones and litter and sitting with his back leaning against the stone banister was a man. The stranger was skeletal. His amber colored face looked like a rock with eyes and three lower small holes."

Josiah excitedly rattled the questions, 'Who are you? What are you doing here? Where am I? Can I help you?'

The rapidly fired questions exhausted the unknown man. He laid his head on a stone step, closed his eyes and said, 'This will be my deathbed.'

'What are you saying? You can't die here. Why are you here?'

The stranger opened his eyes and muttered, 'Young man, when you feel your insides turn cold and the shadow of death dims your vision, it doesn't matter if you are dying in a peaceful meadow or face down in the mud or stretched across cold stone steps. I think the finality is always the same.'

Josiah squatted near the man and asked, 'Can I help you, sir? Why are you here?'"

Michael lowered his voice and said, "The dying man's breathing became very shallow and his words were said barely above a whisper.

'Young man, all men and I presume woman have a feeling deep in their mind of a predetermined heroic destiny and many wait their entire lives for a sign. Well, for better or worse, I didn't wait.'"

Michael was surprised to see that his whole family, even Silva, were attentively listening to his story.

"The amber colored man closed his eyes and his breathing stopped. Josiah was going to feel for a pulse when the stranger's eyes ripped open and he stuttered, 'There's an angel waiting for you further down this roadway to Hell.'

Josiah had never seen a person die; but he knew the man had stopped living. He touched the stranger's face and it had already turned colder than his stone deathbed. The only person that could give him answers or soothe his fears or dole out some encouragement was now dead. He didn't feel any sorrow or anguish for the dead man, only disappointment.

He slowly started down the stairway and as the anger in his heart and mind grew, the faster he traveled down the steps. He kept asking himself life-questions. Questions like: 'Why can't everyone live a life of peace and contentment. Why did God create death? Why did he create suffering? Why didn't the world's governments stress more fraternity and equality?'

His anger and confusion grew and his speed down the stairway became a leaping sprint. It felt good to labor for breath. Running, brisk exercise, or hard work with a repetitive cadence had always been meditative for Josiah. The harder he breathed the fewer negative emotions were swirling around in his mind or in his heart.

Suddenly he saw, sitting on the right-sided banister, a person. He lost his balance, tripped and collapsed to the steps; but his eyes remained on the angel. The dead man had said an angel was waiting. The light of the moon had silvered everything, but the apparition had a golden light.

Slowly and quietly he approached the angelic woman sitting on the banister. She was gazing at a path that diverged from the stairway and disappeared into a chaos of rocks and boulders."

Michael looked at his audience. Michael J had tucked his legs up onto the chair, his arms wrapped under his thighs and his chin was resting on his knees. Silva was on the couch, in the same position, except her forehead was resting on her knees. Their eyes were closed.

He wondered if they were sleeping or listening. Gabriel, as usual, was fidgeting in his chair. His good wife, elbows on the table, her hands supporting her red lipstick smile and beautiful blue eyes was smiling.

"Josiah quietly approached the angel; his eyes investigating every detail. His vision from behind was of a woman with sandy hair, a shiny satin or silk shirt, men's dungarees and work boots.

When he was a short distance from the woman, he cleared his throat and in his best manly deep voice said, 'Hello! Hello, do you need any help?'"

"The woman turned her head slowly to see the rude intruder on her meditation."

'FiFi! FiFi Pullman, is that you?' yelled an excited Josiah.'

The young woman coolly and without a whiff of emotion said, 'Do I know you and why would I need your help?'

In a wounded condition of ruffled dignity Josiah snapped, 'We both attend the Jesuit Academy.'

The young woman that Josiah had always thought was impossibly beautiful, said one word, 'Oh.'

Humiliated and offended Josiah growled, 'Why are you here?'

In a creamy rich voice, she elegantly asked, 'Why are you here?'

Determined to remain a gentleman he snarled, 'My family has fallen on hard times and I'm on this mission to find anything, gold, diamonds, lucky charms, anything that might help them.'

The girl that had made him obsessively infatuated with her beauty turned to continue her examination of the divergent pathway and said in an indifferent tone said, 'And I will give thee the treasures of darkness and hidden riches of secret places.'

Barely able to control his anger he yelled, 'Isaiah, I believe Chapter forty-five. I'm here for my family and I would gladly forsake my place in Heaven to help them.'

More to herself than to Josiah, FiFi quietly said, 'A bible-reading, family-loving pilgrim from the land of savages.'

'Isaiah also said the screech owl shall rest in Edom,' shouted Josiah.

The beautiful young woman turned her attention, once again, on Josiah. Her eyebrows were arched in anger. When she replied, she chose her words carefully and spoke slowly. 'Hopefully you're too ignorant....to understand that Biblical passage.'

Josiah was glad that he had provoked a reaction. 'Oh yes, the Jesuits have taught me well. You didn't answer my question. Why are you here?'

FiFi raised her chin so that her eyes were looking down her nose in disdain at the uncultured boy. In a voice, thick with anger she countered, 'I love to sail forbidden seas.'

Josiah laughed, 'Melville, I believe. I'm in your English literature class. I sit the third row on the boys' side of the class.'

The angry emotion expressed on FiFi's face changed to confusion. It was unusual for someone to scoff at her mighty principles.'

'Please leave if you are only here to best me. You seek treasure. I seek knowledge and truth. I'm not interested in debating you, though, I must admit you probably would be a worthy challenger.'

Josiah didn't take any pleasure in knocking the princess from her throne. FiFi's wealthy family was from Connecticut. Land was cheap in the South and her father had bought three plantations and moved his family into the biggest house on the bayou. The young girl had been removed from an urban environment and forced to live in a small, poor, rural bayou community in the South. She accused her father of trying to ruin her life. Her anger and resentment were expressed by her aloofness, her perceived superiority and her general contempt for the South.

Josiah walked closer to FiFi and said, 'I'm not interested in being a challenger. I don't want to best you. I just want to find help for my family. I would be much obliged if you could help me. I don't want to fight. I don't want to debate. I don't want to argue.'

Regaining her composure, after Josiah's plea for help, she turned and pointed to the white brick symbol embedded in the red brick of the pathway. 'That symbol looks like a direction arrow pointing to the correct route.'

Josiah walked closer to inspect the symbol and his conclusion was not what FiFi had been expecting.

'That's not a direction arrow. The correct route is forward. Ignore the periphery, the distractions, always push forward.'

'Her anger was back. She couldn't believe anyone would so easily dismiss her theory. She could feel a heat rise up to her voice. FiFi angrily countered, 'That's absolute rubbish. How can you have a fixed conviction in a place that's totally foreign.'

"FiFi was extremely pale, but now, Josiah could see her cheeks were fiery fighting red. He couldn't think of a response, he was dazzled by the slender princess. She had prominent gray-blue eyes, straight white teeth, fierce nostrils and thick shoulder length hair that framed her smooth face. She rolled her eyes in dismissiveness and angrily muttered words to herself. He wasn't really listening to her ranting monologue. He could see the girl in his dreams and fantasies for the past six months was totally different from him. She had golden hair; he had unruly, wavy, black hair. Her skin was creamy white; he had a farmer's tan. Her blue eyes demanded attention; his brown eyes were quiet. She was outspoken; willing to forcefully express her opinions. He was a respectful listener. He started to repel her attack, but they both froze when they heard voices coming from the pathway.

The narrow red brick trail disappeared into a jungle of boulders and from this chaos three men loudly emerged. They were carrying rifles and were wearing gray uniforms. The three men didn't seem excited to find two fellow travelers.

'How do there! Good day to you,' bellowed the leader of the threesome, 'If it is day, I couldn't tell which. My name is Captain Enoch Bourgeois.'

Pointing to the others in his group he proceeded to introduce them. 'This is Sergeant Micah Molaison and Private Dump Ledet.'

The Captain turned to face Josiah, but his eyes drifted in FiFi's direction. FiFi's beauty captured the army of three. The three arrivals stared mute. She regained her haughty composure when she realized she now controlled three wishful dreamers.

FiFi decided she was in charge and would speak. 'Gentlemen tell us your brave story. Where is home and what is your destination? Sing us your heroic adventures. What treasures do you seek?'

The Captain stood before FiFi as a perfect gentleman. He removed his floppy hat stuck with a long trailing red feather as its cockade. 'Madame, as I have said before, my name is Captain Enoch Bourgeois. We three are members of the Louisiana Regiment commanded by Major General Mansfield Lovell. Our mission is not for treasure. We simply seek counsel from the Rougarou. The damn Yankees had blockaded our coastline and captured New Orleans. A conjure woman brought us to a door located in a tomb. She said if we found the Rougarou we could ask him to help our cause.'

FiFi twisted her mouth, swallowing like she had tasted something she disliked. She questioned, 'You men are soldiers in the Southern Army of vagabonds and cowards?'

The three men dressed in gray looked as though they'd seen a swamp witch. You could see contempt in the crinkle of the Captain's lips. He protested, 'Madame we're no cowards. We have gallantly fought in many battles to stop the northern aggression.'

FiFi snapped back, 'Northern aggression?' The granddaughter of a Yankee turned towards Josiah and with a majestic glance and a severe stare ordered him to explain to the rapscallions that the Civil War was over.

Mildly embarrassed he spoke respectfully to the confused soldiers. 'The War ended in sixty-five. The Yankees won. They banned the term War of Northern Aggression. History books now call the conflict The Civil War and accuse the southern states of starting the nightmare. The Northern armies burnt down cities, destroyed factories, farms and railways. What they couldn't steal they destroyed. The Federals occupied the South for many years. The South had always struggled against the Eastern nobility. Now their contempt has grown and regard themselves as the Masters of the South.'

FiFi threw up her hands and let out a big theatrical groan.

The Captain was too stunned to speak. The Sergeant asked, 'Who are you. Are you sure of this tragic news?'

Josiah walked closer to the stunned and dejected soldiers. 'My name is Josiah and when we walked through that door in the tomb it was Nineteen Seventeen. The War has been over for fifty years. We're now fighting a war in Europe.'

The Sergeant ignored FiFi and spoke to Josiah, 'It felt like we were here for weeks, but in my gut, I knew something was wrong. Time in this place doesn't seem to exist. There was never a need to eat or drink. This trail is just a diversion. We found a few people on this trail. Most were dead, but the few that were standing, agreed that we had taken the wrong path. It led to a land in mourning. Everything was dark, gray and gloomy. There were no celestial guides to offer directional assistance. The only light was from that cold unmoving moon and that distant fifolet.'

Josiah looked at the distant puny yellow light and wondered if that was his destination or another distraction.

The Private spoke for the first time, 'We met a man dressed in ancient armor. He said he had been a companion to King Arthur. He said his name was something like Gavin. There must be other doors leading to this world, because we've met others that were from the other side of the world.'

The Captain regained his composure and resume his role as leader of the group. He chose his words cautiously, 'If the war is truly over as you have said. There is no need for us to continue on this quest. We should go home to our families.'

Josiah warned the three men that the world had greatly changed in the last fifty years. There were horseless carriages called automobiles. Men could fly in machines called airplanes.

FiFi had a need to further insult the sad soldiers, 'Yes, the world has changed, but where you are going it's still the land of intellectual dwarfs.'

The Captain raised his fist in righteous wrath and angrily replied, 'As Eve, and as Pandora, so shall this shrewish disciple of Satan bring calamity and grim misery.'

FiFi yelled, 'How dare you insult me.'

The soldiers ignored the pompous young woman and began their long journey home. The men in gray had the slouchy demeanor of the defeated as they walked up the endless stairway.

FiFi's angry eyes followed the retreating soldiers. After a few moments, she noticed Josiah staring at her. 'FiFi, what you see as elegance and nobility, most see as vulgarity. You've been given the opportunity to dream for most of your life, but life is not a dream.'

Josiah started walking down the stairway. He would continue his journey alone."

Gabriel leaned across the table to whisper to his father. "Pops, don't stop for me. I gotta go pee."

Michael needed a break from storytelling and said, "Yeh! Go! I'm gonna take a break and get some more coffee."

Michael J looked at his mother and moaned, "Mom, I'm still hungry."

"MJ, you had two bowls of cereal an hour ago."

Hearing his growing son plead for more food, Michael volunteered, "I'll cook pancakes."

On guard for possibly being volunteered as a helper, Jennifer sternly warned, "Don't forget! The cook is also the dishwasher and the stove and table cleaner."

Michael laughed, "I never make a mess."

Jennifer gave the teasing smile that always made Michael want to steal kisses.

"If the children weren't here, I'd give you the proper answer that remark deserves."

Silva was still sitting on her private property; but she was smiling. Michael J was searching the kitchen cabinets for pancake ingredients. Gabriel walked back to the table struggling with his pants zipper.

The Story (Sunday Afternoon)
The Caillouet family retired to the family room after gorging themselves on pancakes. Michael had let his kids eat as many pancakes they could swallow. He had melted thin chocolate pieces on Gabriel's pancakes. Michael J and Silva covered their pancakes in sliced ruby red strawberries and freezer-frosty whip cream with a drizzle of cane syrup. Jennifer wanted crepe thin cakes folded over warm melted butter and crunchy sugar.

There had been a brief debate about after-lunch entertainment. Michael had won the contest and insisted on a Sunday afternoon nap in his lounge chair that was usually occupied by belligerent trespassers. The Saints were on a bye week, so the TV would remain blank and the story would continue after a Sunday nap.

When Michael felt an alien sensation on his ear he fell out of a black void. He often thought that the unconsciousness of death and his deep sleep were the same. He opened his eyes and saw his youngest lightly tracing his finger on his Dad's ear. Gabriel whispered, "Pops wake up, its story time."

Eight eyes were staring and he wasn't sure of what had happened. Silva was guarding her untouchable side of the couch. Her two brothers and mother were scrunched together and piled up on the other end. Disoriented, Michael was serious when he asked, "What year is it?"

"We were debating if you were alive, laughed Jennifer. You started out with heavy breathing, then you went into the snorting and grunting stage. Then, as usual, you went silent. We weren't sure if you were still breathing, so we sent Gabriel to feel if you were cold. We allowed you two hours of escape and now its story time." Jennifer beamed her mischievous smile, "We're waiting for our entertainment."

Michael sat up in his chair, rubbed the sleep from his eyes and wordlessly walked to the kitchen for a cup of coffee. When he nestled in his comfortable chair, he took a sip of his coffee and said to himself, "Let's see where did we leave our happy couple. FiFi insulted the soldiers and shattered Josiah's image of her. He had a long journey and he couldn't spend any more time bickering with a princess that lacked the simplest empathy.

Michael looked at his audience and said, "That's where we stopped. Right? So..."

"He started down the walkway, prepared to complete his journey alone. At first, Josiah didn't realize that FiFi was following only a few steps behind him. For a long period of immeasurable time they walked in silence, each with their own thoughts. In the beginning, when they talked, they turned on one another with minimal provocation. Heated arguments grew from simple observations made by either traveler. He was tired of her caustic wit and her constant need to prove the infallible correctness of her thoughts. She grew angry with his long periods of silence and his agile tongue that often left her speechless.

Josiah had felt that FiFi's beauty had given her an air of inaccessibility. FiFi had barely noticed Josiah in their literature class. She hadn't seen him as someone of interest. But now on their shared journey Josiah learned that FiFi was not inaccessible, in fact, she seemed lonely. She could see clearly that Josiah was brilliant, her equal. They both learned to listen and to consider the other's viewpoint. They began freely discussing their feelings, their thoughts, and their confusions. FiFi gave a tedious book-long speech on the misinformed actions taken each day by people, institutions and governments. Josiah's response was that there's a price for knowledge that most people are unwilling to pay and so ignorance often rides the horse to inferior victories. He quoted his father as saying that every morning each person had to put on his coat of hope and determination. Determined each day to accomplish his or her goals and the eternal hope that their accomplishments were good for themselves and others. FiFi started to laugh and cry. She had meticulously crafted her lengthy opinion and Josiah had beautifully answered her philosophical question in three sentences. She lagged behind so that she could secretly exam the young man that she was excited to be with on her exploration.

The stairway had flattened into a wide roadway. The road was free of litter, human bones had been neatly stacked on the edges of the roadway and corpses in various stages of rot had been given their own roadside section. They were deep in conversation concerning the huge quantity of bones and who or what could be cleaning the road when they heard someone talking. They could see a man pushing a large janitorial cart stuffed with oddly shaped brooms and mops talking to himself. Josiah and FiFi broke into a jog to catch up with the man shouting a monologue. When they caught up with the stranger, he was so involved in his peerless conversation he failed to notice them.

The skinny young man had long wild black hair and his short beard was an impenetrable black mass of coarse hair. He wore faded blue jeans, leather sandals and a tight green denim vest was buttoned over a loose gray jersey.

'Sir! Sir!' spoke Josiah trying to get the man's attention.

Josiah noted that the bearded man wasn't much older than him. He couldn't tell if the young man was singing or loudly talking to an imaginary friend.

When the noisy young man noticed Josiah, his light brown eyes widen, he broke into a huge smile and responded, 'Haaay man. What's up dude?'

Josiah introduced himself and FiFi. He explained to the young man that they were on a journey searching for the Rougarou. He asked the friendly, smiling, young man if he could help them. Could he tell them which direction they should travel? FiFi asked how far they must travel to meet this Rougarou. They both asked him why there were so many dead people. Why did they never feel any hunger or thirst or fatigue.

'Thank God you speak English,' answered the smiling hairy young man. 'The last two times I met travelers, I had no idea what language they were speaking and was relieved when they journeyed on.'

FiFi and Josiah were standing like attentive students waiting for answers. A mischievous smile spread across the young man's face and his eyes turned visionary as he spoke.

'I can't give you factual or proven answers; but I can give you my sensible theories and a few credible reports that other travelers have told me.'

'Well what are you waiting for? To the best of your abilities give us some answers,' yelled FiFi.

The young man was already captured by FiFi's beauty. His big friendly smile turned into a silly grin. He was mute. He stood in a hypnotic daze.

'Speak!' ordered an impatient FiFi.

Verbally shaken out of his trance the young man pointed to the tiny, distant, yellow spot in the sky.

'I'm pretty sure that yellow light warms the lands that you are seeking,' responded the young man.

Josiah asked, 'What makes you come to that conclusion?'

FiFi's attractive face had given the young bearded man amnesia. He had forgotten someone was to his left. Josiah's sudden words startled FiFi's lovesick victim.

The young man boasted, 'I've traveled down into the cold dark Valley of Conflict, safely crossed the black and dangerous Field of Struggles and finally climbed out of the far side of the valley into the Land of Lights. I've met many fellow wanderers and most have agreed that the spec of yellow light in the sky is the direction that everyone must travel towards.'

'But you haven't actually spoken to anyone that has seen this mythical creature,' grilled FiFi.

The young man shook his head no, but before he could answer, FiFi rapidly shouted more questions. 'Where were you going? Where were you coming from? Please, tell me your story.'

The young man collected his thoughts for a moment and then began his story.

'When I explored in the Land of Lights, I found such beauty and awe. A discovery should be shared. So, I decided to return home to find someone to experience with me the wonders of this New World. But for the first time in my life I had a vision; my mental confusion melted away. I knew I was not to explore the New World. My destiny was to clear the pathway through the Field of Struggles so that explorers like you can reach the Land of Lights.'

'Lucky the man that can magically see his destiny. But why are you here?' barked FiFi.

'After I graduated from high school, I was so confused. Many of my classmates were excited to enroll in college. I wasn't interested in college. My girlfriend wanted to marry and start a family, but again, I was not interested. My father wanted me to become a welder and I told him I was not interested. I was confused and bored. I knew I needed a change. I needed to get away from everyone so I could think. I had heard the stories about this place and the doorway in the tomb. Most people don't believe the stories because so very few, if any, have returned from this world. So, in 1972, a year after I graduated, I entered the tomb.'"

'1972!' yelled both Josiah and FiFi.

'We just entered the tomb a few weeks ago and it was 1917,' explained Josiah.

'I've met twin sisters that said it was 2017 when they entered this world from an ancient Pharaonic tomb. Twice I've met a man dressed in knightly armor. He said that he knew King Arthur. I don't think time exist in this world.'

'What is your name?' asked Josiah.

'Why are there so many dead people, bones,' FiFi quickly shouted.

'The battles that take place on the Field of Struggles often spills over onto the pathway. When combatants die, their bodies are left where they've fallen. Sometimes the mounds of slaughtered soldiers are so high they block the pathway. Some of the dead are wanderers or explorers like you. Some die soon after entering this world and others roam for centuries. I don't know what determines longevity. I have a theory. Some people are born with the will to fight, to achieve, to live and others are just born to be the background, the framework of minor characters.'

The young man turned to Josiah and said, 'My name is WawaWain.'

'Oh, you poor man. How could your parent's burden you with such a foolish name,' blurted FiFi shaking her head?

WawaWain laughed and said, 'I like my name. I've known many a canine to answer to your name.'

FiFi's jaw tighten, her nostrils flared and her gray-blue eyes showered contempt on WawaWain.

Josiah started to giggle and then the giggle erupted into a loud laughter. Wawawain joined in the laughter. FiFi stood there watching Josiah. That was the first time she saw him laugh. She started to laugh, not at the absurdity of her name, but at the happiness she felt for Josiah.

When the giggles subsided, Josiah asked WawaWain.

'If you're going to the Valley of Conflict, maybe we can travel with you?'

'Of course, Dude!'

'I got two questions; well, maybe three,' snapped FiFi.

'If you entered the tomb 1972, fifty-five years after Josiah and I; how have you arrived here before us? Second, how do you know the names of this valley and this field? Are there signs saying you have arrived at such and such valley? The third question is why do you say dude.'

'I only chatted and compared notes with explorers traveling in my direction. I was relentless in my exploration of this world. I didn't loiter. In your case, it's obvious that you are a debater, a litigator for your opinions. So, I traveled faster than you. Of course, that's only my theory. Remember I don't think there is time, as we know it, in this world.'

Josiah saw FiFi put her hands on her waist and her chin rose a little higher. He could see she was poised for a fight, but remained silent.

WawaWain was oblivious to the fire he was stoking. He continued his answers without concern for FiFi's ego.

'When the explorer Ferdinand Magellan saw a peaceful and calm ocean, he named it Pacific. When the explorer WawaWain came to a valley and could hear screams, curses and crying coming out of the darkness he named it the Valley of Conflict. When this explorer came to the narrow valley floor and witnessed two opposing armies fight, he named it the Field of Struggles.'

'So, you are self-appointed or officially designated by some higher authority. Mr. Magellan was given the authority to name newly discovered lands and oceans by the king of Spain. You can give a name to everything you see. You can give a title to every pebble under your foot. But without proper authority, it means nothing,' challenged FiFi.

Josiah could see that the smiling WawaWain was ready for battle. He quickly repeated the third question in an effort to prevent the impending conflict.

'What about the word dude?'

WawaWain answered Josiah's question, but continued gazing at FiFi.

'Dude is just an informal, friendly greeting that was popular in the early seventies. The formal would be, hello sir, and the informal would be, hey dude.'

Josiah turned to walk down the pathway and said, 'We do loiter too much. It's time for me to resume my mission.'

He walked down the road that had turned into a narrow, paved pathway and the two others followed. He could hear FiFi loudly groan, 'I must be the luckiest woman in the world. Now I have two barbarians as traveling companions.'

Eventually WawaWain and FiFi continued their contentious conversations and heated debates. Every time Josiah asked a question or gave an opinion, FiFi would smother WawaWain with an avalanche of questions. It was her attempt to make Josiah jealous or at least angry. She showered her traveling companion with attention, ignored Josiah and dominated any conversation when he tried to talk. Josiah thought she was being an immature girl that was frightened when she wasn't the center of attention. Instead of competing, Josiah decided to listen in on the vast array of topics the two debated. Wawawain liked to study history and found FiFi's stories and explanations of early Twentieth Century America to be fascinating. She rattled on and on about her excellent abilities on a dance floor. She demonstrated a few dance steps and made sure Josiah saw her. She listened with polite skepticism when she was told about the lunar landings. FiFi often looked in Josiah's direction to see if she'd made him jealous or angry. She told WawaWain that she had often deliberated if it would be liberating to be stupid. 'If you don't know, then you don't care and all is well. Living in a sweet ignorant bliss.' She looked directly at Josiah when she'd made the statement, but he wasn't listening. He was frustrating her, making her angry. That's how they traveled until the Valley of Conflict was before them."

Michael eyed his audience and saw that they were attentively listening. He took a sip of his cold coffee and continued his tale.

"After walking for an amount of time that no human invention, such as a clock or calendar, could measure; the trio came to the edge of a precipice and saw before them a darkness that filled a valley.

'What is this?' asked FiFi.

WawaWain answered, 'This is the Valley of Conflict.'

As he spoke, they could hear moans, screaming and angry shouting emanating from the darkness.

'This black river of darkness is a time-span of nothingness. You have to follow the trail down the side of the valley to see the Field of Struggle. Nothing can be seen from here. Only fiendish sounds reach the rim of the valley. On the valley floor, there is a brief moment of twilight. This is when most of the atrocities of battle occur,' explained WawaWain.

He pointed towards the horizon and said, 'Do you see that distant faint pinkish strip of color. That's your destination. This valley is my destiny. I am to be a guide for travelers similar to the boatman Charon.'

FiFi hissed and replied, 'That's nonsense, you cannot abandon us. You are our traveling companion. I couldn't endure traveling for eternity with Josiah. He has no tongue, he doesn't appreciate the spirit of a debate, he always must rush to victory.'

She saw that Josiah was smiling, but his answer was going to put her into a rage.

A smiling Josiah spoke loud and clear, 'I'm always intrigued….and entertained by the comedy of your childish behavior. Your privilege life has robbed you of good common sense.'

FiFi took a step towards Josiah and with a clenched fist and a red face yelled, 'The word barbarian was invented for crass people like yourself. And!'

WawaWain walked between the fighting couple and said, 'This is not a good time to fight. We will shortly embark on a very dangerous passage through the Valley of Conflict.'

Hearing the words Valley of Conflict, FiFi remembered she had to change the name.

'Listen, you have to change the name. Valley of Conflict is so backpage boring. At least think about the Chasm of Screams or the Gorge of Blackness or maybe the March of Hell or the March of the Hellish Night or Screaming Cavity, anything, but The Valley of Conflict. It's such a dull name. It's a title that would remain unopened on a shelf.' FiFi gave an audible sigh and slowly shook her head, thinking how witless men could be.

WawaWain and Josiah were intently walking the edge of the darkness searching for the path that led across the valley.

WawaWain halted his search, looked up at FiFi and in his usual genial attitude jested, 'Hey Babe! If we get across this hellhole; you can name it whatever you wish.'

FiFi saw Josiah pointing at her and with a huge smile, silently mouthed 'Hey Babe.'

'Hey Baaabe? Hey Babe! My name is FiFi Pullman, you hairy savage,' exploded FiFi. She then directed her wrath on Josiah. 'A gentleman friend would not allow a rude fool to address his companion in such a familiar manner.'

No one heard her words because WawaWain and Josiah found the path and had descended into the darkness to explore.

When the explorers emerged from the darkness, Josiah grabbed FiFi's hand and led her to the edge. He explained that they would descend only a few feet and would sit until their eyes adjusted to the darkness. A moment before stepping into the black pit a shadow of worry spread across FiFi's face. Josiah assured her he would be by her side and he'd keep her safe. The three ventured down the path and sat until their eyes could recognize outlines of shapes. When they descended further down the narrow path the air became cooler and it had a machine-created artificial smell.

The path narrowed until they had to cautiously walk in a single file. On their right was a wall of stone and to their left was the edge of oblivion. A number of times the foot of one of the explorers would miss the edge and sink into the waiting nightmare. A moment of fear and then a friend's steady hand saved their lives. The thick black air was slowly moving. FiFi said that she thought they were inside a sinister cloud.

The further downward they crept the air temperature rose and the sounds coming from below were sharper. Sounds that would go unnoticed in daylight brought fear and a creeping hysteria in the darkness. By the time the trail became wider and less steep the temperature had become jungle hot and thick with flying insects.

WawaWain motioned to his companions to sit and whispered that they should only speak in hushed tones. He explained that they were perched above the Field of Struggle. He described how the ensuing battle could possibly pour onto the trail and they had to be prepared to move to a more secure spot. He gave a chilling description of how the constant battles occasionally rushed up onto the stairway they had just traveled. This explained the numerous skeletal remains that had lined the stairway.

FiFi peppered WawaWain with whispered questions. She wanted to know who or what was on the battle field below. She needed to know why the combatants were fighting. Why the screams, where were these fighters from and was this crossing going to be dangerous.

WawaWain sat between FiFi and Josiah so that both of his companions could hear his whispered explanation. He warned them that there were brief periods of twilight and during this time they would witness acts of savagery they would never forget. He explained that there was a small army of men with faces painted red and naked of clothing and weapons. He didn't know who they fought for or why they were fighting. He just called them the Red Army that came from his right. Then there was a huge army of blue-faced naked men without weapons that came from the left. He went into detail describing his previous journey to the Field of Struggles. He had hurried down the trail towards a bleak light and a chorus of yells, shouts and screams. When he'd gotten to approximately this same spot he was frozen with fear. He stood in confusion and horror as a scene of slaughter revealed itself. He'd stayed on this same spot to study the havoc that he had witnessed. He could tell them, with certainty, that the battles only took place when the weak light appeared. The warriors on each side were naked and carried no weapons. They looked exactly the same, except one army came from the right with faces painted red and the other larger army with faces painted blue came from the left. Hundreds, maybe thousands were ripped apart and killed during each battle. He had regularly saw a peculiar action taken by members of the Blue Army. He'd seen on many occasions, veterans of the Blue Army, paint their faces red and join the army on the right, replenishing the Red Army's losses. Some battles were verbal; two masses of warriors, shouting distance apart, screaming curses and jeering at the opposition. But the primal ferocity of most battles brought a cold terror to his stomach.

WawaWain explained that when the battle was over and the field once again cloaked in gloom was when they would make a frantic dash across the bloody battlefield. They sat in silence in the darkness with a building wild apprehension.

Without warning, a gray light rushed across the condemned valley floor and a galloping mass of naked, red faced warriors were racing with the light. The three witnesses could hear the dull thud when the army from the right slammed into the Blue Army and then the savage screams and the frightened moans began. The sounds were terrifying. Fifi had never before seen a naked man, but it was the ripping apart of flesh and the savage horror that would not let her look away. The warriors twisted off limbs of their enemy or bit down into the neck until a fountain of blood sprayed the combatants. Eventually the gray light slowly retreated to the right and the armies withdrew into the darkness. The three travelers could see in the dying light, warriors limping and crawling away from the battlefield. An immense accumulation of slain warriors blocked their route across the field and there were mountains of skeletal remains of former warriors scattered everywhere. They realized that the valley floor had been a killing field for eternity. An unending war fought for unknown reasons.

When the last living warrior had left the battlefield, WawaWain started down the path and motioned to the others to follow. Before rushing across the battlefield, he stopped to whisper that they must cross the field before the light returned. FiFi and Josiah didn't hear a word that he had softly spoken. They were gagging and dry heaving. The thick choking vapor of rotting flesh had overwhelmed their senses. WawaWain grabbed his companions and pulled them onto the battlefield. He told them that their brain would adjust and the smell would become just a nuisance. He stressed that if the light returned when they were in the middle of the crossing they would become as lifeless as their surroundings. FiFi and Josiah reluctantly followed him.

They had to climb over mounds of tangled corpses and whenever their feet actually touched down on the path, they sank ankle deep into a black muck. The couple had thought the muck was mud until WawaWain explained that it was the crushed bones of past warriors mixed with the blood of current casualties. The clouds of flying insects landed on bloodied warriors and fed at the open wounds. The insects were blood drinking vampires that didn't bite the living. They had either lost that ability or never had it. The aftermath of competing armies was banquets for the insects.

They struggled across the field for hours or maybe years, but finally the edge of the valley floor was near. With her face painted black, FiFi grabbed WawaWain's arm and inches from his face declared the battlefield had been officially rename the Field of Horror. They were near to where the path would start rising out of the hot reeking hell they had crossed. There was a sense of relief. Soon they would be safe. But suddenly there was a fourth voice. The companions froze, they slowly turned searching for the ghost voice. Josiah was the first to see a pair of pleading eyes looking up from the black muck. He called out to the others to help him free the owner of those eyes from the muck and the tangled frozen dead. WawaWain spoke with authority and commanded Josiah to leave the savage. There was no time to be the Good Samaritan. He could faintly hear the pounding of the advancing Red Army. He grabbed FiFi's hand and they raced to continue their exodus. The rumble of the advancing armies grew louder and they could see a faint strip of gray light in the distance to the right. By the time they exited the battlefield the chaos of attacking armies was furiously loud, a thunderous explosion. They glimpsed back down the path expecting Josiah to be close behind; but he was missing. They looked out onto the dimly lit battlefield and saw Josiah working to free the warrior.

FiFi started screaming and ran towards the battlefield. Once again, WawaWain grasped her hand and pulled her up the path yelling that they must climb higher. She was being led up the path but her focus was down below on the battlefield. She collapsed when she saw the warring armies swallow Josiah. WawaWain held his companion in his arms and he carried her higher and higher.

WawaWain gently released FiFi when he'd felt they had reached a safe distance from the battlefield. She fell to her knees and looked up at rescuer. Her forehead wrinkled and her bottom lip pushed out in preparation for a cry. She pleaded with him to help her pray.

She prayed, she begged, she cried, she screamed, 'Please, please, I've never asked, nor shall I ever again! Please God!'

When her prayers and crying became less intense, WawaWain asked her if she felt a slight craving for food. He told her he couldn't explain their lack of hunger during their journey through the darkness; but he knew they were now in a different world.

Everything that they saw, tasted or heard would be exquisite. Each new day would intensely excite their senses. They had crossed over from the other side and were now in a world that would lure them to the Land of the Rougarou.

FiFi hadn't heard a word that he'd spoken. She looked at WawaWain and he could see a gray shadow of worry had shrouded her face. She told him she could go no further without Josiah. She said she thought she would have him forever and that there was no point in living in daylight if Josiah was in darkness. She mumbled that when Josiah was near, she felt a cozy warmth that covered her, protected and comforted her.

The first time he had explored this mystery world of golden light, he knew he had to share this land of bounty and beauty with someone he loved. On his return journey, he had an epiphany. The revelation detailed how he would guide travelers down the valley trail, then ferry his passengers across the black pit of chaos and then lead the explorers into the promised land. His first attempts would be rudimentary, but eventually his vision called for a bridge that would span the dark river of struggle and there would be a token charge. An affordable price for services; because everyone knew, things that were free are never appreciated. But then fate brought FiFi to him. He had to find out if there was an ounce of a chance FiFi was his true destiny. During their journey, they spoke for ages. They laughed and debated, sang and teased. They were students that taught. He had never enjoyed anyone's company as much as FiFi's. He exulted in her presence. But the few times Josiah joined the conversation he noticed FiFi never prepared a response, instead she listened, she studied, she digested his every word. Her smiles were always friendly and inviting; but she looked at Josiah with appraisal and admiration. Now he knew, he couldn't compete with Josiah even with the friendly assistance from Mr. Death. He started down the trail, his last act of appreciation would be to bring the body of his friend to his friend for burial.

FiFi bathed and washed her clothes in a nearby meandering, cool stream. She satisfied her hunger by eating a foreign fruit growing on vines and she prayed and begged. There had been so many battles she had become immune to the deafening roar of another drifting up from below. She was startled out of her meditation by movement on the trail. In an instant a warrior stood before her. She wasn't frightened, she was ready for death. She studied her potential murderer. He was tall with long sinewy limbs. There were splotches of gray powdered bone meal covering his naked body and long brown hair. A swollen jagged wound on his thigh had crusted over and an internal organ was ballooning out of a wound on his side. His face was painted red. The fighter took a few steps toward FiFi and began growling, yelling and chanting a mournful, tragic, black dirge. While singing his black song, he danced in a menacing manner holding in his empty hands a spear and a shield. He stopped his song and dance as suddenly as he'd started and then stepped aside so that FiFi could see what he'd brought her. She saw WawaWain holding Josiah in his arms. She ran towards them; her shattered dream was before her, waiting for her help. The warrior trumpeted a roar as he ran past the reunited companions. He was eager to kill men with faces painted blue.

WawaWain explained to FiFi that he'd found the warrior dragging Josiah up the trail. Josiah had been barely conscious when he'd found him. He'd asked WawaWain if FiFi was safe and when he had been given a satisfactory answer, he drifted into the void.

WawaWain told FiFi that nothing died in this mysterious world. The same flower bloomed every day. Fruit picked from trees grew back the next day and wounds healed quickly. He only partially believed his assurances that Josiah would survive if he still had a flicker of life. Fifi cradled Josiah's head in her lap, brushed away the ash and dried muck from his face and hair while WawaWain gave his personal interpretation of this world's magic.

He suddenly stopped talking. FiFi froze; Josiah had opened his eyes. The heat of life had not gone cold. Mr. Death had withdrawn his help. WawaWain could see the veil of sadness disappear from FiFi's face. He knew all was lost and told FiFi it was best that he was going back down to the battlefield to fulfill his destiny.

Puzzled, FiFi begged that he couldn't leave. Who would talk to her, argue and debate her? She admitted she loved Josiah, but he was half mute. She sobbed and asked who would sing with her.

He thought her face looked as fragile as a porcelain cup.

She screamed, 'You're wrong!'

WawaWain saw her tears, her anguish.

Again, she screamed, 'You're wrong! This is not your destiny. Why are you punishing yourself? Is it a penance, an atonement for the past? Why?'

He could hear FiFi yelling, screaming and crying as he quickly walked down the path. Once again, he had lost the competition for love. He walked and cried and cried and cried."

Michael woke from his concentration on storytelling. He could hear Jennifer calling his name.

"Michael, we need to feed these hungry bellies and get these guys cleaned. School tomorrow, so we need to get things ready for the morning chaos. Let's all eat and shower and then finish the story."

Michael J., always hungry, asked, "What are we going to eat?"

"I can make lots of scrambled eggs and buttered toast and chocolate milk," answered his mother.

Michael countered, "We still have pancake batter. Why not some more pancakes?"

The two boys cheered. They were in favor of eating pancakes.

"I don't know Michael. We had cereal, pancakes, then ice cream while you were napping and now some more pancakes."

Michael J., the dealmaker, responded, "Mom we can eat salad for the next two days." He raced into the kitchen to set the dishes and the utensils on the table.

Silva rose from her protected area of the couch and told her Mom, "I'm going to take a quick shower while you feed the savages. I'll eat eggs or pancakes; either is fine with me." She slowed as she walked by her Dad's chair. She was smiling, but her gaze was focused on the floor. "Dad I'm really enjoying your story."

Gabriel walked over to his Dad and rubbed his forearm. "Pops, I don't understand everything, but I really like your story. It's better than watching football."

Michael cooked pancakes for his family. He didn't eat; he was still feasting on compliments.

The Story (Sunday Evening)

The Caillouet family had fed on pancakes and showered. Silva was again protecting her half of the couch. She seemed less wrathful in her pink nightgown. Michael J. and Gabriel wore matching pajamas. Jennifer wore her satiny wine-colored PJs. The ones Michael liked because of the cool silky feel on the backs of his hands while the palms of his hands felt the warmth of his wife's skin. For a moment, Michael considered finishing the story the next evening.

"OK guys, when we left for pancakes, WawaWain had left to fulfill his destiny to keep the path to the land of the Rougarou clear of dead warriors, litter and anything else that blocked the path. Josiah and FiFi were once again alone. They rested by the cool clear stream and made plans for their continued journey. So…!"

"Josiah told FiFi that his only worry on the battlefield had been for her safety and he would be forever indebted to WawaWain for bringing her safely out of the chaos. He admitted to himself that he was glad the competitor for FiFi's attention was gone, but he did miss WawaWain.

FiFi's cheeks blushed when she explained her feelings for Josiah. She told him that she saw him as someone that was confident and steady. Someone that wouldn't flee when there was a problem and she knew that sometimes she could be the problem. She said that she realized that he needed periods of peace and serenity and she would give him his needed time to quietly plot, plan and dream; but she needed lively conversation, contentious disputes, song and dance.

The couple bathed and swam in the cool stream and feasted on the abundant edible fruits, vegetables and flowers. For the first time, they discussed their families, their insecurities, their fears and their dreams. When they continued their quest to find the Rougarou they were in love.

The sights of this foreign world were hypnotically surreal. There was a time cycle in the new land. Each new day began with a golden, sparkling light and the entire day was like a perpetual dawn. Everything was silvered each night by a large full moon and for many nights they witnessed the Goddess of Night admire her reflection in a large blue lake surrounded by gray mountains. The further they traveled from the Field of Horror the sweeter the air became. Sweet and crisp air filled each breath.

The terrain of the magical land continually changed. One day they would be hiking a path through waist high, lush, emerald green grass sprouting cannonball size, crimson and gold flowers that housed tiny, pink wooly critters. The next day the path could be zigzagging through a mist laden forest. Squat trees with cranberry-red umbrella foliage drizzled sweet rain. On another day, the explorers would trek along the path shaded by towering trees with red, brown, gold or rust colored leaves floating down like colored snow. Birds feathered in an array of black and blue tints darted from tree to tree, then hovered in groups whistling a joyful undersong to accompany the majesty of the day. The birds didn't have beaks. They puckered red lips to sound their cheerful tunes.

One morning, FiFi and Josiah were finger combing each other's night hair when they heard a thrumming vibration. They cautiously followed the path. Small puffs of white clouds streamed along the trail, and floated between and wrapped around their legs and the trunks of the trees. They halted when they reached the forest edge. Where the forest ended, began a vast sea of flowering plants. Jade green stalks shouldered large metallic-gold flowers that reflected the sun's glitter. The vibrations they heard were from the beating wings of bee-sized humans. The gold covered creatures were mining the flowers for a golden substance. When Josiah and FiFi followed the path through the green and gold field, the miniature winged humans were excited to see the visitors and settled on their shoulders and in the hair of the couple. The excited gold miners tunneled through Josiah and FiFi's hair, tickle kissed their cheeks, smeared the gold substance on their lips and clung to their ears so they could whisper enchanted secrets. The vibrations and soft whispers awoke their senses to rapture and serenity. They sang, they danced, they celebrated and they fell deeper in love. Had they walked up to and crossed the threshold of death and entered Heaven? The threshold of death, the dark and dangerous valley they had successfully navigated had been renamed by FiFi. She named it for their almost forgotten companion: The Valley of WaWa.

The sun rose and fell thousands of times during their journey through Paradise, but everything has an ending. When their path emerged from the sea of flowers, it continued into a very different world. A foul fume assaulted them as they follow their path. The heavy smell of sun-cooked oily tar made it difficult to breathe. They had left a land of joy that hummed with activity. But now, their path snaked through an eerie stillness; a barren land of packed, firm sand, the color of raw sienna. Black bark trees naked of leaves were monuments to death. The sun shone brightly, but the lonely landscape looked to be in shadows. The couple experienced hunger and thirst for the first time. They followed their path through the featureless land until the need for nourishment forced them to consider ending their journey and returning to the Land of Flowers. They assured themselves that they would come back with sufficient provisions. But, before they could start on their retreat, they heard a distant voice yelling for help.

In the far distance, they could see someone standing on the path waving his arms and shouting for assistance.

Josiah and FiFi trudged towards the person pleading for help. When they were within talking distance, the couple could hear the man saying, 'I need help! My friend is stuck in the comede and I need help to pull him free.'

Dizzy and weak from hunger and thirst and exhaustion, the volunteers halted in confusion, when they were vaguely able to see the man. But, was he a man? The individual begging for help was a slender, but muscular, pole of flesh. He had flippers instead of feet. He had no legs. Short stunted arms and tiny hands pointed to the friend in distress. He was colored in various ranges of the color red. His flippers and bottom third were dragon-fire red which faded to mauve, then hot pink, then coral pink, then fleshy pink. The very top of its head was once again colored in dragon-fire red. The face was human. He had small ears and a tiny mouth. His nose and eyes were abnormally large. The only facial difference from humans was the goggles grown to protect the big eyes.

'Pull down that small dead tree,' commanded the stranger, pointing to a dead shrunken black bark tree standing next to the path, 'then lay it across the comede so my friend can pull himself free.'

'I'm too exhausted to knock down a tree. I'll walk over and try to pull him free,' muttered a delirious Josiah.

'No!' screamed the big-eyed stranger. 'The comede will capture you, suck you down and devour your flesh.'

'I can't walk on the sand,' questioned Josiah?

'No!' screamed the panicked stranger.

Josiah took off his shirt and trousers and tied his clothing into a rope of rescue. He flung one end to the drowning victim and together Josiah and FiFi pulled him to safety. The couple collapsed to the path, while the two strange man-creatures frantically wiped the sand from the victim.

'We're starving,' Josiah angrily cried.

The screamer opened his faded blue satchel that he wore high across his chest, pulled out a shiny, golden flask, handed it to his rescuers and said, 'Drink!'

He explained that the flask contained an elixir obtained from the golden men, the miners of flowers. He told the couple that the miraculous potion was a cure-all for sickness, hunger or thirst.

"After the couple had regained their strength, their first questions were: 'Who are you? What are you? Where are we?'

The odd-looking men continued brushing sand off of the victim. The one that had asked for help, turned to face Josiah and FiFi and told the couple that his name was Samuel. Then pointed to the one that had been recused, and, who was still picking sand from his body, was called David. A chuckle barely escaped his small mouth and said, 'Most of our acquaintances call us Sam and Dave, The Time Serpents.'

After the strangers finished their cleaning, they both relaxed in a semi reclining position. Samuel did most of the talking. He said, that he and David had escaped from the same world the couple had departed. He explained that in the history of humanity, during chaos and peaceful civility, a class system always quickly formed. In its simplest form, the most physically powerful ruled. In a more complex society, the true Crown was invisible to the masses. The Crown rules the nobility that controls the mob. When he and David escaped, multinational corporations ruled by the patrician class, took control of the media. They knew that the one that controls the media, controls the message. The corporate elite, hidden in their lofty secretive chambers high above the peasants enforced their message of a weak military and illegitimate, corrupt governments. The message convinced the common man that segments of the population were their enemies, taking the focus off of the ruling class.

Samuel said that because of their youthful ignorance and stupidity, they became voices of discontent. The ruling class insisted on absolutism, total fealty to the Crown's message. They escaped to different lands, but the tyrants were always in pursuit or lying-in-wait.

Eventually they fled to the empty deserts of North Africa, but, the relentless pursuit continued. One night when capture was imminent, a lone stranger dressed in sun bleached rags, walked out of the cold desert night and asked for shelter near their campfire. He helped them drink the last of their coffee and told them about a nearby oasis. He told them the oasis was mentioned in many centuries-old stories because of a massive dead tree. The dead tree was still standing, but the giant tap root had rotted away leaving a dark underground passage. The stranger said that in the folklore of the desert tribes, anyone who braved the journey and traveled into the vein of the Father would find horror or Paradise.

Their choices were imprisonment or the mysteries of a black hole. They convinced the stranger to lead them that night to the special oasis. When they had reached a grove of trees bordering a pool of water the sun was not yet visible but its warmth could be felt. The dead colossus towered over the other trees and at its base was a yawning black hole. So, on a Spring morning in 2053, they took a different direction in their life's journey.

'Wait! Wait! You said 2053. We entered this world over a century earlier. I don't understand,' interrupted a confused Josiah.

Samuel assured the rescuers that he'd try to explain their new world as best as he could. He revealed there were a few doors in their former world that when opened led to this new world, which most call Tonta'Mer. He said there were a few major paths that could be traveled, many dead ends and many side trails, some that led nowhere and others that led to miraculous wonders.

He told the attentive couple that time did not exist before or after the Wound. The Wound was where the unending game of war was fought in the dark valley. He told the couple that he and Dave have been to the Wound many times to pick up passengers. He said that their friend, WawaWain, was still clearing the path of rubbish and dead warriors. He had also opened clinics on both sides of the valley to care for the injured. Samuel called him a missionary for peace. A kind earnest man with trivial success. He always asked if Sam and Dave had seen his friends FiFi and Josiah. He said that the definition of a real man was Josiah and that angels of grace were with the beautiful FiFi.

'Has it been that long since we last saw WawaWain. He was a wonderful companion and we both miss him. What you call the Wound, FiFi and I call the Valley of WaWa,' praised Josiah.

Samuel was not finished giving his quick tutorial. He said the world the couple had known, no longer existed. Their family and friends had died long ago. Time in their old world sped on, while they had slavishly followed the main path, when many side trails led to Paradises."

It was FiFi's turn to interrupt, 'But we are searching for the Land of the Rougarou. We were told that he grants wishes and that he could return us to our families.'

A rich, but sympathetic voice came from David's tiny mouth. He said they were in the Land of the Rougarou. Everything around them had been created by and ruled by the Rougarou. The comede, which I'm sure you think is sand, but is actually tiny carnivorous parasites. The Purgamen Comedentia, created by the Rougarou, trap their prey and nibble at the flesh. The Rougarou's army search these fields for victims and if the unfortunate is still living, they are then brought to the master. These fields were once green with grass and trees and then the Rougarou unleashed his predators. He does grant some wishes, but very few. The fulfilled wishes are bait. He chums the desires of people. Those granted wishes lure more victims.

Samuel continued the narrative. He made clear that the Rougarou tolerated the tiny gold men because he needed their elixir to nourish his army of savages. But is a menace to everyone else. No one considers him an enemy to be destroyed. He's like a dangerous venomous snake that is a small blemish on the beauty of this world. He's a creator of suffering and chaos. We don't hate him. We don't want to destroy him. His immoral conduct gives value to our principles. He plants turmoil, hatred and danger. Our defense against his depraved evil attitude makes us stronger. You might say we need the Rougarou and his dark world.

Samuel proceeded to unfold the answers to Josiah's questions. He said that when he and Dave first arrived in Tonta'Mer they aimlessly explored and by chance entered a community of scholars and thinkers. The mantra or the community code was that the brain was the Temple of Possibilities. If you could think or picture something, the brain could find a solution. He said they had always liked speed and, so, studied various possibilities of traveling their immense new world at an unprecedent speed. They found a simple solution that required a difficult or impossible application. Their project called for creating a controllable atom with an excess of internal energy. They didn't focus on proton repulsion, instead, limiting their trials to magnetism or forces of attraction, a stronger energy. Together Sam and Dave, with help from the community, successfully genetically engineered their bodies to utilize their discoveries. It was a gradual process, but, their brain and bodies eventually evolved into flying machines. Whenever they wished to travel at high speeds, they leapt up and turned and twisted their bodies. They repeat these actions until they are able to corkscrew their bodies while in the air. Once they are able to perform the corkscrew maneuver, their bodies are prepared to travel at a high speed. Because of the corkscrew maneuver, others called them Time Serpents. They can travel anywhere in Tonta'Mer further and faster than anyone or anything. The duo gave travelers, explorers and the lazy, rides for a small fee. They had been bringing two passengers to see the Rougarou when the riders insisted on an immediate landing. An immediate landing is an uncontrolled landing that led to a crash. The passengers became feast for the Comede and Dave would have been next if Josiah and FiFi hadn't miraculously appeared. Because of their heroic deeds Sam and Dave offered to give the couple free transportation to any destination."

Michael paused for a moment to check if he still had the attention of his audience. His children were wide-eyed and attentive, but his wife was eye talking to him. Her expressive eyes could picture her emotions and thoughts. He knew when she was happy because her eyes sparkled and when she was angry, he could feel the heated stare. When she was sad her eyes frowned at the corners and when she was trying to get his attention her eyes became big cat-eye marbles. If one brow was arched it was her plea for help, to rescue her from a boring conversation or an embarrassing situation. He could tell that her eyes were yelling at him to hurry and finish his story. He took a deep breath, thought for a moment about an appropriate ending and then continued his tale.

"Josiah and FiFi accepted Sam and Dave's offer and said that they would be most appreciative of a quick journey to the house or dwelling of the Rougarou. The Time Serpents said a meeting with the Rougarou was a waste of time and probably dangerous. Together, in unison, they described many wonderful paradises and exotic lands that were waiting for a couple of young explorers. But Josiah was not in this new world for himself; he was on a mission to help his family and FiFi knew the only place she wanted to be was standing next to and helping Josiah.

So…., when the Time Serpents realized they could never change the minds of their rescuers, they reached into their satchels and pulled out garments. They gave Josiah and Fifi long thin metallic green coats, thick red gloves and bulky blue caps with ear flaps that tied under the neck. Sam explained that they needed to wear the clothing because it would get very frosty during transit. While the couple got into their flight garments, Sam and Dave attached collapsible saddles to their backs. Each saddle had an enclosed compartment for the passenger.

Dave explained the preflight procedures in a routine manner. He said that he and Sam would leap into the air and twist and turn. On their third vault into the air, they would go higher and twist in a corkscrew motion, thus the name Serpents. After this third jump the couple were to jump into the enclosed compartments and prepare for the ride of their life.

Josiah and FiFi stood in their flight suits and watched the odd pair make strange strained facial expressions. Then one mighty leap into the air and then another. When the pair landed after their third jump, Josiah and FiFi scrambled into the saddles and buckled the doors closed. Sam and Dave flung their comical-looking bodies into the air three more times and each time they did a graceful corkscrew maneuver. Then for a long moment they just floated and then the next moment they were racing below the clouds. The blue horizon turned pink then orange and then disappeared. They soared through the cold glory of darkness with pinpricks of starlight zigzagging above.

The nose dive landing had been frightening, but safely accomplished. Josiah quickly jumped out of the saddle compartment and ran over to help free FiFi from her saddle. He was excited. He was close to completing his mission.

Dave pointed to a door that was not connected to walls. It was a huge free-standing bronze door that cast a long shadow. In the distance could be seen a number of fire tornadoes and the sunlight was a harsh glare, but near the door was nothing unusual. In a solemn voice, Dave said, 'Behind that door is the one you seek. He's been waiting a long time to meet you. We will remain near these portals to mischief, as long as we think there is a chance that you will return, so that we can deliver you from this evil land.'

Josiah and FiFi walked into the gray shadow of the door. Most of the door was caked in black grime and a dark yellowish spidery fungus. The only part of the door that its bronze composition was evident, was the area surrounding the small door-pull. That part of the door was shiny, greasy and marked with dirty fingerprints. The door, maybe ten feet tall, looked immovable; but when Josiah yanked on the door-pull the massive monstrosity swung open without much effort. The air that escaped from the darkness smelled like the vapors from a charnal house. The couple held hands as they cautiously took their first steps into the hideous black. They took small steps, testing the ground before them, making certain there was not a bottomless pit waiting for them. They advanced slowly, constantly reassuring each other as they tried to ignore the choking stench and the warm humid air hanging around them draping their hair and shoulders with clinging stifling wet air. They froze when they heard rapid pounding footsteps. Without warning the young couple were ripped away from each other. FiFi felt her damp hand slide out of Josiah's grip. She could hear him struggling, fighting the unseen forces. She was screaming his name as she was roughly lifted into the air and carried deeper into the darkness. She heard Josiah yell her name, but it was distantly faint and muffled. The forces that held her aloft raced at whippet speed. Her porters slowed after entering a cavern lit by dancing flames confined to a fire pit. FiFi was gently put on her feet and when she looked across the filthy cave, she saw him standing in the shadows. She was shocked, struck mute. Her trembling mind assessed the situation. Her mind's voice shouted, 'My Lord, he exists. The Rougarou exist.'

Before her stood a man-wolf. He didn't have a snout like a canine; but his lower face was stretched tight to confine bone crushing teeth. His face was covered in dirty black and coffee-brown wiry hair. He stood on two feet like a human, was tall and muscular. At the ends of his hairy human hands were cracked and worn claws coated in dried blood. His only clothing was torn baggy trousers. The dancing flames cast a brief lazy wave of light on the creature's face, then undulated to a gray shadow; a swaying repetition of light and dark. The fire light illuminated the face of a menacing killer.

The creatures first words were part laughter, part growl, 'FiFi, My Love, I see you have met my associates.'

FiFi's eyes slowly scanned the walls of the cavern. In the shadows were creatures just like the one that had spoken. Some were missing an eye; others had a hand or a leg missing. Others had large patches of fur ripped away replaced with wrinkled and cracked scars. They wore only their matted and dirty fur. It was obvious that each had been beaten, probably in battles for supremacy.

When FiFi spoke, her voice betrayed her. Her high-pitched plea quivered in fear.

'Please don't hurt me or Josiah. How do you know my name?' After that pleading attempt to speak, her focus was not on the creatures, but on the enemy within her. She knew she had to defeat Mr. Fear if she was to rescue Josiah. A smile spread across the creature's face, 'For centuries, I've patiently waited as you journeyed to me and now My Love has arrived.'

FiFi felt her inner will gradually taming Mr. Fear, 'For centuries! Sir that's not possible. I've had breath for less than a score of years.'

The creature began to pant like an excited dog.

'Please My Love, call me Ootah. You and your companion never realized that in this paradise the war against time has been won. Time has been defeated. You are now in a world without end.'

The Rougarou licked his lips and continued, 'I watched you descend the steps that led from your earthly hell. I was grateful for WawaWain's ability to safely get you through the Black Valley. I watched you bath in the stream while you waited to see if your companion survived his stupidity. I fell in love with you and waited. Finally, you have arrived and now I will make you my queen. You will be by my side as I rule this land and conquer new territories.'

FiFi could feel terror as Mr. Fear fought her for control as she asked the question, 'Mr. Ootah, am I in Hell?'

The creature stood tall and gave an excited half laugh, half canine yelp. He looked around at the others to assess their fear and in a snarling roar said, 'No, My Dear! This is not Hell, though I do know the proprietor of that establishment. We occasionally have business dealings.'

Still battling Mr. Fear, FiFi mustered her own snarling voice and yelled, 'Where is Josiah? I demand that you bring him to me.'

'Let me tell you the obvious, My Love,' the monster's lips formed a cruel smile as he spoke in the measured cadence of someone considering carefully what he said. 'Your Josiah is not here for you. He's on a mission for his family. He doesn't love you and will never be able to provide for your needs. I adore you and will give you everything you desire.'

'I will give you a choice. Become my queen and I will send the boy back to his family with incredible wealth that his family no longer needs. If you refuse to be my queen, I will allow you to leave my realm, but you will never see the boy again. I might sell him to the greatest villain in history. Together we can live and love forever. We can rule for eternity.'

'Eternity,' shouted FiFi, 'You fool! You ignorant dog! Even eternity has an ending.'

Along the walls of the cave erupted yelps, growls and nervous laughter.

FiFi was winning her battle with Mr. Fear and now had to gain control over Miss Anger. She realized anger had given her the courage to yell at the creature. She also knew that unrestrained anger was as dangerous as paralyzing fear.

Ootah slammed his furry hands on the trestle table that separated him from FiFi. The only sound that echoed in the vast cavern were his blood-stained claws raking the table top.

'My Dear,' the creature said as his lips separated to reveal large stained teeth, 'Your friend's journey has been for naught. His father survived the war and when he returned home, oil was found under the farm and the family became incredibly wealthy and with no help from your witless friend.'

'My Love, happiness is a fragile condition. I will do everything in my power to feed your happiness. Anything you desire will be yours and once you become my queen, I will send that silly boy back to his family with gold they no longer need. You need someone like me. Only someone like me can make you happy and satisfied.'

FiFi closed her eyes. She could feel Miss Anger savage Mr. Fear. The knots of uncertainty and confusion evaporated in the whirlwind of her anger. When FiFi opened her eyes, she was ready to fight. In a clear calm echoing voice, she did battle.

'Mr. Ootah, I am flattered you wish me to be your queen. But I will not be forced to make a Faustian Bargain with a savage. I kindly ask you to return Josiah to my side, unharmed and with the knowledge of his family's good fortune. It had been rumored that if someone ventured to this mystery world, it was not necessary for that someone to return home for his loved ones to profit from his or her journey. You have just put truth to what we had thought were wishful prayers. Sir, I thank you for lifting the burden of making a decision. We have Time Serpents waiting to bring us to our destiny. Since we are free from our responsibilities to our families, together, Josiah and I can now explore new worlds.'

'My Love, I may be a savage, but I'm no Mephistopheles. I'm not asking you to make a bargain. I'm asking you to be my queen so that I can serve you. But, My Love, there is an if. If you refuse to be my queen, you will be free to leave my kingdom alone. You will never see your weak friend again, nor will his family. His eternity will be Hell.'

FiFi could feel her anger-heat building in her chest, her brow became damp and her fists clinched, ready for a fight. There was scorn in her fearsome glare. Her voice was soaked in venom and sneering sarcasm when she warned the monster.

'Mr. Ootah, you are making a fatal mistake. No one is immune from disaster. I will journey to the Dark Valley as you have named it and when I return to this evil dung heap, I will be leading an army, maybe two. A red army and the other blue. I will give them a reason to unite and to fight for a noble cause. I will have them destroy everything in this wicked land. You will wish you had chosen an honorable path.'

FiFi turned her back to the Rougarou and marched towards the darkness from where she had come, but, before disappearing into the black void she gave the creature an over-the-shoulder scowl and said, 'When I'm finished here, if my Josiah is not standing next to me unharmed, I will sell you to the Devil.'"

Michael made an audible sigh, then a yawn and said, "Well ladies and gentlemen that is the end of a very long story."

Gabriel blurted, "But Pops, did she come back and save Josiah."

Michael had a quick counter, "Why don't you think about it and then write down some thoughts and next weekend you can continue the story."

Jennifer stood up and stretched and said, "OK, no more, it's time for bed. School and work tomorrow. Come on, we'll pick out some school clothes before you go to bed."

Before his mother herded him off to bed Michael J, put his hand on his Dad's arm and asked, "Dad what is a Faustian Bargain?"

Jennifer put her arm around Michael J's shoulders to escort him to bed and gently said, "Nope! Not tonight, that's a question to ask while your Dad is fixing breakfast in the morning."

Jennifer and her two sons hustled down the hall, but Silva remained on the couch. Michael couldn't decide if she looked angry or puzzled.

Michael's confused teenage daughter softly said, "Dad, did this man really tell you this story?"

Michael sat next to Silva and spoke cautiously to his quick-tempered daughter.

"Oh yes. Mr. Landry told us this story and so many others. I wish I could remember all of them."

Often when Silva felt sorry for herself, she would have a silent cry. She was sitting next to her Dad. She was embarrassed because tears were racing down her cheeks and she didn't know why her heart felt so heavy.

"Why don't we have storytellers like this old man?"

"Oh, today, that's all we have is storytellers. Every time we turn on the TV a story is being told. Even commercials are mini stories.

Movies, books, magazines, online sites, the daily news and even music have stories trying to grab our attention. Maybe we have too many storytellers and sometimes it's hard to tell if the story is fiction or nonfiction. The hard thing for all of us is to filter out a lot of the noise. There are people, organizations, media corporations and even governments that want us to see the world as they would have us see it, whether it's correct or fake. These people are only interested in their agenda. They know that the power to define a situation is the ultimate power. We have to wisely choose our story tellers. The world is becoming tribal because of the vast amount of conflicting views."

Jennifer walked into the living room yawned and said, "OK guys it's time to turn out the lights. Let's go Silva."

Silva turned to her Dad and gave him a tight hug.

"Thanks Dad. Thanks for a good Sunday."

Silva abandoned her fortress and went to her bedroom. Jennifer raised her eyebrows, smiled and said, "Well, you're something else Mr. and yes I agree it was a good Sunday."

Jennifer gave her husband a hug and kissed his neck and said, "Don't forget, you didn't cook breakfast this morning and so I expect something other than pancakes in the morning."

www.ingramcontent.com/pod-product-compliance
Lightning Source LLC
LaVergne TN
LVHW021700060526
838200LV00050B/2442